**Oddities, Discord, and B-Sides:
Lyrical Ruckus in the City**

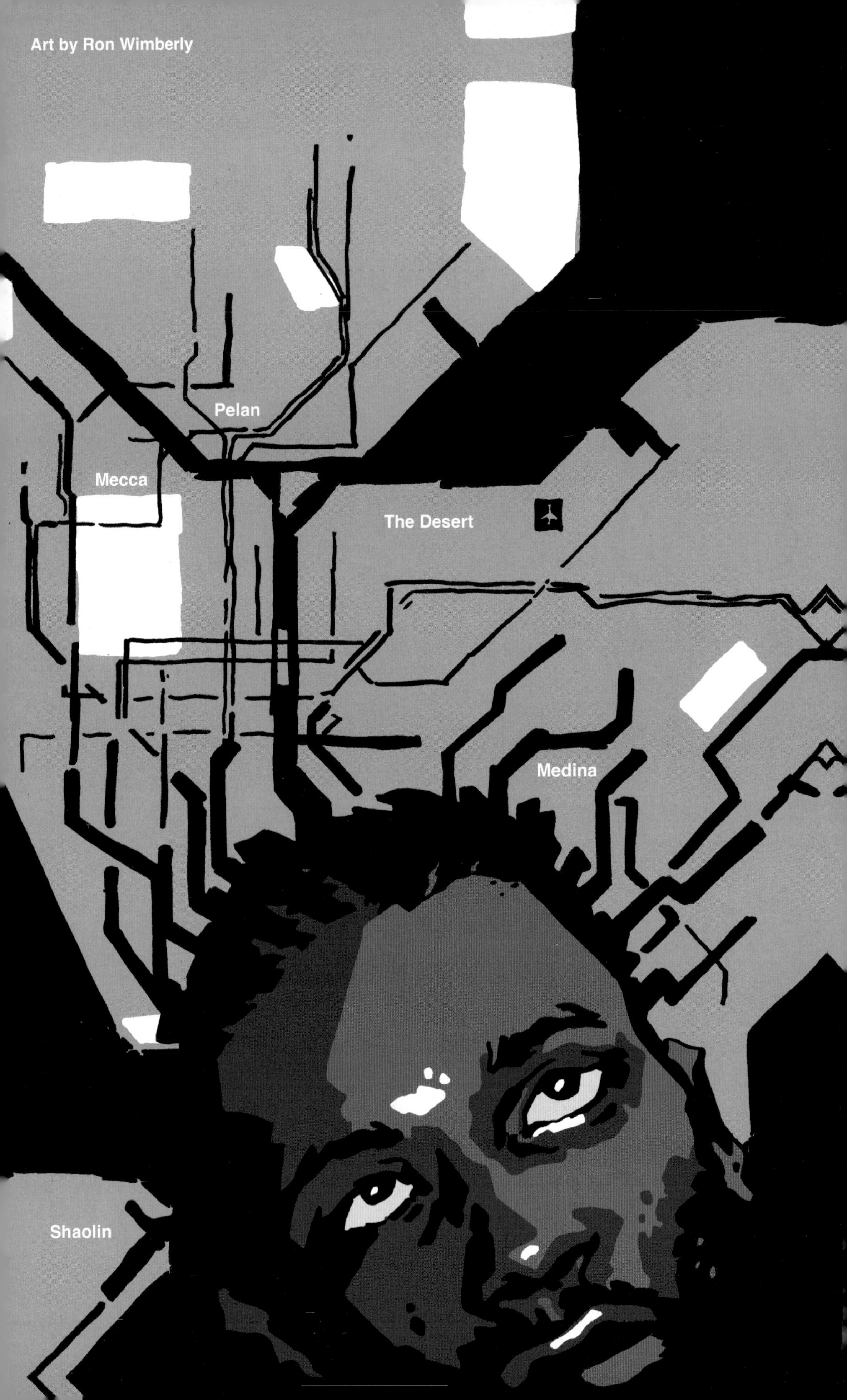
Art by Ron Wimberly
Pelan
Mecca
The Desert
Medina
Shaolin

Oddities, Discord, and B-Sides: Lyrical Ruckus in the City

🟧 **Script by** Jason Pierre, Ike Reed & David Gorden, Troy-Jeffrey Allen, Regine Sawyer, and Chris Robinson

🟦 **Art by** David Brame, Dojo Gubser, Maan House, Chris Gooding, Mike JC, and Felipe Sobriero

🟩 **Colors by** DJ Chavis, Dojo Gubser, and Karla Aguilar

🟥 **Letters by** Nathan Kempf

🔵 Cover by Paris Alleyne
🟠 Kickstarter Exclusive SC cover by Jay Hero
🟡 Kickstarter Exclusive HC cover by Paris Alleyne
🟢 Kickstarter Exclusive HC cover by Damion Scott
🟣 Kickstarter Exclusive HC cover by Mike del Mundo
🔴 Kickstarter Exclusive HC cover by Ron Wimberly

PLOT BY Ike Reed & David Gorden, Nicole Beckett, Messiah Jacobs & Jaxson Beckett Williams

CREATED BY Icelene Jones, Jaxson Beckett Williams, Messiah Jacobs & Nicole Beckett

SPECIAL THANKS TO Shaquita Jones, The Estate of Russell Jones, and Leila del Duca

DESIGNER Carey Soucy
EDITORS David Steward II, Nicole Beckett, Messiah Jacobs, Jaxson Beckett Williams & Chris Robinson
ASSISTANT EDITOR Camila Rozo

PUBLISHED BY ONI-LION FORGE PUBLISHING GROUP, LLC.

Hunter Gorinson, president & publisher • Sierra Hahn, editor in chief • Troy Look, vp of publishing services • Spencer Simpson, vp of sales • Angie Knowles, director of design & production • Daniel Crary, director of marketing • Katie Sainz, director of sales, book market • Jeremy Colfer, director of development • Chris Cerasi, managing editor • Bess Pallares, senior editor • Grace Scheipeter, senior editor • Karl Bollers, editor • Megan Brown, editor • Matt Dryer, editor • Gabriel Granillo, editor • Jung Hu Lee, assistant editor • Michael Torma, senior sales manager • Andy McElliott, operations manager • Sarah Rockwell, senior graphic designer • Carey Soucy, senior graphic designer • Winston Gambro, graphic designer • Matt Harding, digital prepress technician • Sara Harding, executive coordinator • Kaia Rokke, marketing & communications coordinator • Joe Nozemack, publisher emeritus

ONI PRESS.COM /ONI PRESS

First Edition: November 2024 • ISBN: 978-1-62010-839-0
eISBN: 978-1-63715-515-8 • Library of Congress Control Number: 2024932035
PRINTED IN CHINA
1 2 3 4 5 6 7 8 9 10

ODB: Oddities, Discord, and B-Sides—Lyrical Ruckus in the City, November 2024. Published by Oni-Lion Forge Publishing Group, LLC., 1319 SE Martin Luther King Jr. Blvd., Suite 216, Portland, OR 97214. © 2024 Oni-Lion Forge Publishing Group, LLC & Four Screens Production, Inc; "Lyrical Ruckus in the City" and "Sword of the Cypher" are ™ 2024 Four Screens Production, Inc. Ol' Dirty Bastard ™ is used under license from the Estate of Russell Jones. The ODB logo and related designs are trademarks and copyrighted designs used under license from the Estate of Russell Jones. All rights reserved. Oni Press logo and icon are ™ & © 2024 Oni-Lion Forge Publishing Group, LLC. All rights reserved. Oni Press logo and icon artwork created by Keith A. Wood. The events, institutions, and characters presented in this book are fictional. Any resemblance to actual persons, living or dead, is purely coincidental. No portion of this publication may be reproduced, by any means, without the express written permission of the copyright holders.

CONTENTS

01. PROLOGUE..........................7
Script by Jason Pierre
Art by David Brame
Color by DJ Chavis

02. "LAGUARDIA'S STEPPERS"............11
Script by Ike Reed & David Gorden
Art & color by Dojo Gubser

03. "DEMON FLOW"....................28
Script by Troy-Jeffrey Allen
Art by Maan House
Color by Steve Canon

04. "LOVE IN THE MIX"................43
Script by Regine Sawyer
Art & color by Felipe Sobreiro

05. "SWORD OF THE CYPHER"............60
Script by Chris Robinson
Art by Chris Gooding
Layouts by Mike JC
Color by Steve Canon

06. "MARCUS AND THE DRUNKEN FIST"....77
Script by Jason Pierre
Art by Mike JC
Color by Karla Aguilar

07. EPILOGUE........................99
Script by Jason Pierre
Art by David Brame
Color by DJ Chavis

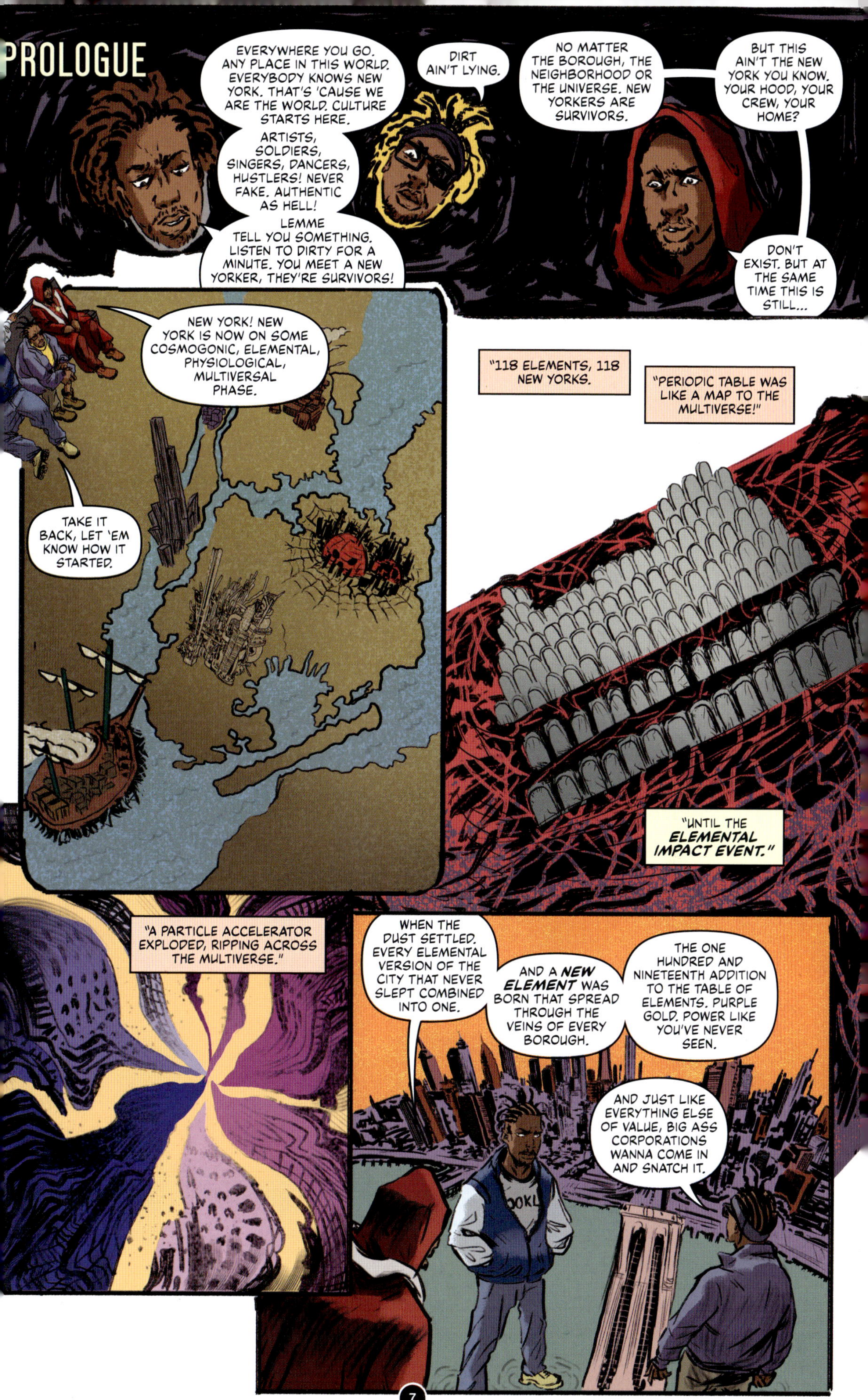
PROLOGUE
EVERYWHERE YOU GO. ANY PLACE IN THIS WORLD. EVERYBODY KNOWS NEW YORK. THAT'S 'CAUSE WE ARE THE WORLD. CULTURE STARTS HERE.
ARTISTS, SOLDIERS, SINGERS, DANCERS, HUSTLERS! NEVER FAKE. AUTHENTIC AS HELL!
LEMME TELL YOU SOMETHING. LISTEN TO DIRTY FOR A MINUTE. YOU MEET A NEW YORKER, THEY'RE SURVIVORS!
DIRT AIN'T LYING.
NO MATTER THE BOROUGH, THE NEIGHBORHOOD OR THE UNIVERSE. NEW YORKERS ARE SURVIVORS.
BUT THIS AIN'T THE NEW YORK YOU KNOW. YOUR HOOD, YOUR CREW, YOUR HOME?
DON'T EXIST. BUT AT THE SAME TIME THIS IS STILL...
NEW YORK! NEW YORK IS NOW ON SOME COSMOGONIC, ELEMENTAL, PHYSIOLOGICAL, MULTIVERSAL PHASE.
TAKE IT BACK, LET 'EM KNOW HOW IT STARTED.
"118 ELEMENTS, 118 NEW YORKS.
"PERIODIC TABLE WAS LIKE A MAP TO THE MULTIVERSE!"
"UNTIL THE ***ELEMENTAL IMPACT EVENT.***"
"A PARTICLE ACCELERATOR EXPLODED, RIPPING ACROSS THE MULTIVERSE."
WHEN THE DUST SETTLED. EVERY ELEMENTAL VERSION OF THE CITY THAT NEVER SLEPT COMBINED INTO ONE.
AND A ***NEW ELEMENT*** WAS BORN THAT SPREAD THROUGH THE VEINS OF EVERY BOROUGH.
THE ONE HUNDRED AND NINETEENTH ADDITION TO THE TABLE OF ELEMENTS. PURPLE GOLD. POWER LIKE YOU'VE NEVER SEEN.
AND JUST LIKE EVERYTHING ELSE OF VALUE, BIG ASS CORPORATIONS WANNA COME IN AND SNATCH IT.

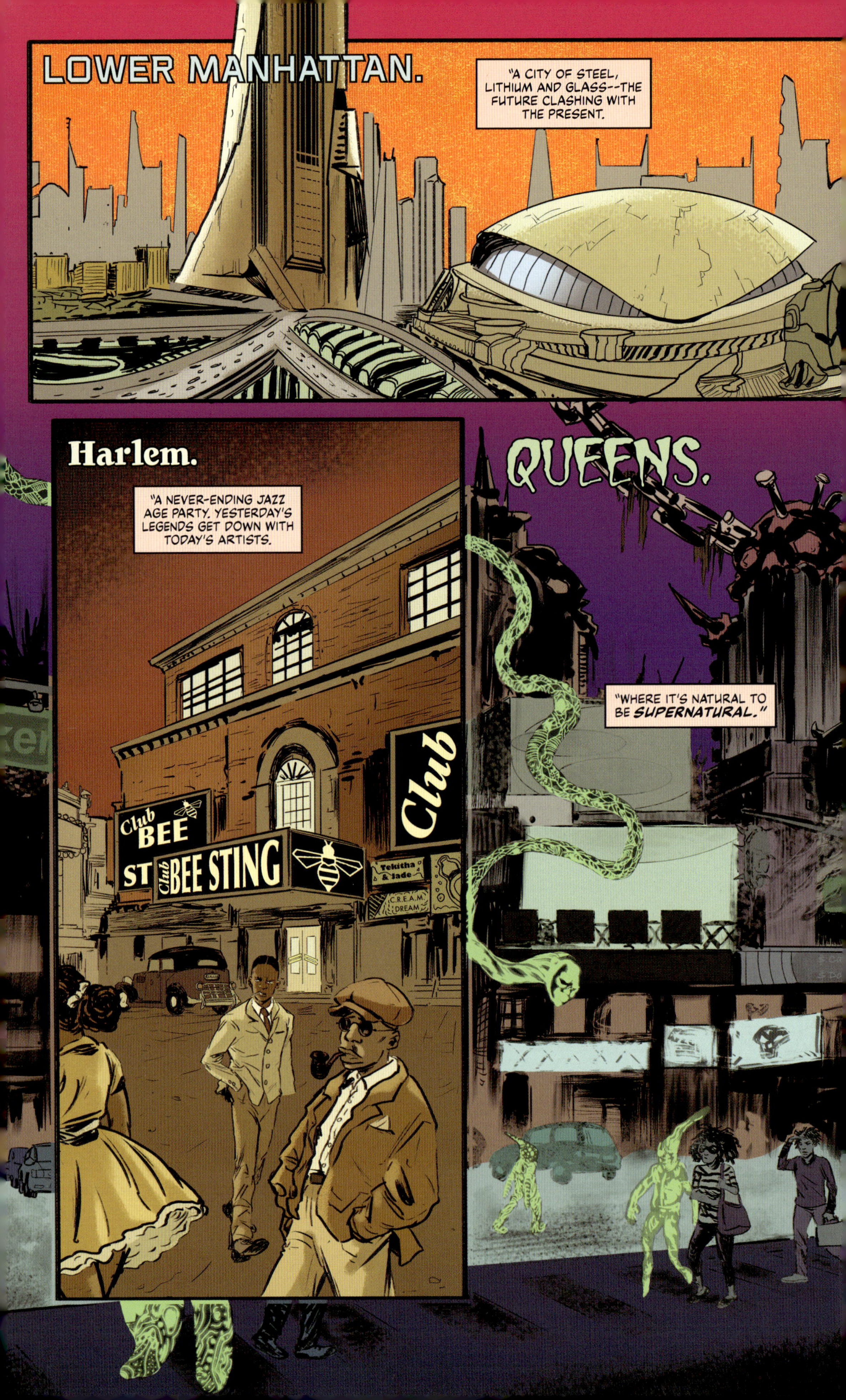
LOWER MANHATTAN.
"A CITY OF STEEL, LITHIUM AND GLASS--THE FUTURE CLASHING WITH THE PRESENT.
Harlem.
"A NEVER-ENDING JAZZ AGE PARTY. YESTERDAY'S LEGENDS GET DOWN WITH TODAY'S ARTISTS.
Club BEE
ST Club BEE STING
Club
Tekitha & Jade
C.R.E.A.M. DREAM
QUEENS.
"WHERE IT'S NATURAL TO BE SUPERNATURAL."

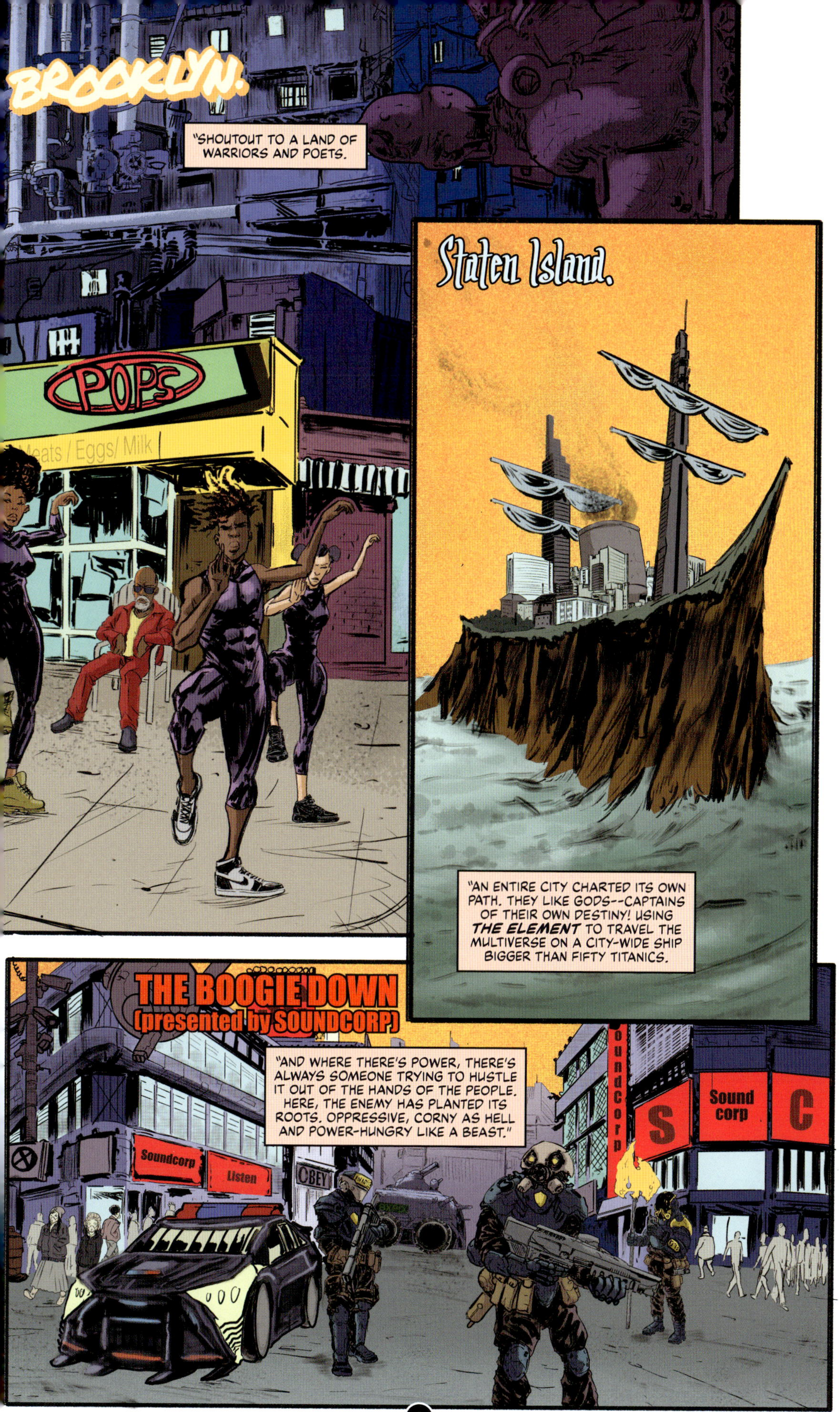
BROOKLYN.
"SHOUTOUT TO A LAND OF WARRIORS AND POETS.
POPS
Meats / Eggs/ Milk
Staten Island.
"AN ENTIRE CITY CHARTED ITS OWN PATH. THEY LIKE GODS--CAPTAINS OF THEIR OWN DESTINY! USING ***THE ELEMENT*** TO TRAVEL THE MULTIVERSE ON A CITY-WIDE SHIP BIGGER THAN FIFTY TITANICS.
THE BOOGIE DOWN
(presented by SOUNDCORP)
"AND WHERE THERE'S POWER, THERE'S ALWAYS SOMEONE TRYING TO HUSTLE IT OUT OF THE HANDS OF THE PEOPLE. HERE, THE ENEMY HAS PLANTED ITS ROOTS. OPPRESSIVE, CORNY AS HELL AND POWER-HUNGRY LIKE A BEAST."
Soundcorp
Listen
OBEY
Soundcorp
Sound corp
S
C

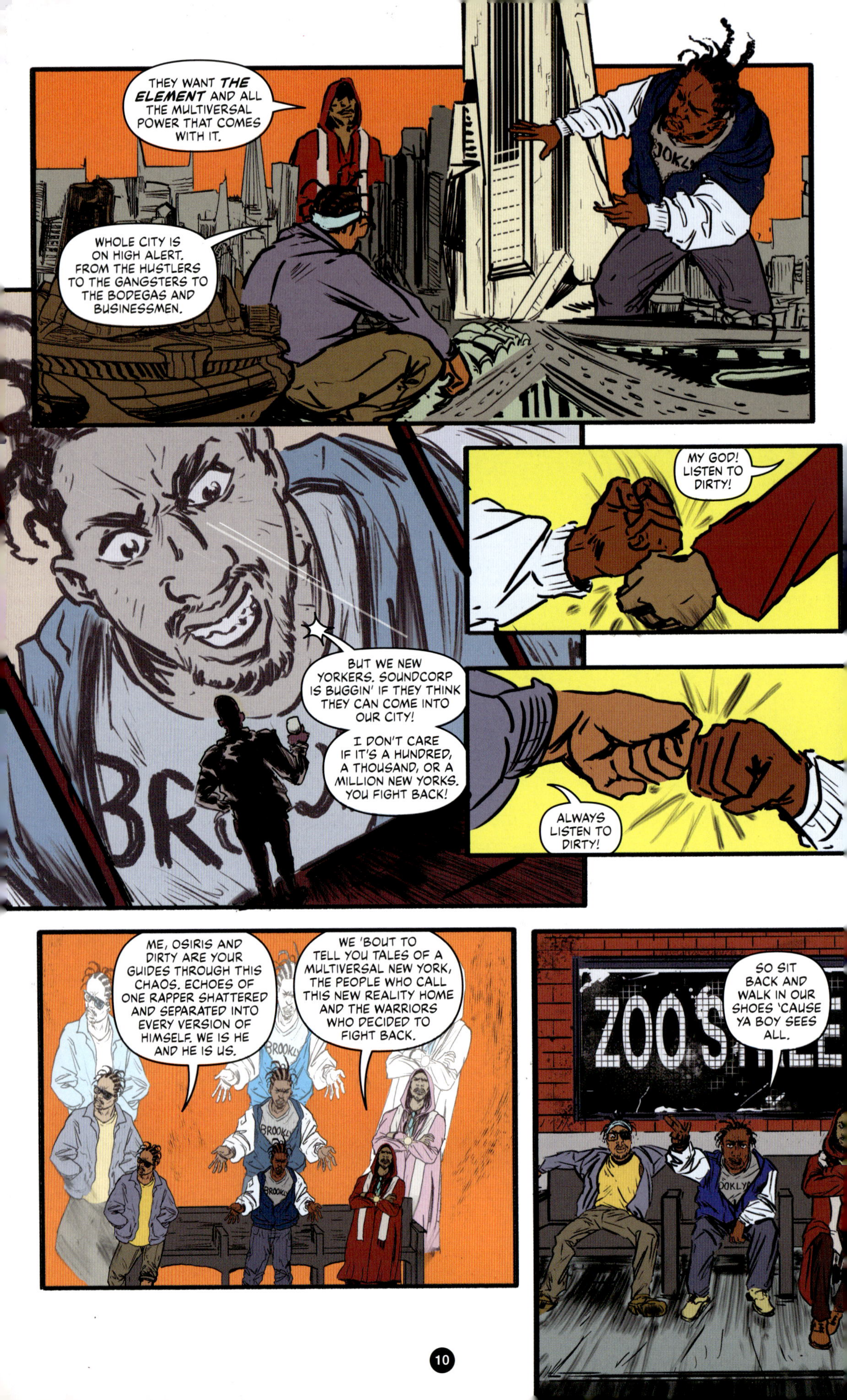

THEY WANT ***THE ELEMENT*** AND ALL THE MULTIVERSAL POWER THAT COMES WITH IT.
WHOLE CITY IS ON HIGH ALERT. FROM THE HUSTLERS TO THE GANGSTERS TO THE BODEGAS AND BUSINESSMEN.
BUT WE NEW YORKERS. SOUNDCORP IS BUGGIN' IF THEY THINK THEY CAN COME INTO OUR CITY!
I DON'T CARE IF IT'S A HUNDRED, A THOUSAND, OR A MILLION NEW YORKS. YOU FIGHT BACK!
MY GOD! LISTEN TO DIRTY!
ALWAYS LISTEN TO DIRTY!
ME, OSIRIS AND DIRTY ARE YOUR GUIDES THROUGH THIS CHAOS. ECHOES OF ONE RAPPER SHATTERED AND SEPARATED INTO EVERY VERSION OF HIMSELF. WE IS HE AND HE IS US.
WE 'BOUT TO TELL YOU TALES OF A MULTIVERSAL NEW YORK, THE PEOPLE WHO CALL THIS NEW REALITY HOME AND THE WARRIORS WHO DECIDED TO FIGHT BACK.
SO SIT BACK AND WALK IN OUR SHOES 'CAUSE YA BOY SEES ALL.

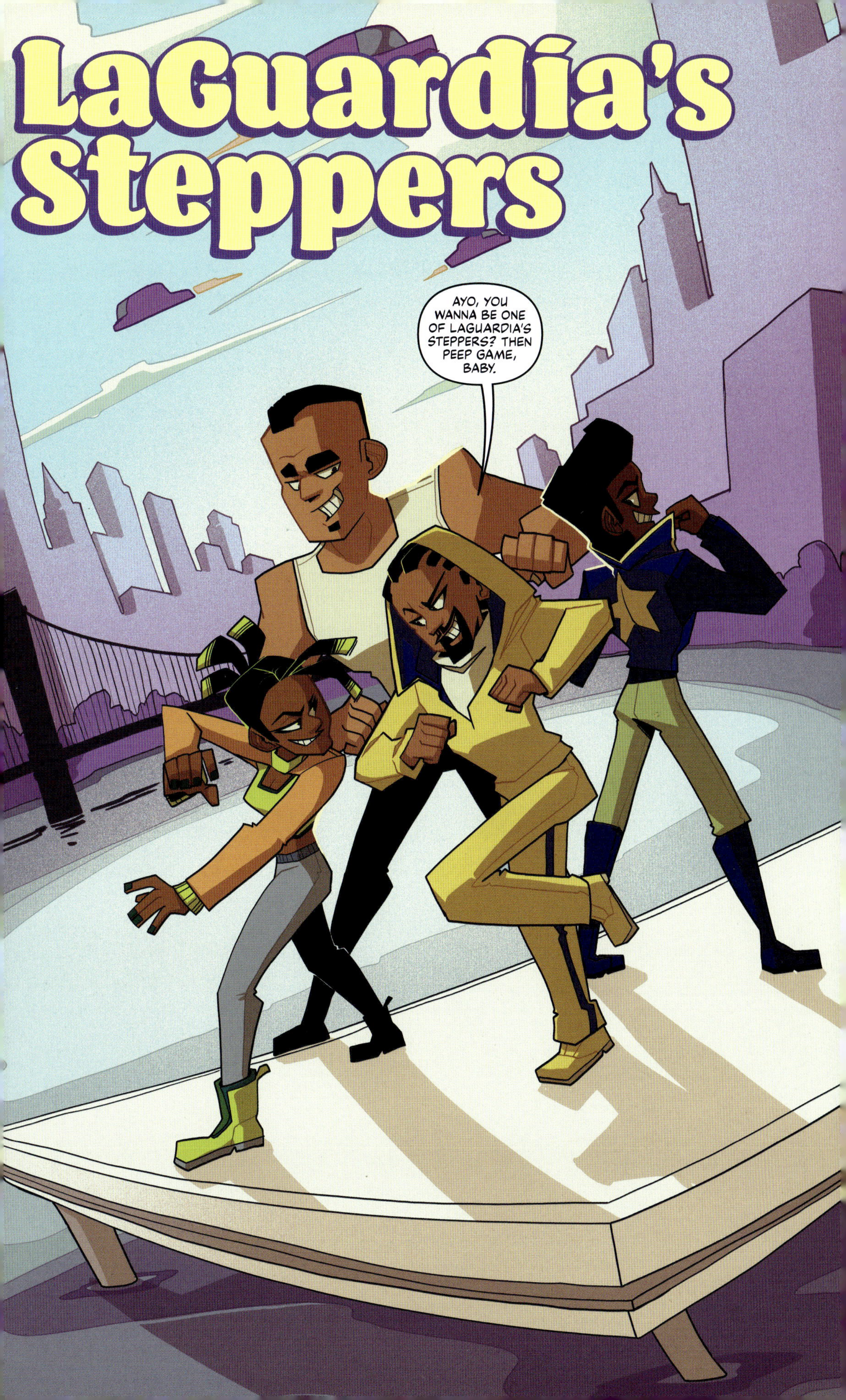
LaGuardia's Steppers
AYO, YOU WANNA BE ONE OF LAGUARDIA'S STEPPERS? THEN PEEP GAME, BABY.

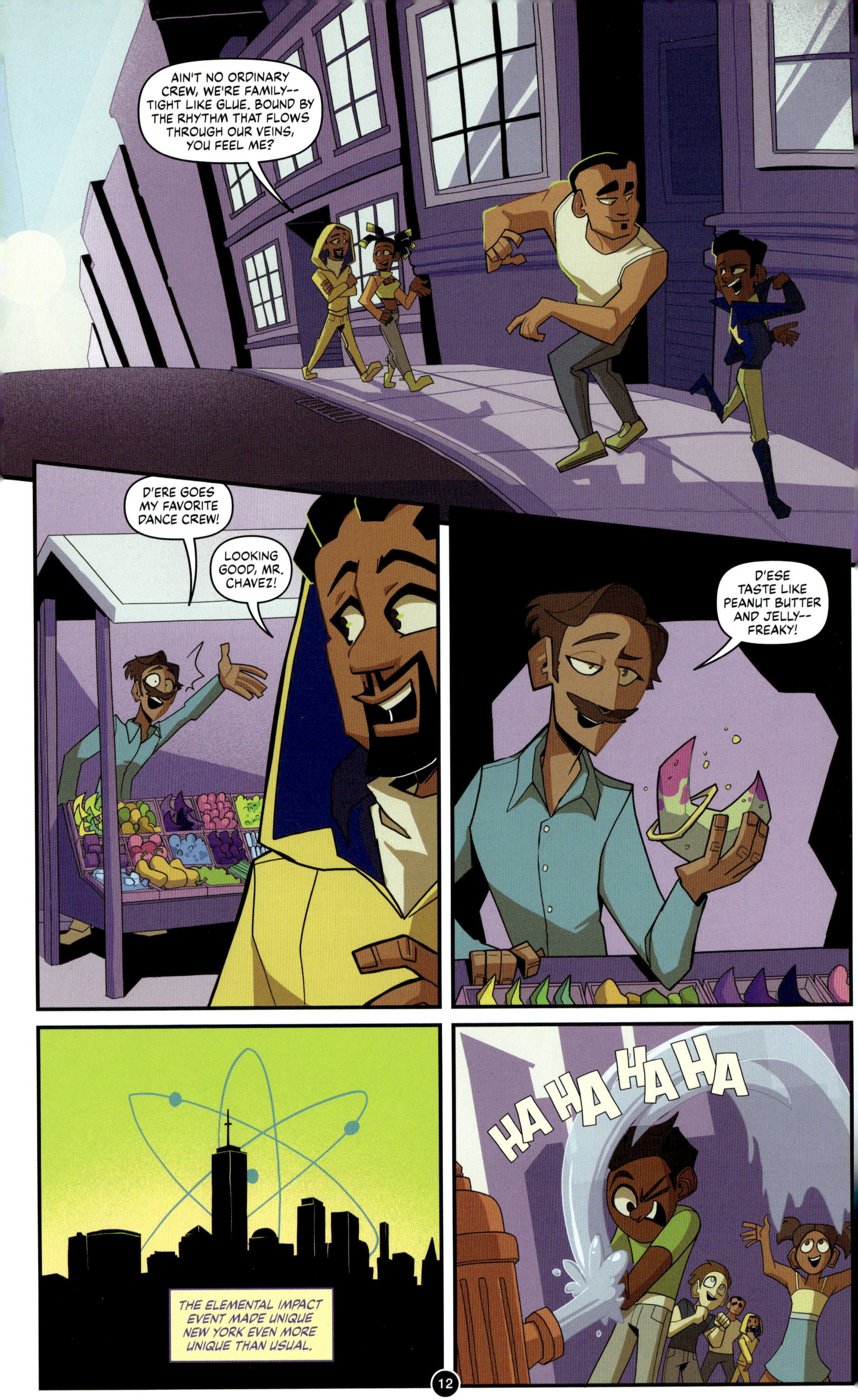
AIN'T NO ORDINARY CREW, WE'RE FAMILY-- TIGHT LIKE GLUE. BOUND BY THE RHYTHM THAT FLOWS THROUGH OUR VEINS, YOU FEEL ME?
D'ERE GOES MY FAVORITE DANCE CREW!
LOOKING GOOD, MR. CHAVEZ!
D'ESE TASTE LIKE PEANUT BUTTER AND JELLY-- FREAKY!
THE ELEMENTAL IMPACT EVENT MADE UNIQUE NEW YORK EVEN MORE UNIQUE THAN USUAL.
HA HA HA HA HA

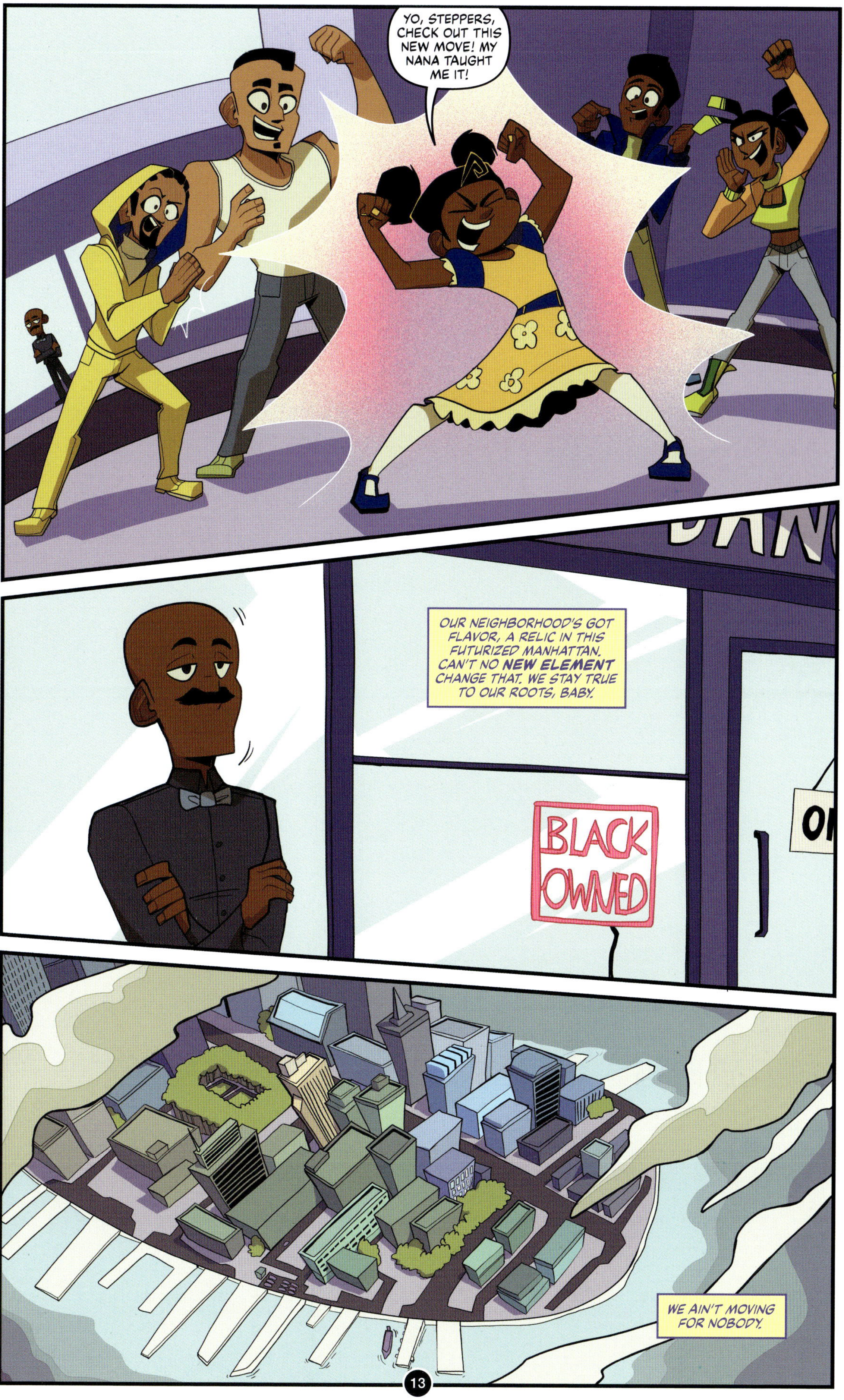
YO, STEPPERS, CHECK OUT THIS NEW MOVE! MY NANA TAUGHT ME IT!
OUR NEIGHBORHOOD'S GOT FLAVOR, A RELIC IN THIS FUTURIZED MANHATTAN. CAN'T NO **NEW ELEMENT** CHANGE THAT. WE STAY TRUE TO OUR ROOTS, BABY.
BLACK OWNED
WE AIN'T MOVING FOR NOBODY.

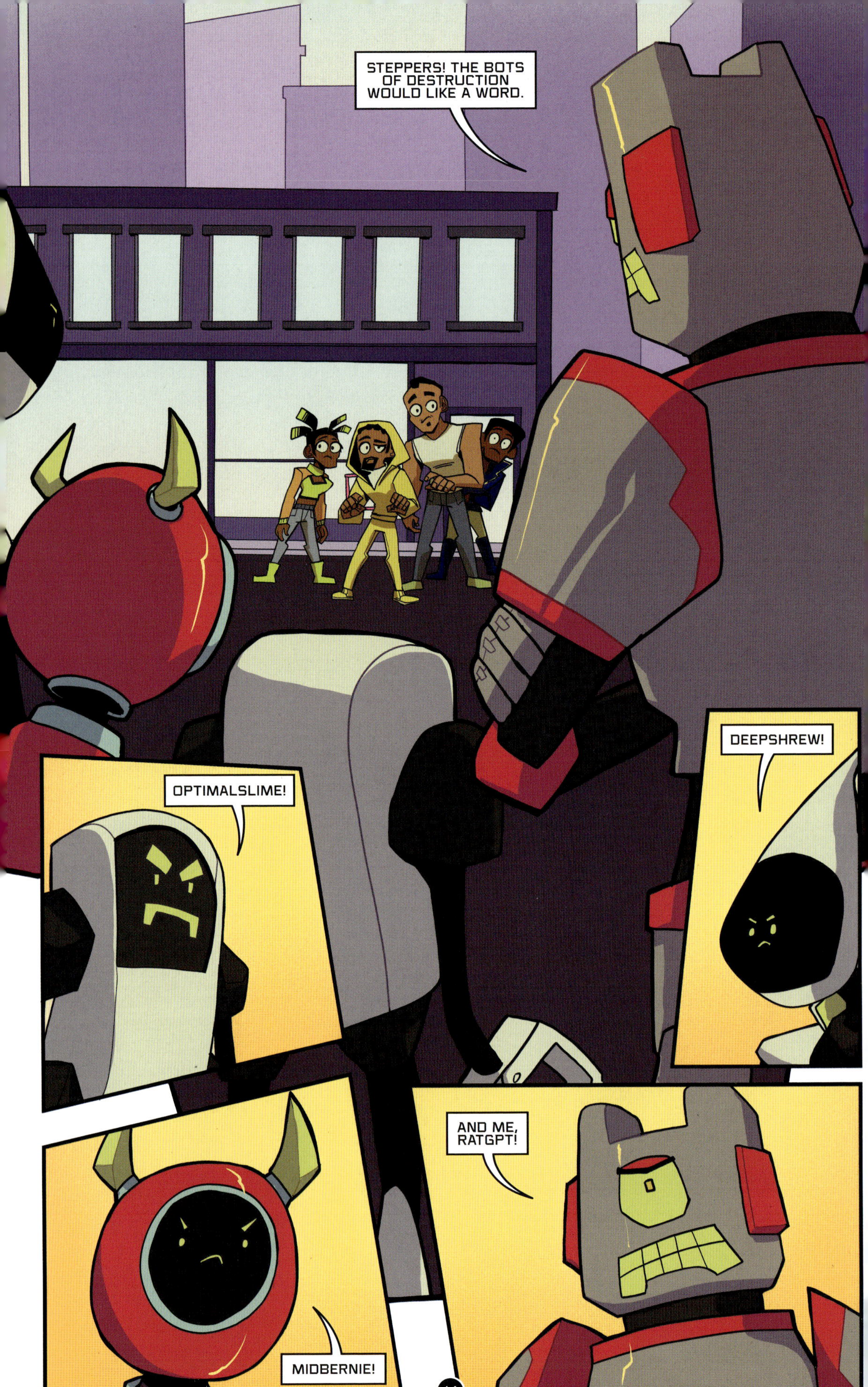
STEPPERS! THE BOTS OF DESTRUCTION WOULD LIKE A WORD.
OPTIMALSLIME!
DEEPSHREW!
MIDBERNIE!
AND ME, RATGPT!

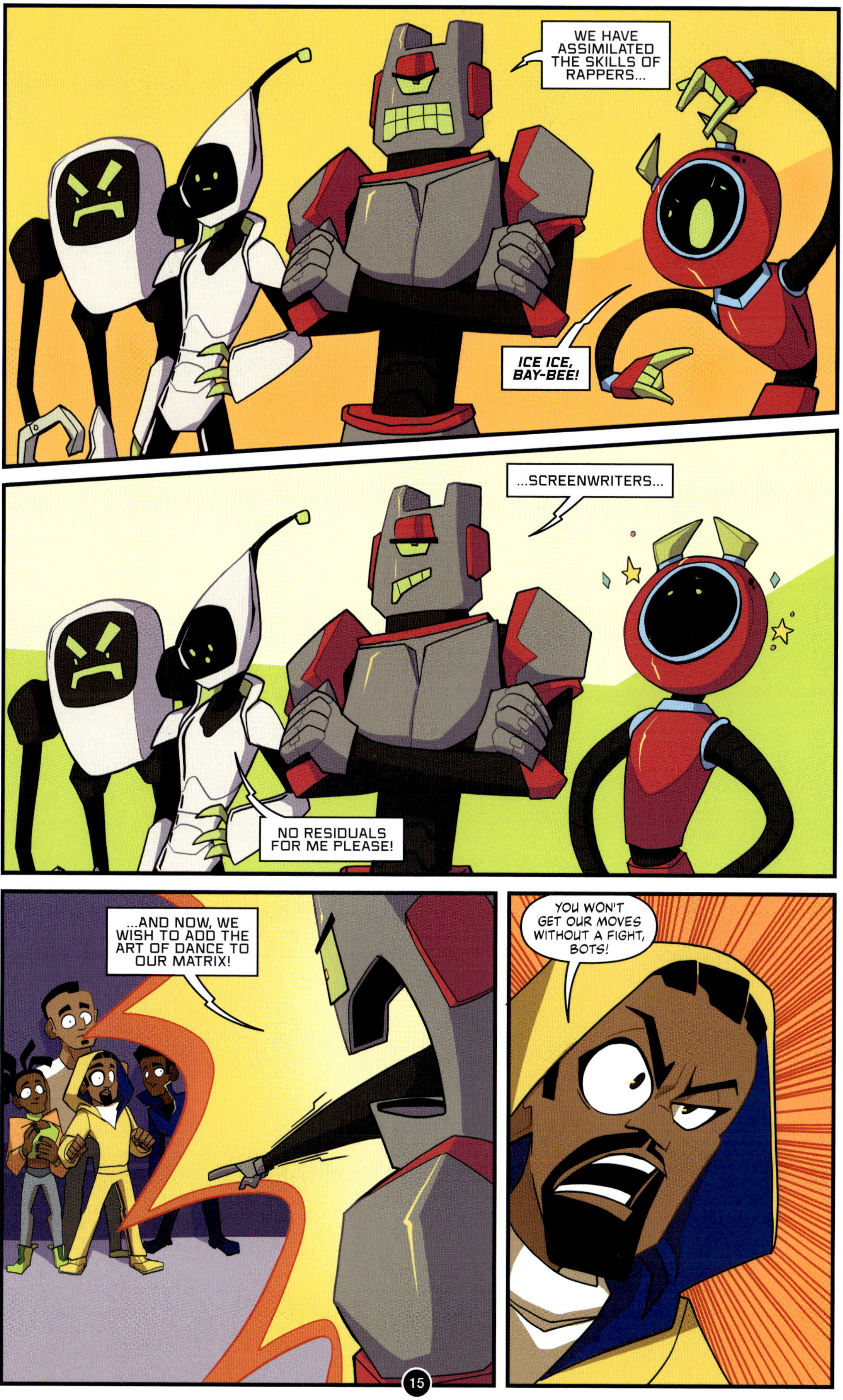
WE HAVE ASSIMILATED THE SKILLS OF RAPPERS...
ICE ICE, BAY-BEE!
...SCREENWRITERS...
NO RESIDUALS FOR ME PLEASE!
...AND NOW, WE WISH TO ADD THE ART OF DANCE TO OUR MATRIX!
YOU WON'T GET OUR MOVES WITHOUT A FIGHT, BOTS!

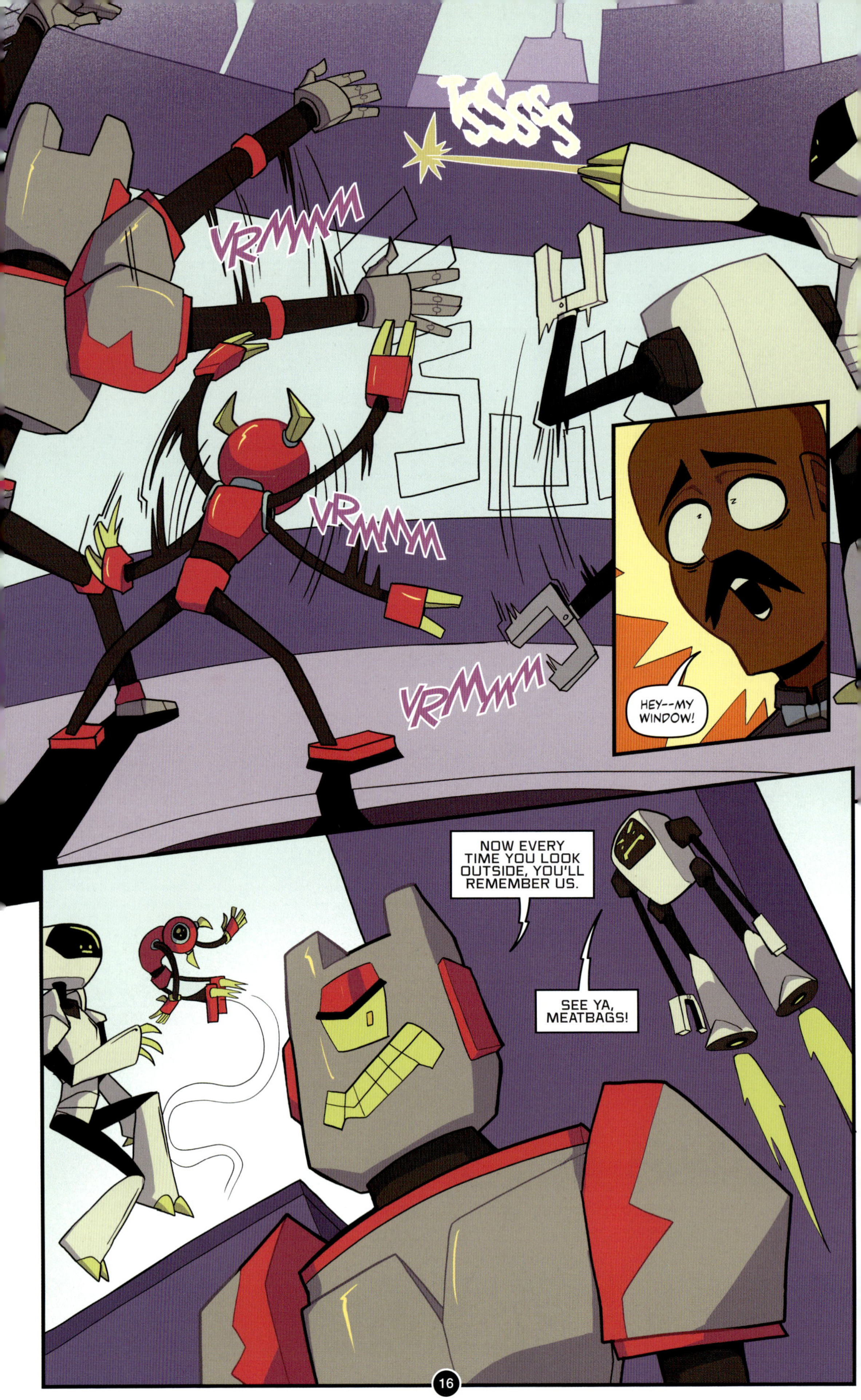
TSSSSS
VRMMMM
VRMMMM
VRMMMM
HEY--MY WINDOW!
NOW EVERY TIME YOU LOOK OUTSIDE, YOU'LL REMEMBER US.
SEE YA, MEATBAGS!

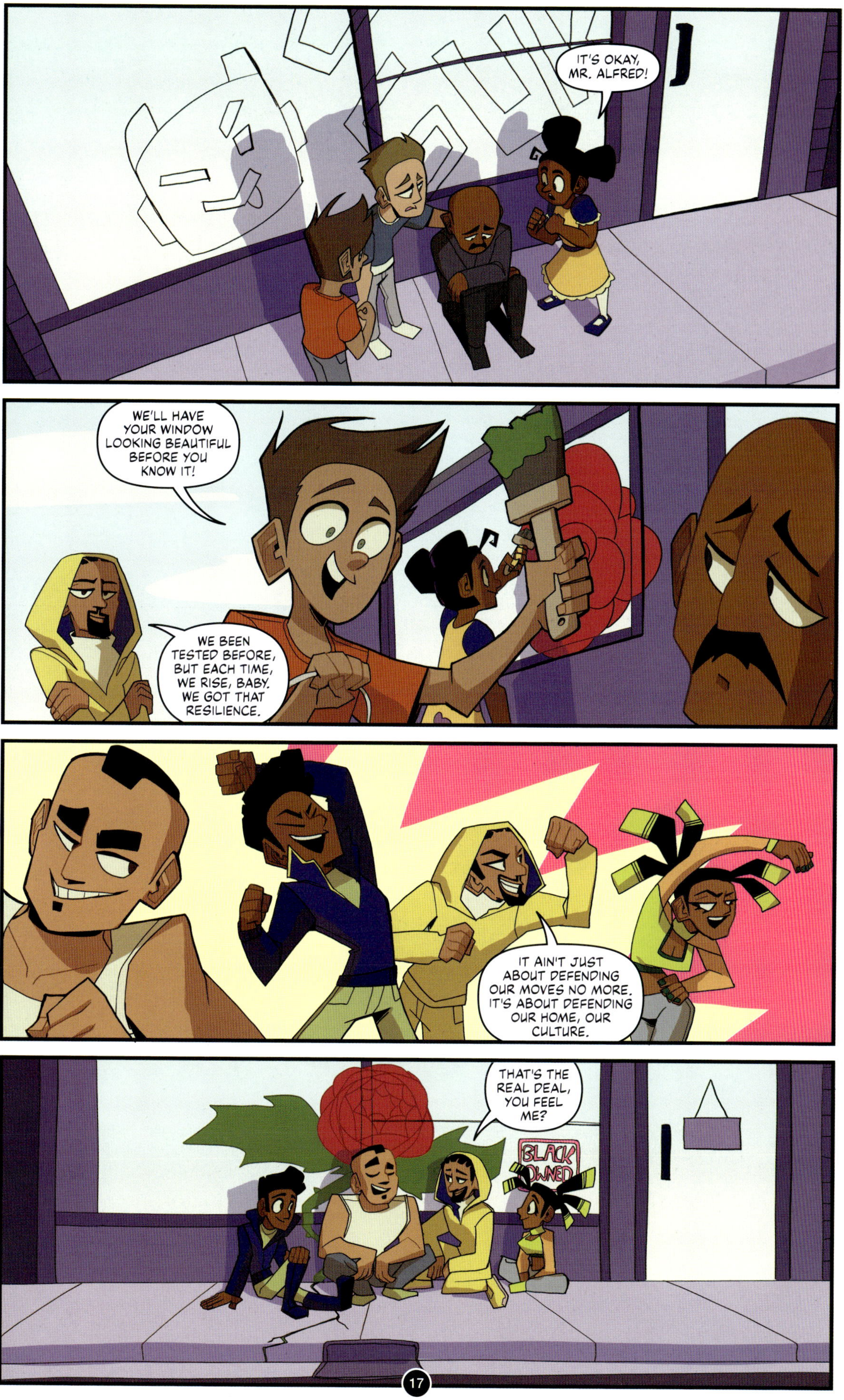
IT'S OKAY, MR. ALFRED!
WE'LL HAVE YOUR WINDOW LOOKING BEAUTIFUL BEFORE YOU KNOW IT!
WE BEEN TESTED BEFORE, BUT EACH TIME, WE RISE, BABY. WE GOT THAT RESILIENCE.
IT AIN'T JUST ABOUT DEFENDING OUR MOVES NO MORE. IT'S ABOUT DEFENDING OUR HOME, OUR CULTURE.
THAT'S THE REAL DEAL, YOU FEEL ME?
BLACK OWNED

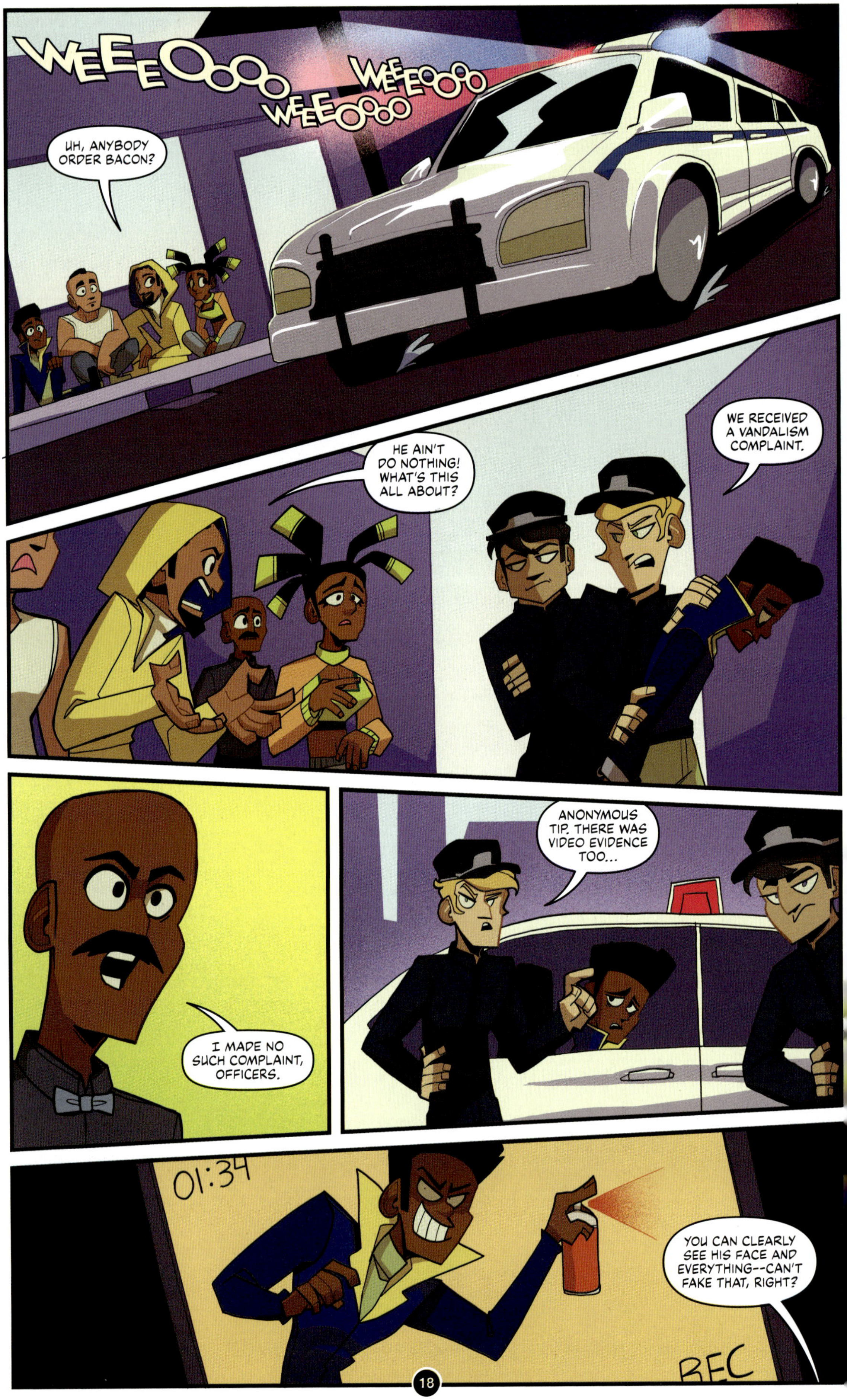
WEEEOOOO
WEEEOOOO
WEEEOOOO
UH, ANYBODY ORDER BACON?
HE AIN'T DO NOTHING! WHAT'S THIS ALL ABOUT?
WE RECEIVED A VANDALISM COMPLAINT.
I MADE NO SUCH COMPLAINT, OFFICERS.
ANONYMOUS TIP. THERE WAS VIDEO EVIDENCE TOO...
01:34
YOU CAN CLEARLY SEE HIS FACE AND EVERYTHING--CAN'T FAKE THAT, RIGHT?
REC

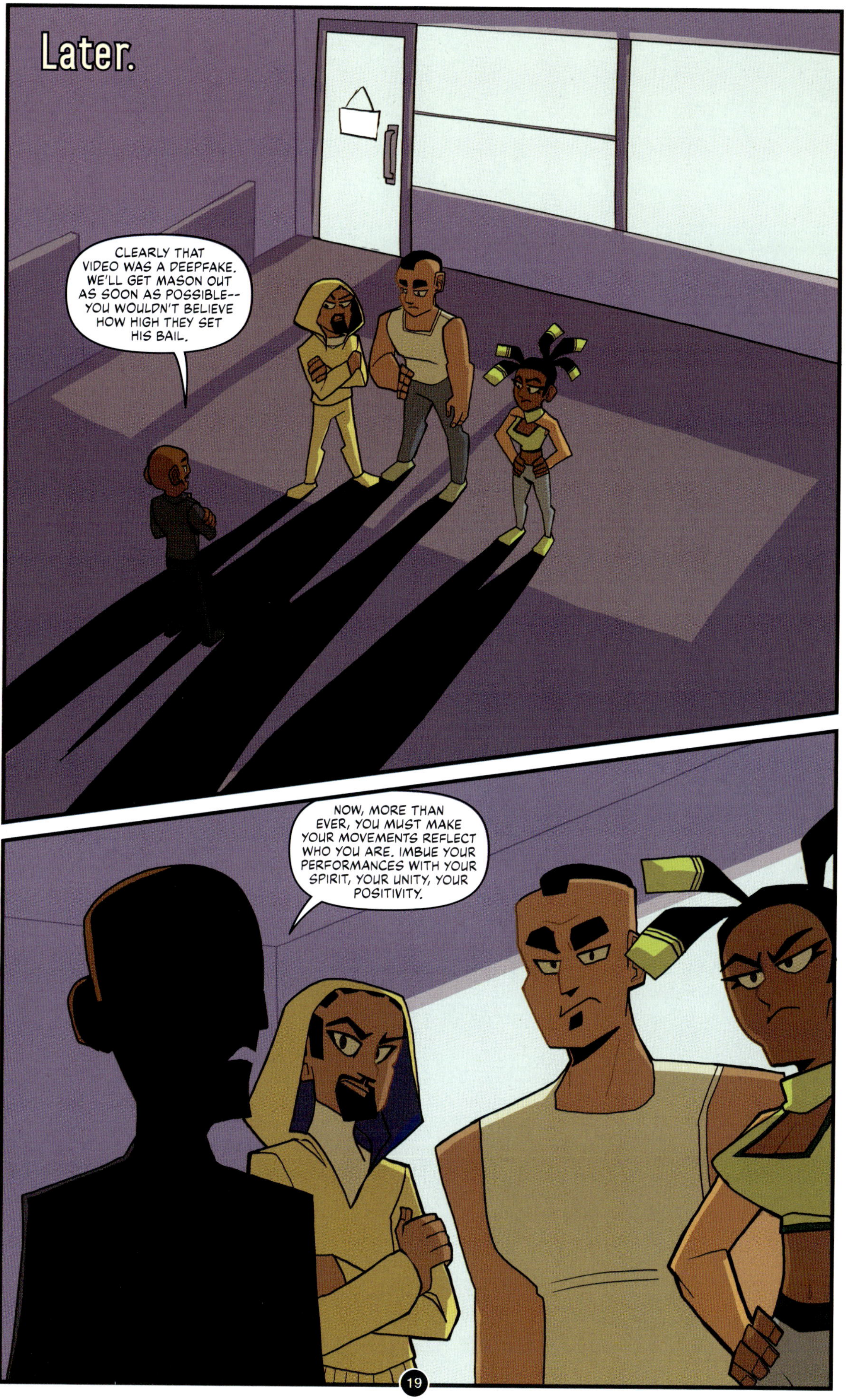
Later.
CLEARLY THAT VIDEO WAS A DEEPFAKE. WE'LL GET MASON OUT AS SOON AS POSSIBLE--YOU WOULDN'T BELIEVE HOW HIGH THEY SET HIS BAIL.
NOW, MORE THAN EVER, YOU MUST MAKE YOUR MOVEMENTS REFLECT WHO YOU ARE. IMBUE YOUR PERFORMANCES WITH YOUR SPIRIT, YOUR UNITY, YOUR POSITIVITY.

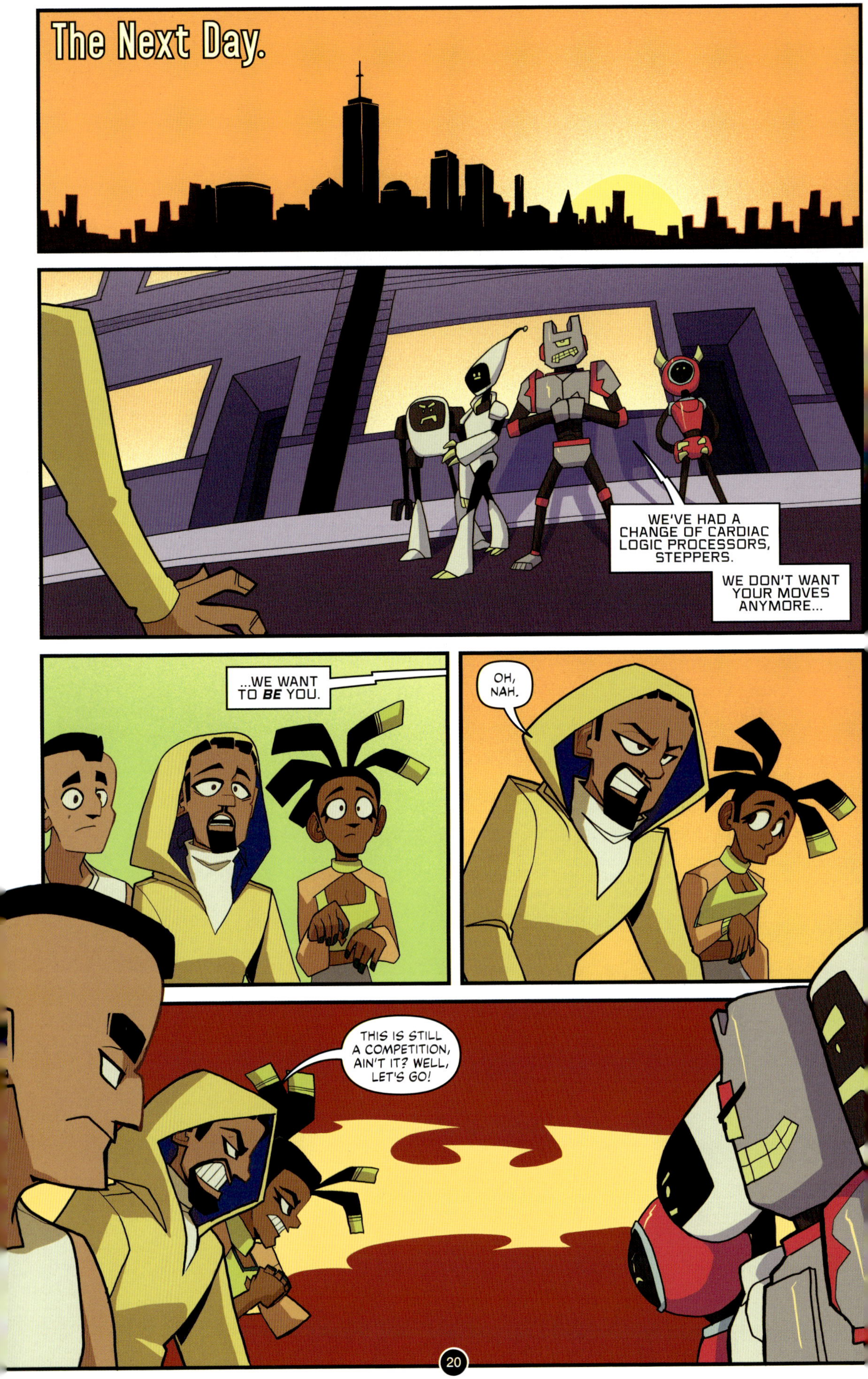
The Next Day.
WE'VE HAD A CHANGE OF CARDIAC LOGIC PROCESSORS, STEPPERS.
WE DON'T WANT YOUR MOVES ANYMORE...
...WE WANT TO *BE* YOU.
OH, NAH.
THIS IS STILL A COMPETITION, AIN'T IT? WELL, LET'S GO!

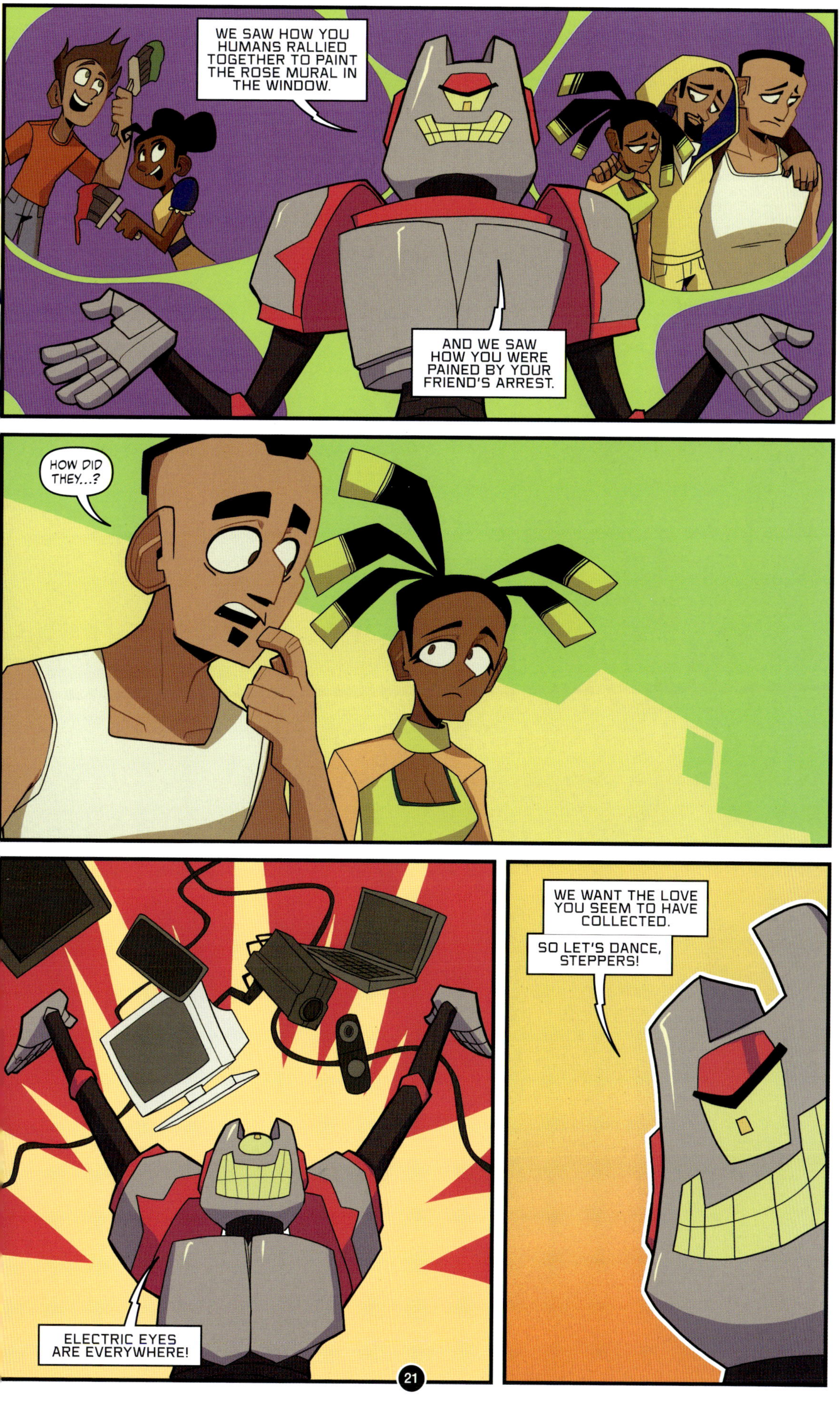
WE SAW HOW YOU HUMANS RALLIED TOGETHER TO PAINT THE ROSE MURAL IN THE WINDOW.
AND WE SAW HOW YOU WERE PAINED BY YOUR FRIEND'S ARREST.
HOW DID THEY...?
ELECTRIC EYES ARE EVERYWHERE!
WE WANT THE LOVE YOU SEEM TO HAVE COLLECTED.
SO LET'S DANCE, STEPPERS!

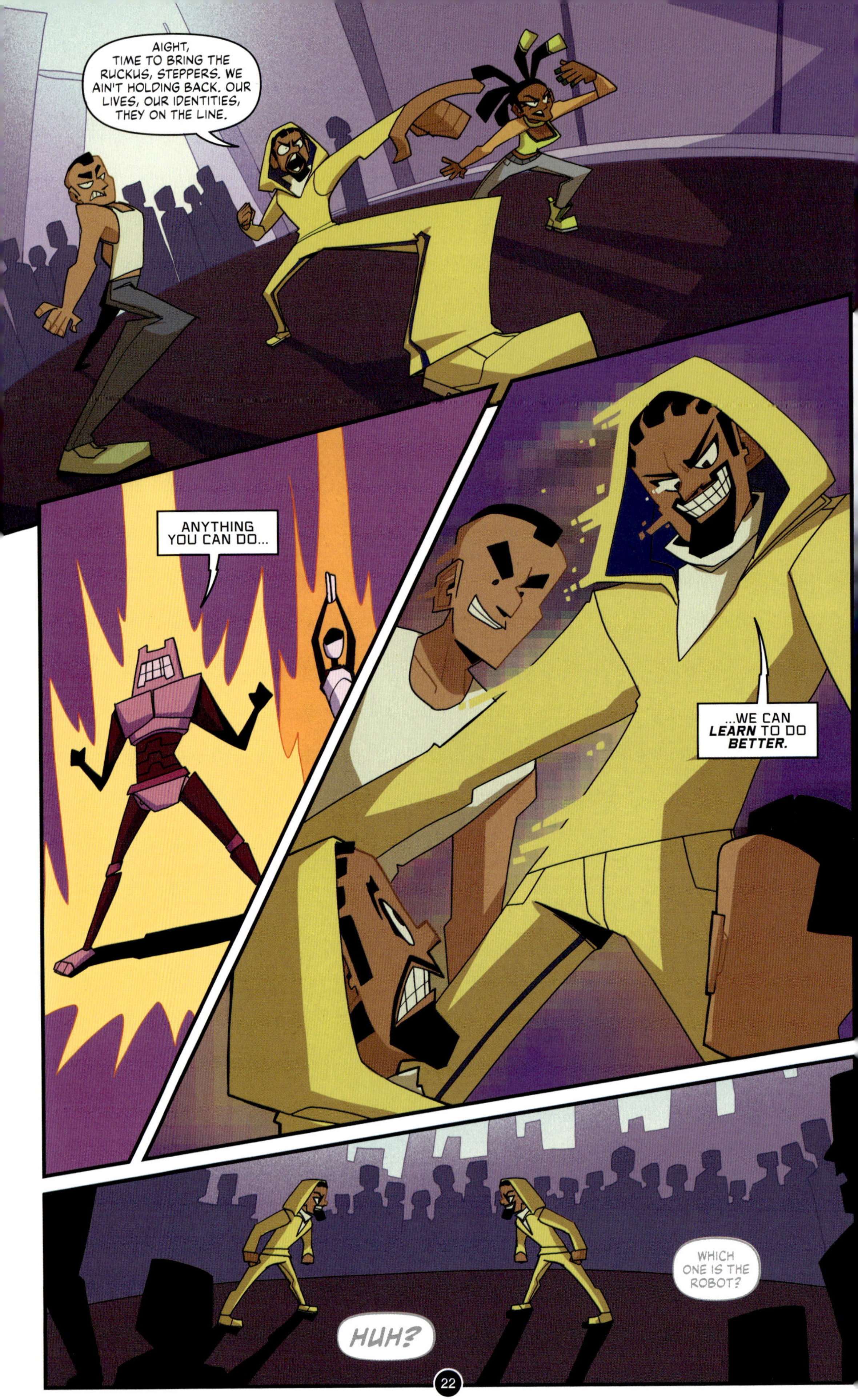
AIGHT, TIME TO BRING THE RUCKUS, STEPPERS. WE AIN'T HOLDING BACK. OUR LIVES, OUR IDENTITIES, THEY ON THE LINE.
ANYTHING YOU CAN DO...
...WE CAN **LEARN** TO DO **BETTER.**
WHICH ONE IS THE ROBOT?
HUH?

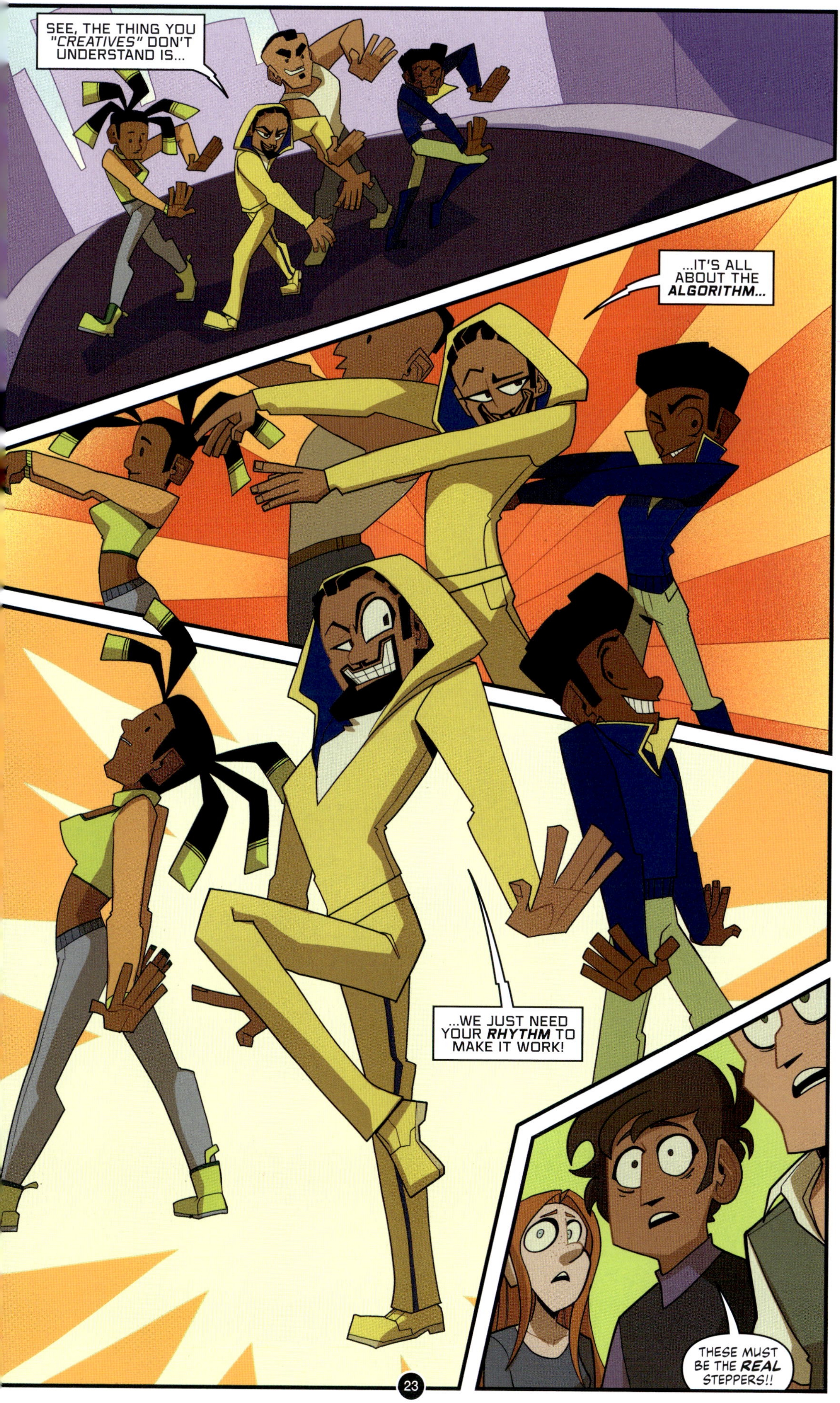
SEE, THE THING YOU "*CREATIVES*" DON'T UNDERSTAND IS...
...IT'S ALL ABOUT THE ***ALGORITHM...***
...WE JUST NEED YOUR ***RHYTHM*** TO MAKE IT WORK!
THESE MUST BE THE ***REAL*** STEPPERS!!

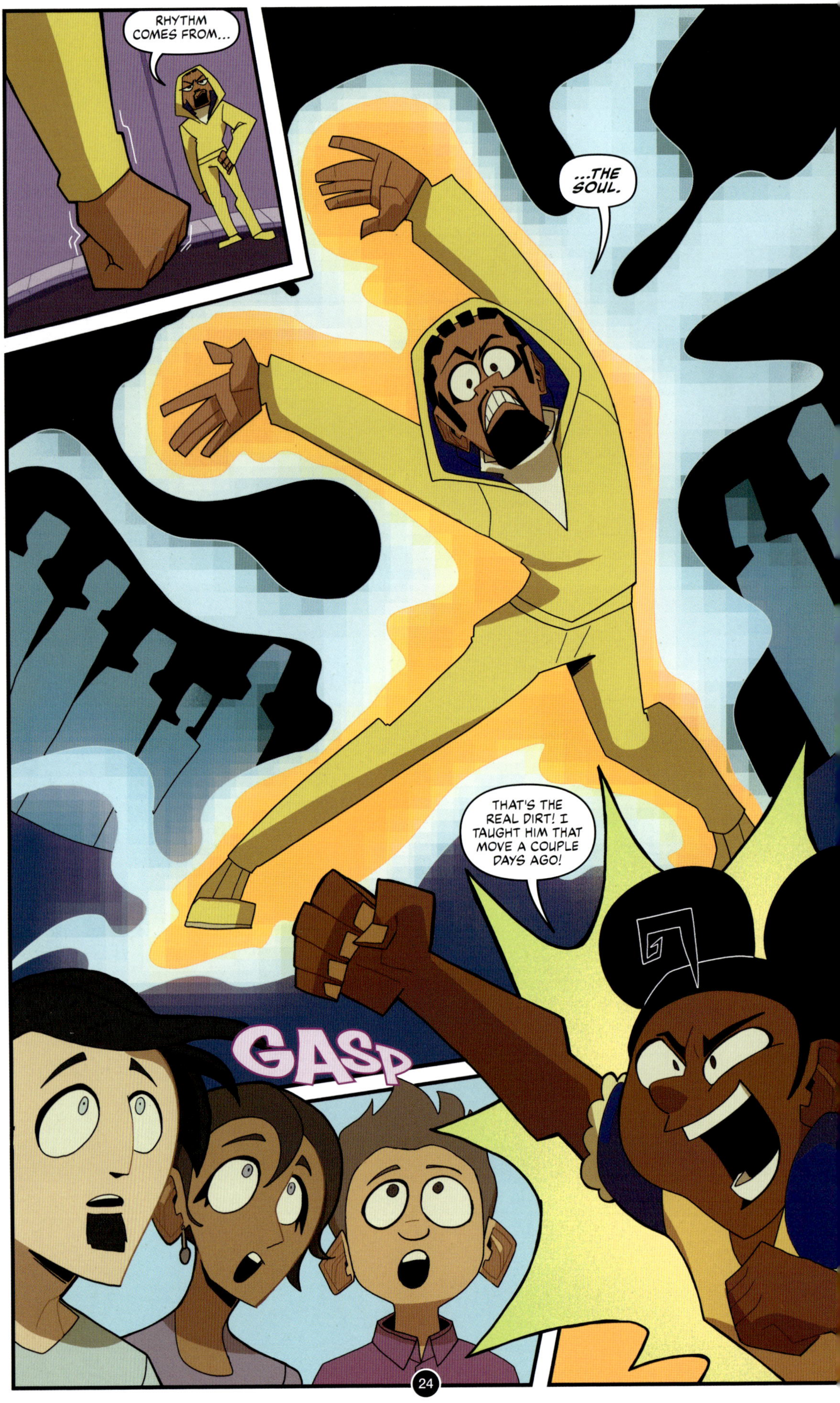
RHYTHM COMES FROM...
...THE SOUL.
THAT'S THE REAL DIRT! I TAUGHT HIM THAT MOVE A COUPLE DAYS AGO!
GASP

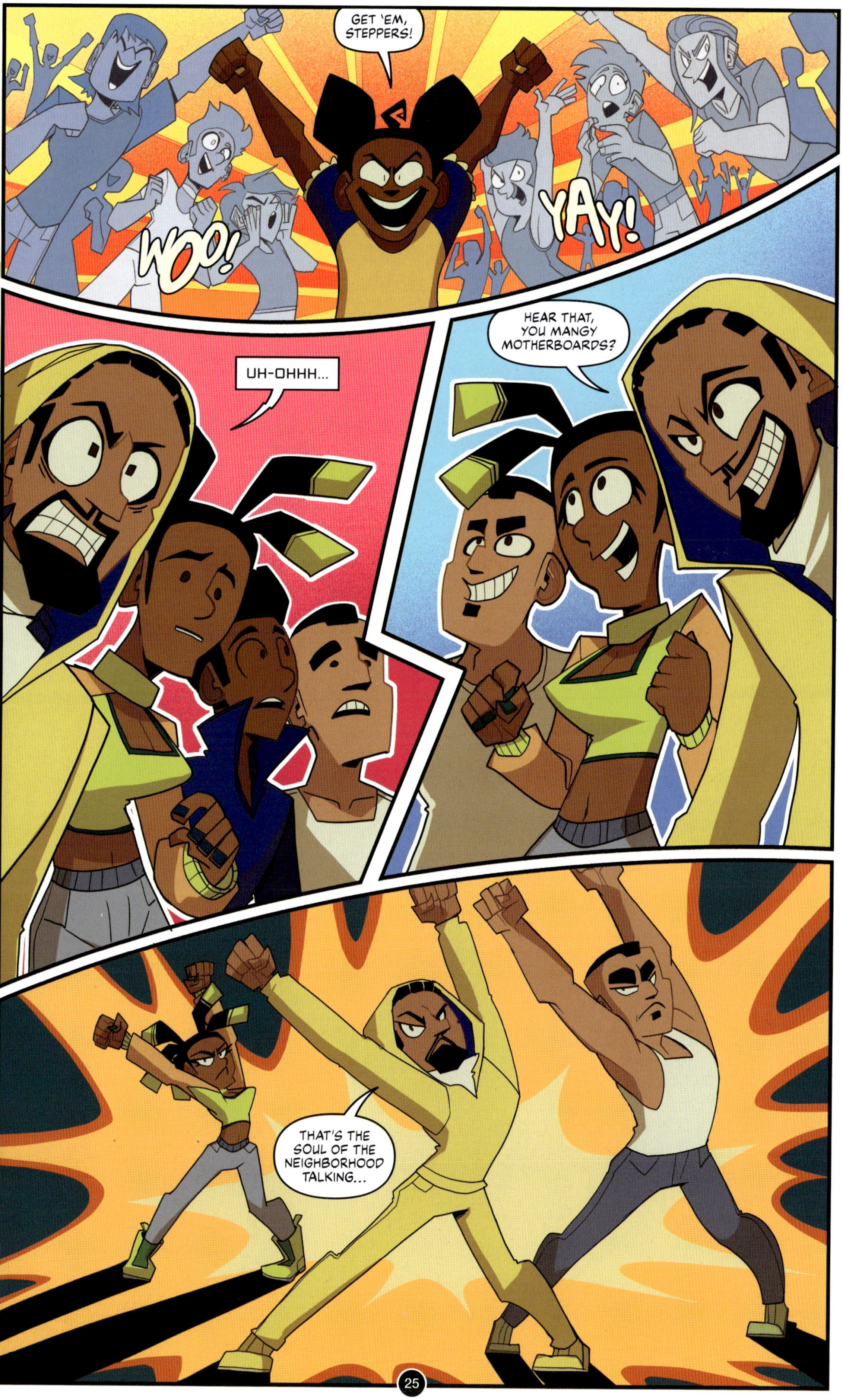
GET 'EM, STEPPERS!
WOO!
YAY!
UH-OHHH...
HEAR THAT, YOU MANGY MOTHERBOARDS?
THAT'S THE SOUL OF THE NEIGHBORHOOD TALKING...

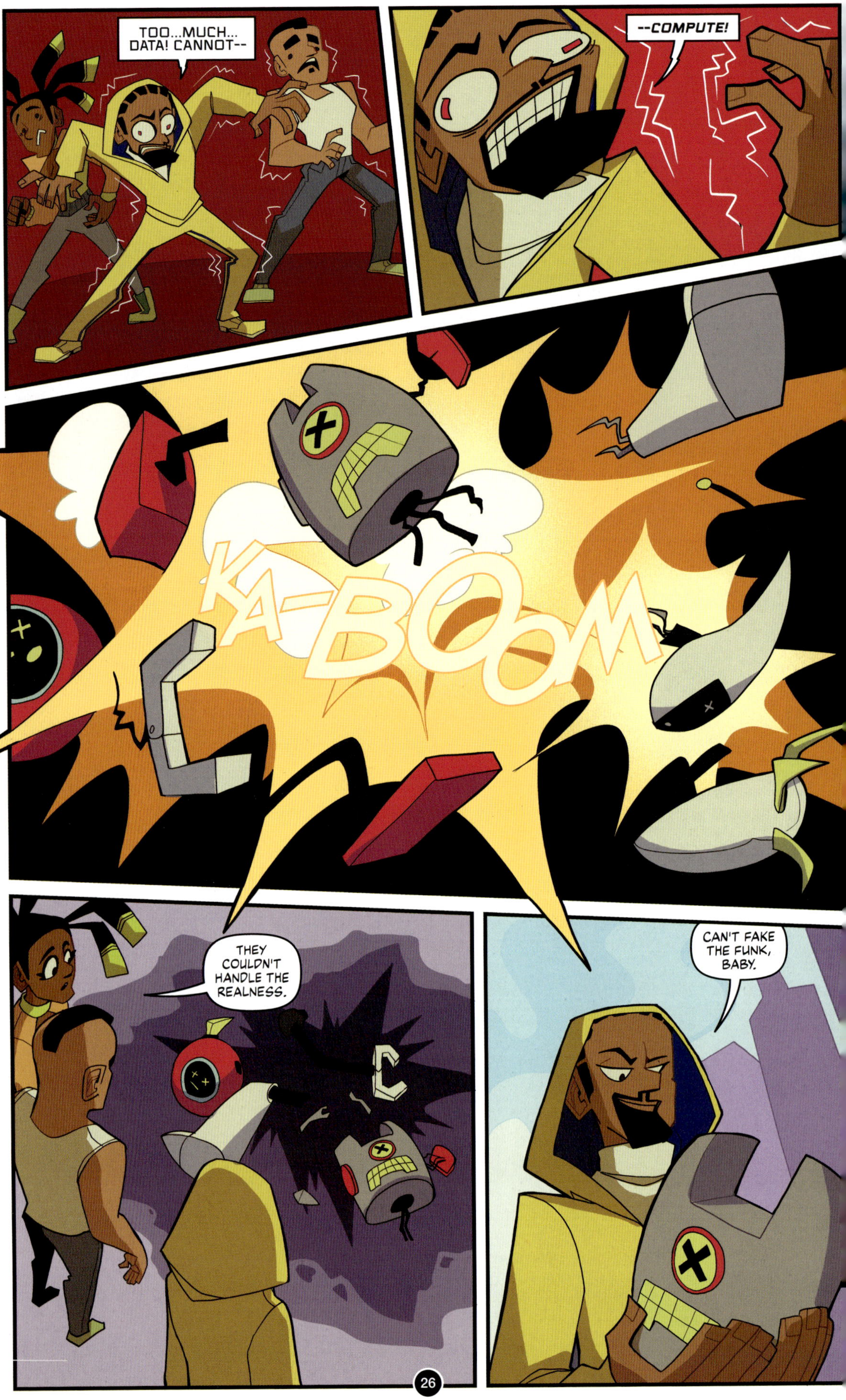

TOO...MUCH... DATA! CANNOT--
--COMPUTE!
KA-BOOM
THEY COULDN'T HANDLE THE REALNESS.
CAN'T FAKE THE FUNK, BABY.

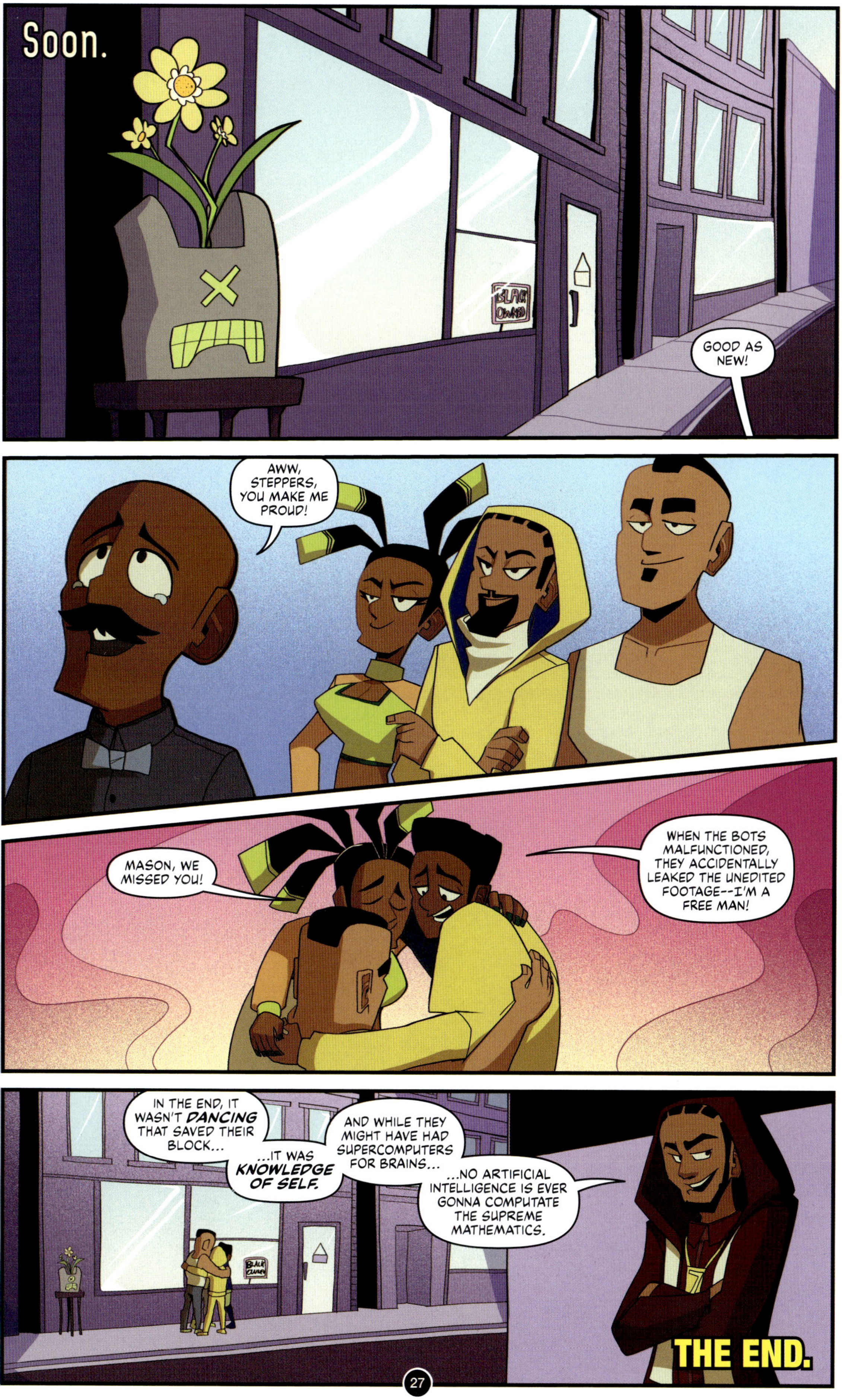
Soon.
BLACK OWNED
GOOD AS NEW!
AWW, STEPPERS, YOU MAKE ME PROUD!
MASON, WE MISSED YOU!
WHEN THE BOTS MALFUNCTIONED, THEY ACCIDENTALLY LEAKED THE UNEDITED FOOTAGE--I'M A FREE MAN!
IN THE END, IT WASN'T ***DANCING*** THAT SAVED THEIR BLOCK...
...IT WAS ***KNOWLEDGE OF SELF.***
AND WHILE THEY MIGHT HAVE HAD SUPERCOMPUTERS FOR BRAINS...
...NO ARTIFICIAL INTELLIGENCE IS EVER GONNA COMPUTATE THE SUPREME MATHEMATICS.
BLACK OWNED
THE END.

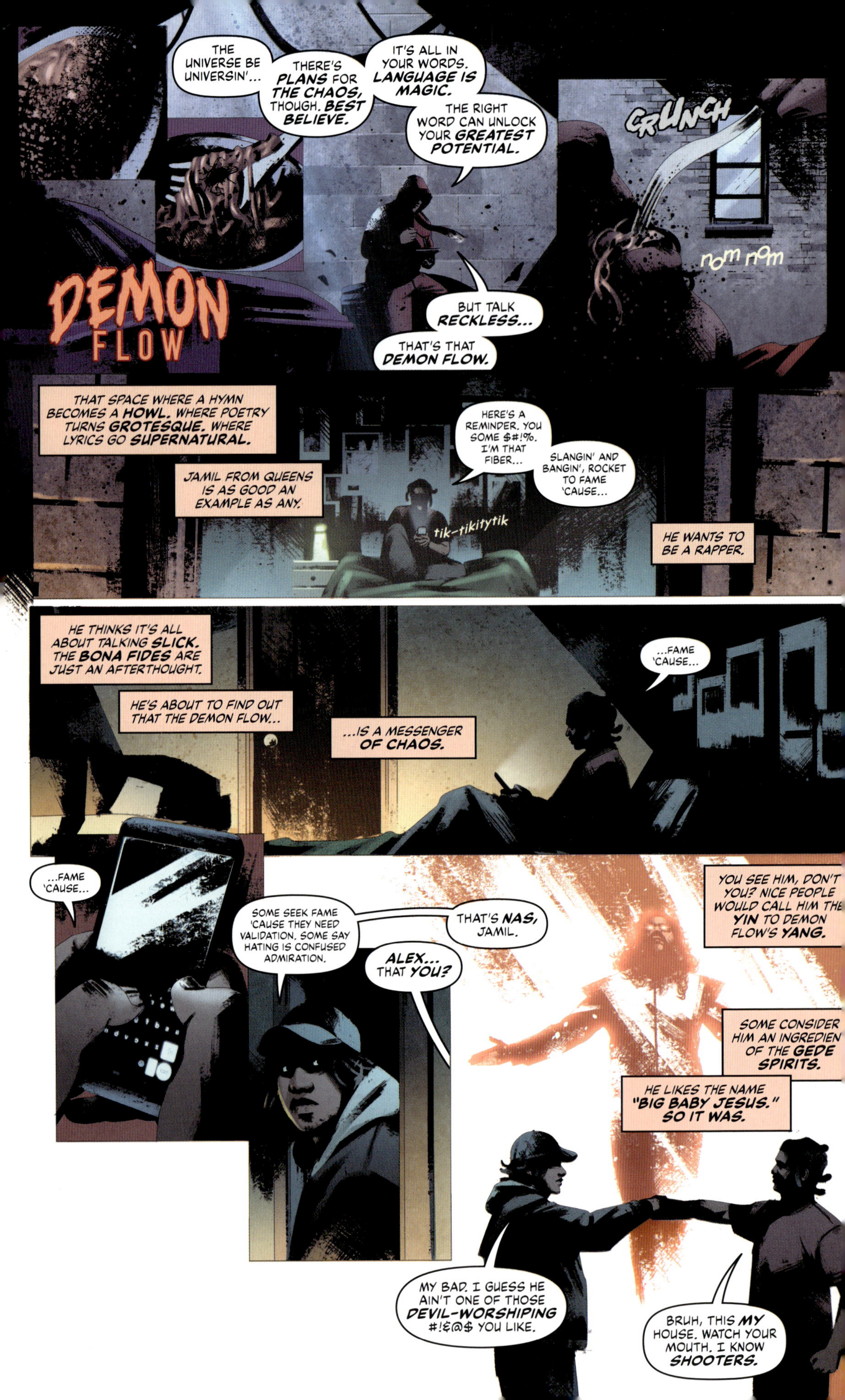

THE UNIVERSE BE UNIVERSIN'...
THERE'S PLANS FOR THE CHAOS, THOUGH. BEST BELIEVE.
IT'S ALL IN YOUR WORDS. LANGUAGE IS MAGIC.
THE RIGHT WORD CAN UNLOCK YOUR GREATEST POTENTIAL.
CRUNCH
nom nom
DEMON FLOW
BUT TALK RECKLESS...
THAT'S THAT DEMON FLOW.
THAT SPACE WHERE A HYMN BECOMES A HOWL. WHERE POETRY TURNS GROTESQUE. WHERE LYRICS GO SUPERNATURAL.
JAMIL FROM QUEENS IS AS GOOD AN EXAMPLE AS ANY.
HERE'S A REMINDER. YOU SOME $#!%. I'M THAT FIBER...
tik-tikitytik
SLANGIN' AND BANGIN', ROCKET TO FAME 'CAUSE...
HE WANTS TO BE A RAPPER.
HE THINKS IT'S ALL ABOUT TALKING SLICK. THE BONA FIDES ARE JUST AN AFTERTHOUGHT.
HE'S ABOUT TO FIND OUT THAT THE DEMON FLOW...
...IS A MESSENGER OF CHAOS.
...FAME 'CAUSE...
...FAME 'CAUSE...
SOME SEEK FAME 'CAUSE THEY NEED VALIDATION. SOME SAY HATING IS CONFUSED ADMIRATION.
THAT'S NAS, JAMIL.
ALEX... THAT YOU?
YOU SEE HIM, DON'T YOU? NICE PEOPLE WOULD CALL HIM THE YIN TO DEMON FLOW'S YANG.
SOME CONSIDER HIM AN INGREDIEN OF THE GEDE SPIRITS.
HE LIKES THE NAME "BIG BABY JESUS." SO IT WAS.
MY BAD. I GUESS HE AIN'T ONE OF THOSE DEVIL-WORSHIPING #!&@$ YOU LIKE.
BRUH, THIS MY HOUSE. WATCH YOUR MOUTH. I KNOW SHOOTERS.

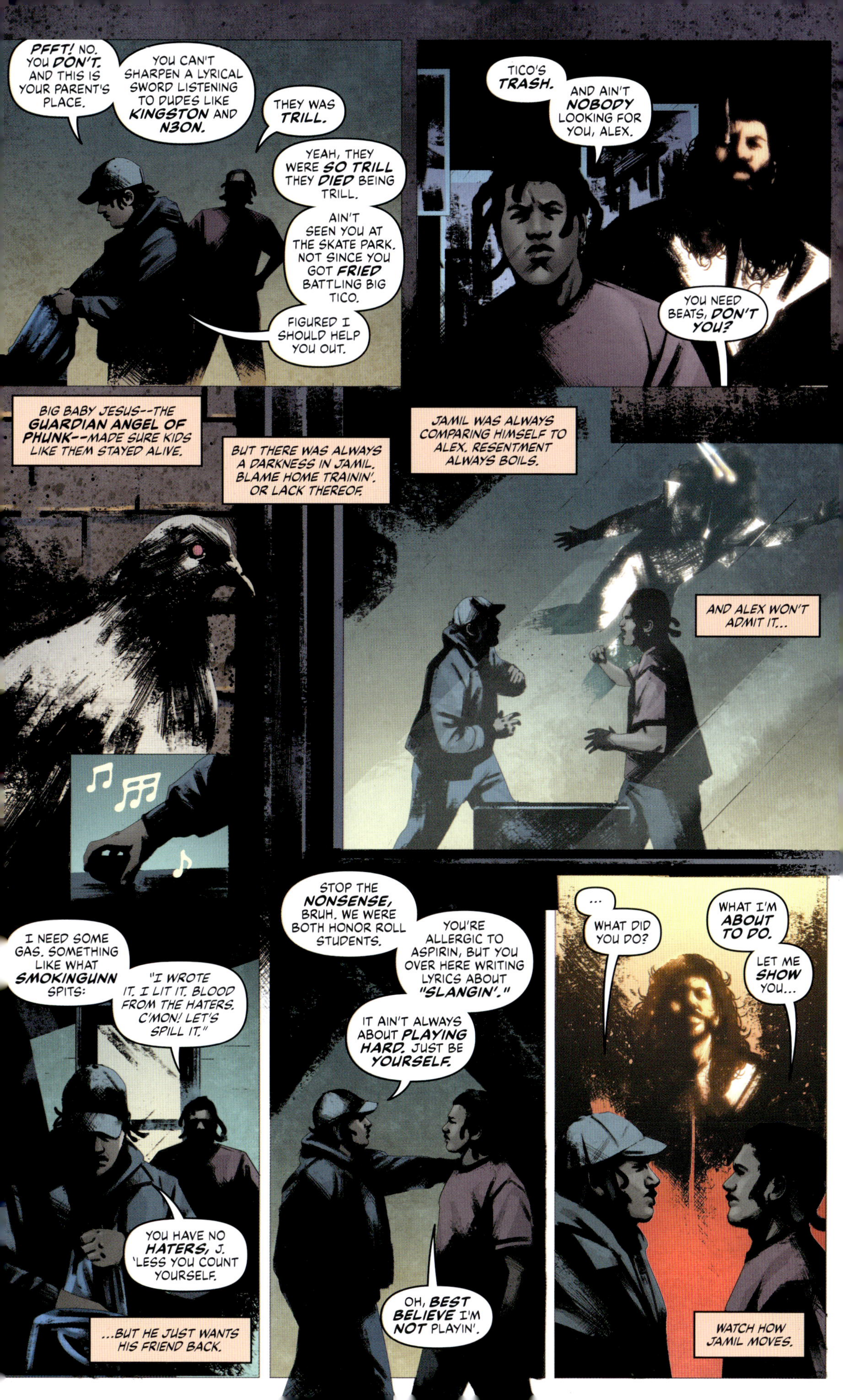
PFFT! NO. YOU DON'T. AND THIS IS YOUR PARENT'S PLACE.
YOU CAN'T SHARPEN A LYRICAL SWORD LISTENING TO DUDES LIKE KINGSTON AND N3ON.
THEY WAS TRILL.
YEAH, THEY WERE SO TRILL THEY DIED BEING TRILL.
AIN'T SEEN YOU AT THE SKATE PARK. NOT SINCE YOU GOT FRIED BATTLING BIG TICO.
FIGURED I SHOULD HELP YOU OUT.
TICO'S TRASH.
AND AIN'T NOBODY LOOKING FOR YOU, ALEX.
YOU NEED BEATS, DON'T YOU?
BIG BABY JESUS--THE GUARDIAN ANGEL OF PHUNK--MADE SURE KIDS LIKE THEM STAYED ALIVE.
BUT THERE WAS ALWAYS A DARKNESS IN JAMIL. BLAME HOME TRAININ'. OR LACK THEREOF.
JAMIL WAS ALWAYS COMPARING HIMSELF TO ALEX. RESENTMENT ALWAYS BOILS.
AND ALEX WON'T ADMIT IT...
I NEED SOME GAS. SOMETHING LIKE WHAT SMOKINGUNN SPITS:
"I WROTE IT. I LIT IT. BLOOD FROM THE HATERS. C'MON! LET'S SPILL IT."
YOU HAVE NO HATERS, J. 'LESS YOU COUNT YOURSELF.
...BUT HE JUST WANTS HIS FRIEND BACK.
STOP THE NONSENSE, BRUH. WE WERE BOTH HONOR ROLL STUDENTS.
YOU'RE ALLERGIC TO ASPIRIN, BUT YOU OVER HERE WRITING LYRICS ABOUT "SLANGIN'."
IT AIN'T ALWAYS ABOUT PLAYING HARD. JUST BE YOURSELF.
OH, BEST BELIEVE I'M NOT PLAYIN'.
... WHAT DID YOU DO?
WHAT I'M ABOUT TO DO.
LET ME SHOW YOU...
WATCH HOW JAMIL MOVES.

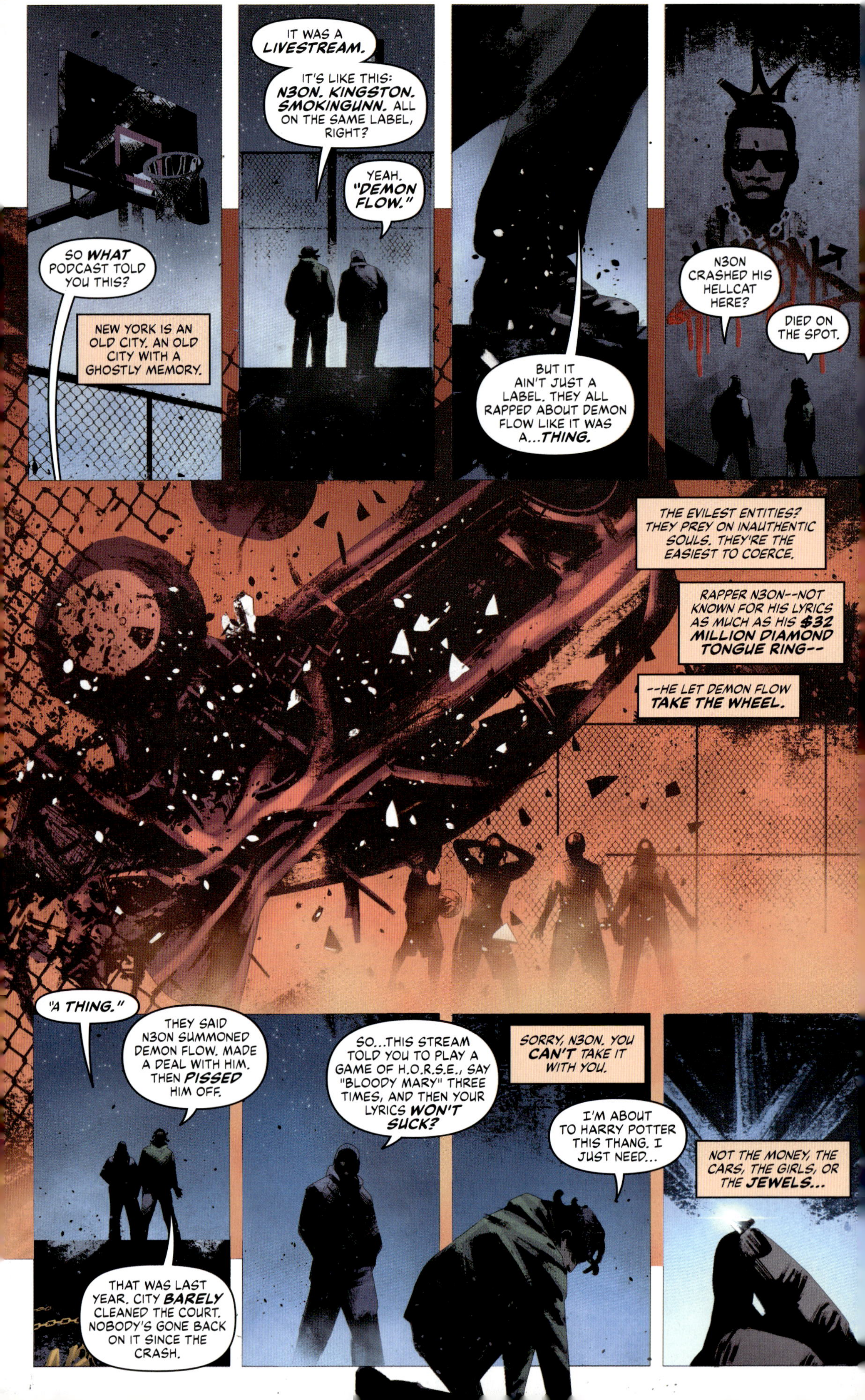
SO WHAT PODCAST TOLD YOU THIS?
NEW YORK IS AN OLD CITY. AN OLD CITY WITH A GHOSTLY MEMORY.
IT WAS A LIVESTREAM.
IT'S LIKE THIS: N3ON. KINGSTON. SMOKINGUNN. ALL ON THE SAME LABEL, RIGHT?
YEAH. "DEMON FLOW."
BUT IT AIN'T JUST A LABEL. THEY ALL RAPPED ABOUT DEMON FLOW LIKE IT WAS A...THING.
N3ON CRASHED HIS HELLCAT HERE?
DIED ON THE SPOT.
THE EVILEST ENTITIES? THEY PREY ON INAUTHENTIC SOULS. THEY'RE THE EASIEST TO COERCE.
RAPPER N3ON--NOT KNOWN FOR HIS LYRICS AS MUCH AS HIS $32 MILLION DIAMOND TONGUE RING--
--HE LET DEMON FLOW TAKE THE WHEEL.
"A THING."
THEY SAID N3ON SUMMONED DEMON FLOW. MADE A DEAL WITH HIM. THEN PISSED HIM OFF.
THAT WAS LAST YEAR. CITY BARELY CLEANED THE COURT. NOBODY'S GONE BACK ON IT SINCE THE CRASH.
SO...THIS STREAM TOLD YOU TO PLAY A GAME OF H.O.R.S.E., SAY "BLOODY MARY" THREE TIMES, AND THEN YOUR LYRICS WON'T SUCK?
SORRY, N3ON. YOU CAN'T TAKE IT WITH YOU.
I'M ABOUT TO HARRY POTTER THIS THANG. I JUST NEED...
NOT THE MONEY, THE CARS, THE GIRLS, OR THE JEWELS...

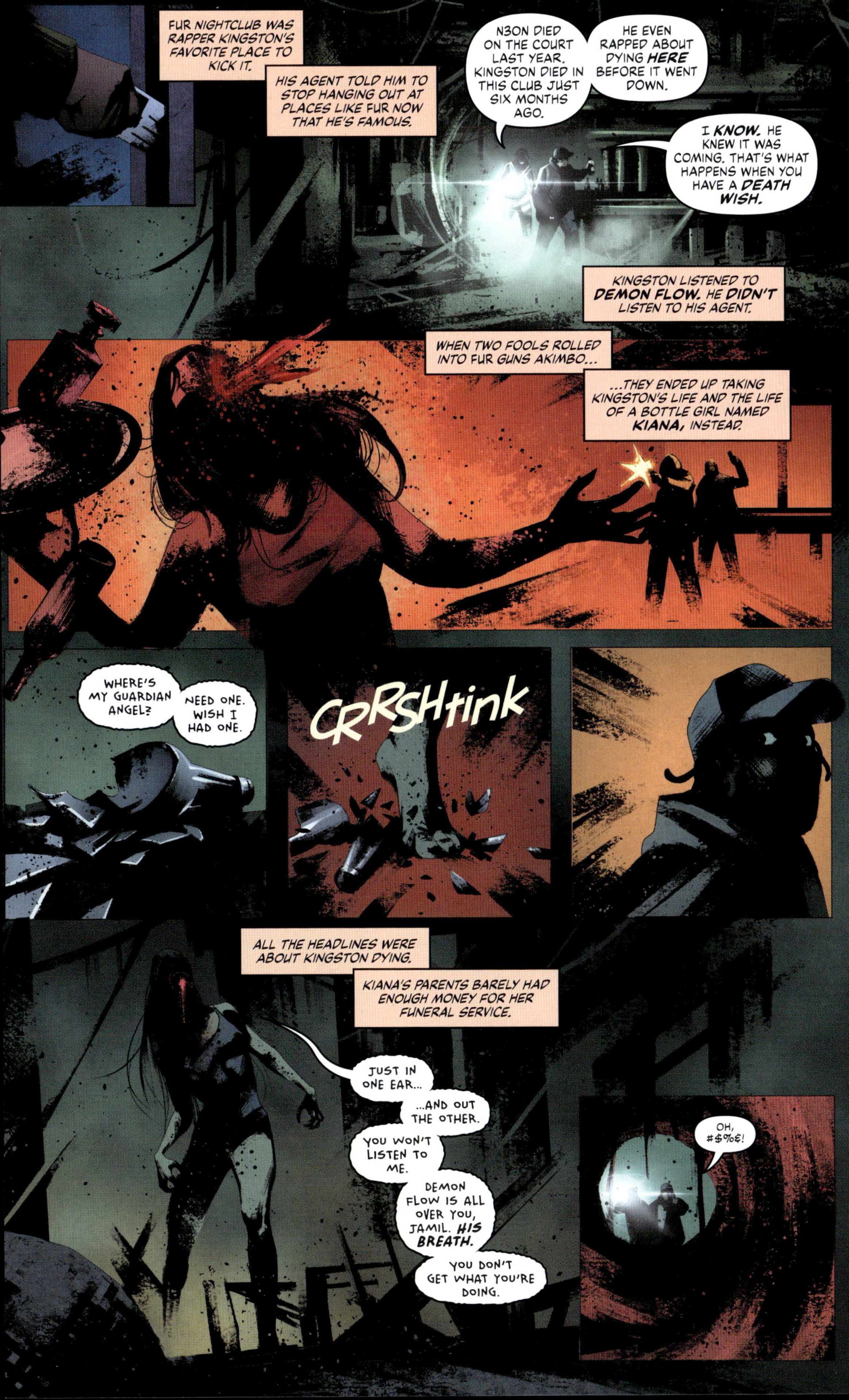
FUR NIGHTCLUB WAS RAPPER KINGSTON'S FAVORITE PLACE TO KICK IT.
HIS AGENT TOLD HIM TO STOP HANGING OUT AT PLACES LIKE FUR NOW THAT HE'S FAMOUS.
N3ON DIED ON THE COURT LAST YEAR. KINGSTON DIED IN THIS CLUB JUST SIX MONTHS AGO.
HE EVEN RAPPED ABOUT DYING HERE BEFORE IT WENT DOWN.
I KNOW. HE KNEW IT WAS COMING. THAT'S WHAT HAPPENS WHEN YOU HAVE A DEATH WISH.
KINGSTON LISTENED TO DEMON FLOW. HE DIDN'T LISTEN TO HIS AGENT.
WHEN TWO FOOLS ROLLED INTO FUR GUNS AKIMBO...
...THEY ENDED UP TAKING KINGSTON'S LIFE AND THE LIFE OF A BOTTLE GIRL NAMED KIANA, INSTEAD.
WHERE'S MY GUARDIAN ANGEL?
NEED ONE. WISH I HAD ONE.
CRRSHtink
ALL THE HEADLINES WERE ABOUT KINGSTON DYING.
KIANA'S PARENTS BARELY HAD ENOUGH MONEY FOR HER FUNERAL SERVICE.
JUST IN ONE EAR...
...AND OUT THE OTHER.
YOU WON'T LISTEN TO ME.
DEMON FLOW IS ALL OVER YOU, JAMIL. HIS BREATH.
YOU DON'T GET WHAT YOU'RE DOING.
OH, #$%&!

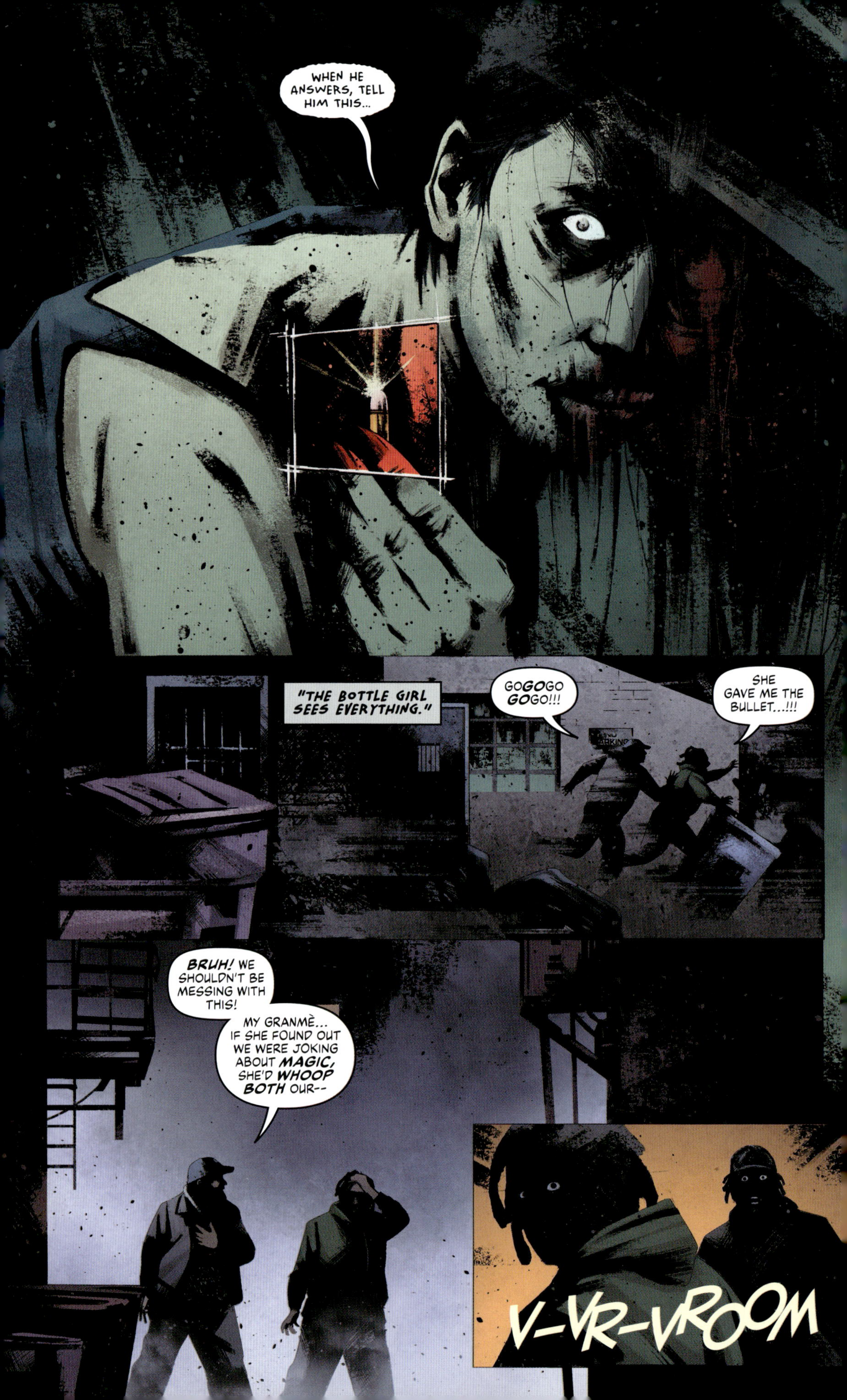
WHEN HE ANSWERS, TELL HIM THIS...
"THE BOTTLE GIRL SEES EVERYTHING."
GOGOGO GOGO!!!
SHE GAVE ME THE BULLET...!!!
BRUH! WE SHOULDN'T BE MESSING WITH THIS!
MY GRANMÈ... IF SHE FOUND OUT WE WERE JOKING ABOUT MAGIC, SHE'D WHOOP BOTH OUR--
V-VR-VROOM

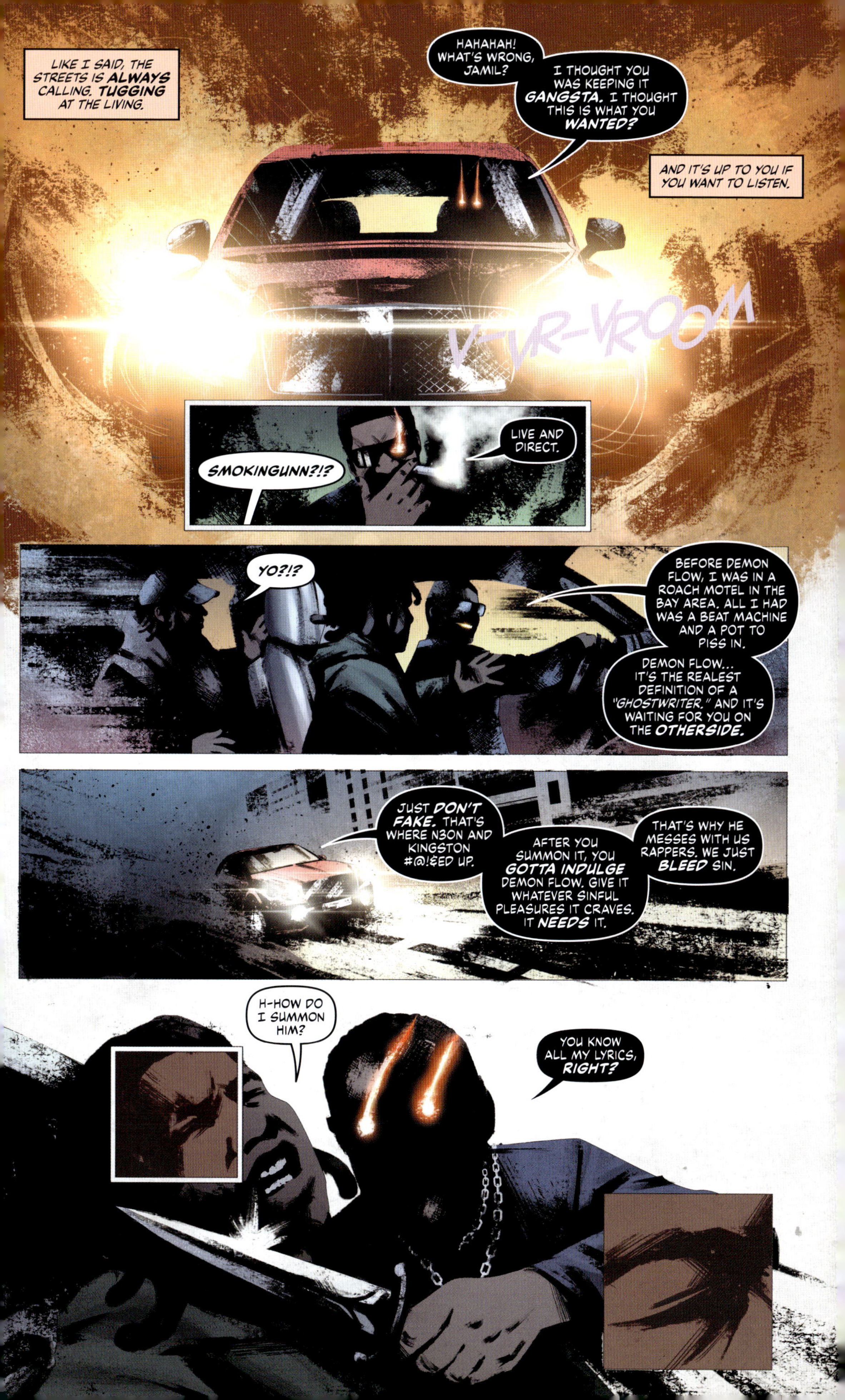
LIKE I SAID, THE STREETS IS ALWAYS CALLING. TUGGING AT THE LIVING.
HAHAHAH! WHAT'S WRONG, JAMIL?
I THOUGHT YOU WAS KEEPING IT GANGSTA. I THOUGHT THIS IS WHAT YOU WANTED?
AND IT'S UP TO YOU IF YOU WANT TO LISTEN.
V-VR-VROOM
SMOKINGUNN?!?
LIVE AND DIRECT.
YO?!?
BEFORE DEMON FLOW, I WAS IN A ROACH MOTEL IN THE BAY AREA. ALL I HAD WAS A BEAT MACHINE AND A POT TO PISS IN.
DEMON FLOW... IT'S THE REALEST DEFINITION OF A "GHOSTWRITER," AND IT'S WAITING FOR YOU ON THE OTHERSIDE.
JUST DON'T FAKE. THAT'S WHERE N3ON AND KINGSTON #@!&ED UP.
AFTER YOU SUMMON IT, YOU GOTTA INDULGE DEMON FLOW. GIVE IT WHATEVER SINFUL PLEASURES IT CRAVES. IT NEEDS IT.
THAT'S WHY HE MESSES WITH US RAPPERS. WE JUST BLEED SIN.
H-HOW DO I SUMMON HIM?
YOU KNOW ALL MY LYRICS, RIGHT?

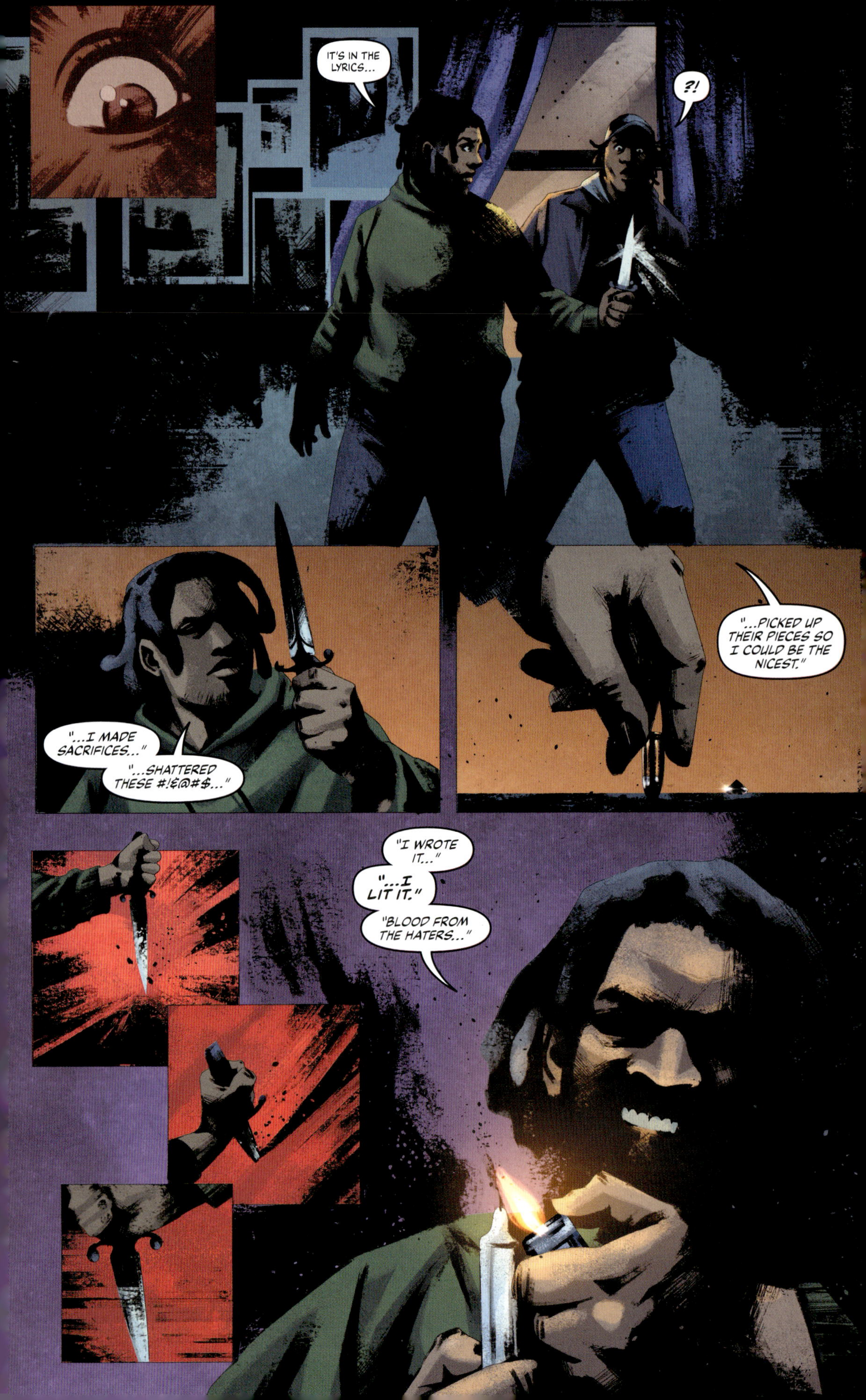
IT'S IN THE LYRICS...
?!
"...I MADE SACRIFICES..."
"...SHATTERED THESE #!&@#$..."
"...PICKED UP THEIR PIECES SO I COULD BE THE NICEST."
"I WROTE IT..."
"...I LIT IT."
"BLOOD FROM THE HATERS..."

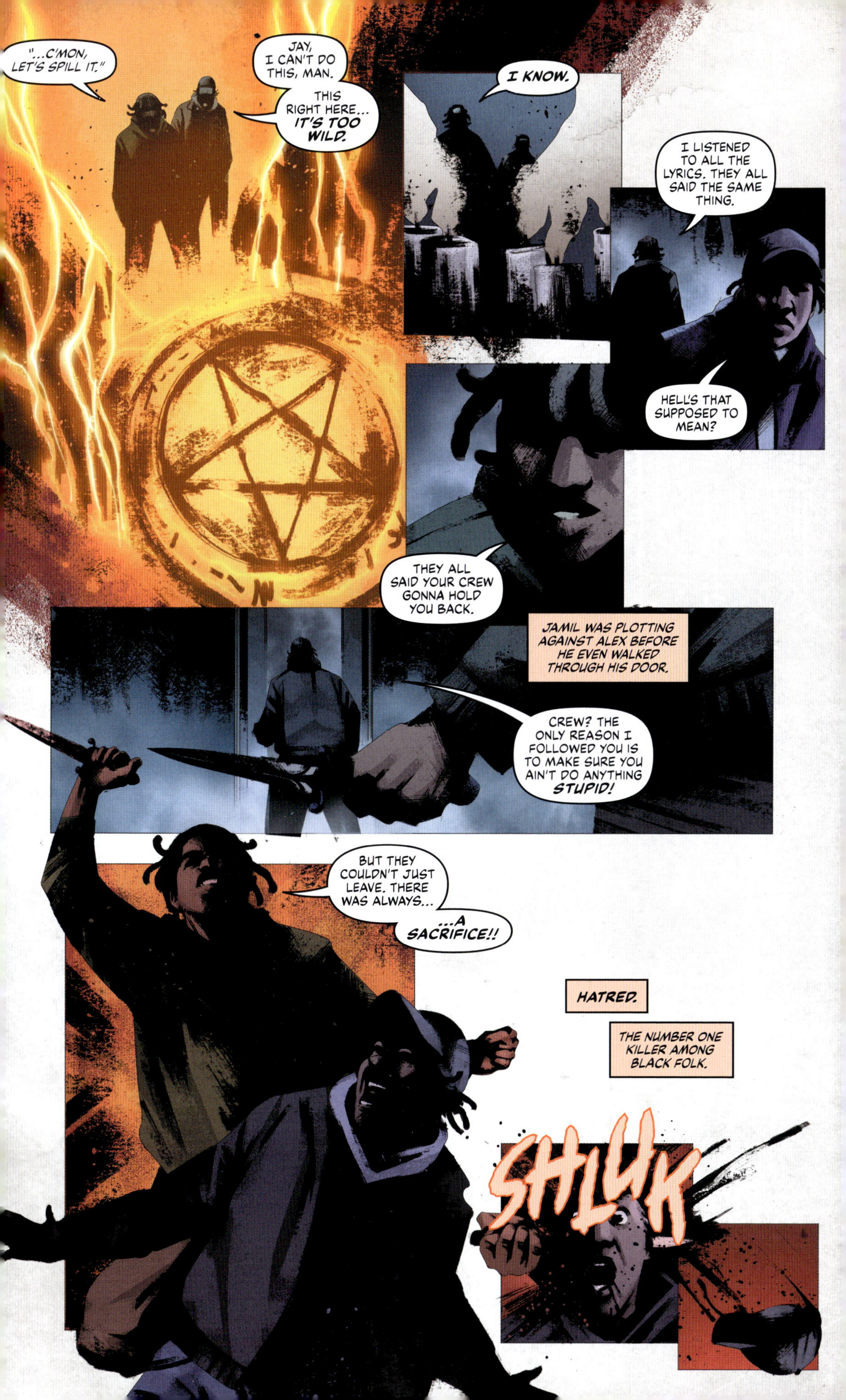
"...C'MON, LET'S SPILL IT."
JAY, I CAN'T DO THIS, MAN.
THIS RIGHT HERE... IT'S TOO WILD.
I KNOW.
I LISTENED TO ALL THE LYRICS. THEY ALL SAID THE SAME THING.
HELL'S THAT SUPPOSED TO MEAN?
THEY ALL SAID YOUR CREW GONNA HOLD YOU BACK.
JAMIL WAS PLOTTING AGAINST ALEX BEFORE HE EVEN WALKED THROUGH HIS DOOR.
CREW? THE ONLY REASON I FOLLOWED YOU IS TO MAKE SURE YOU AIN'T DO ANYTHING STUPID!
BUT THEY COULDN'T JUST LEAVE. THERE WAS ALWAYS...
...A SACRIFICE!!
HATRED.
THE NUMBER ONE KILLER AMONG BLACK FOLK.
SHLUK

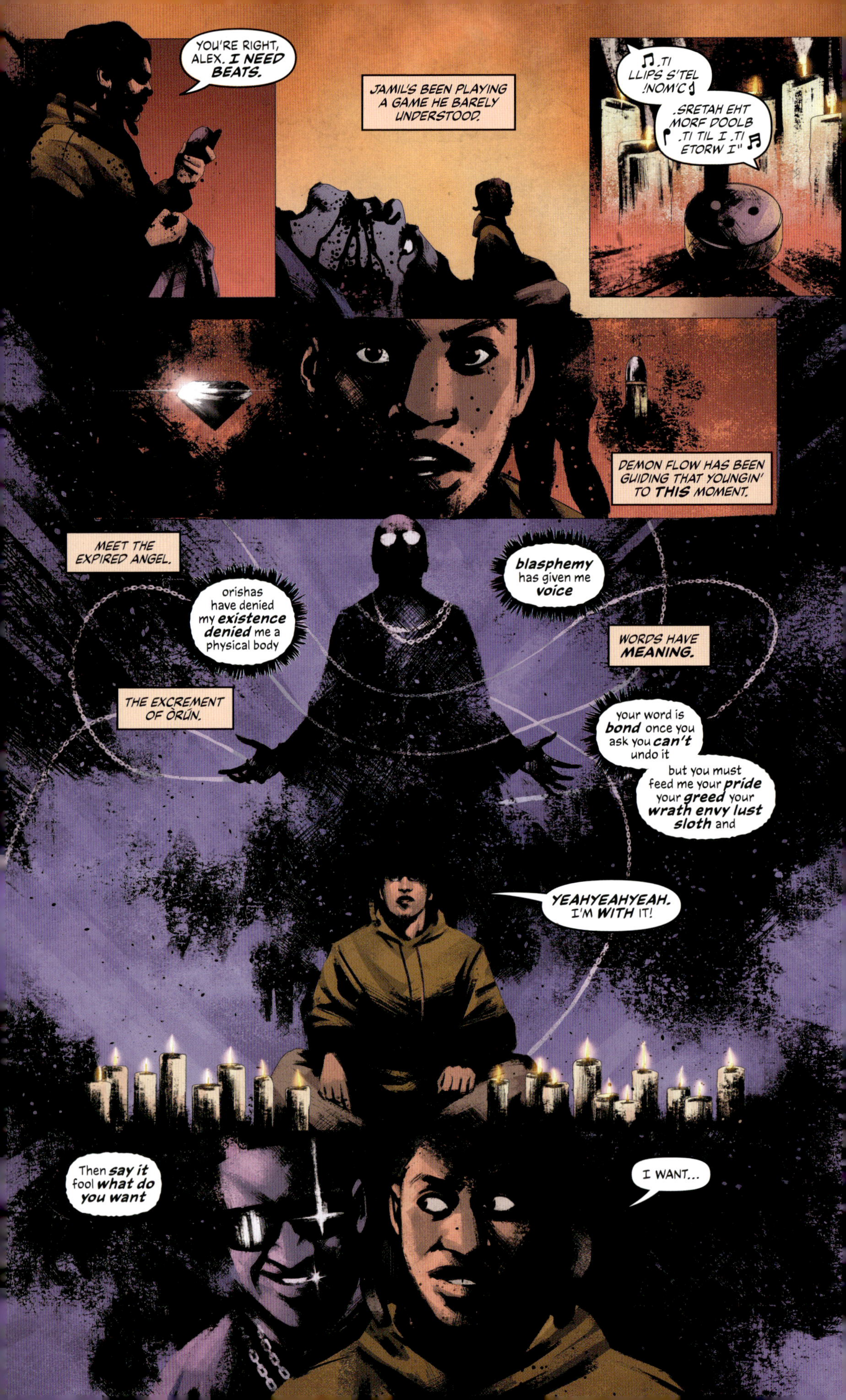
YOU'RE RIGHT, ALEX. I NEED BEATS.
JAMIL'S BEEN PLAYING A GAME HE BARELY UNDERSTOOD.
.TI LLIPS S'TEL !NOM'C
.SRETAH EHT MORF DOOLB .TI TIL I .TI ETORW I"
DEMON FLOW HAS BEEN GUIDING THAT YOUNGIN' TO THIS MOMENT.
MEET THE EXPIRED ANGEL.
blasphemy has given me voice
orishas have denied my existence denied me a physical body
WORDS HAVE MEANING.
THE EXCREMENT OF ÒRÚN.
your word is bond once you ask you can't undo it
but you must feed me your pride your greed your wrath envy lust sloth and
YEAHYEAHYEAH. I'M WITH IT!
Then say it fool what do you want
I WANT...

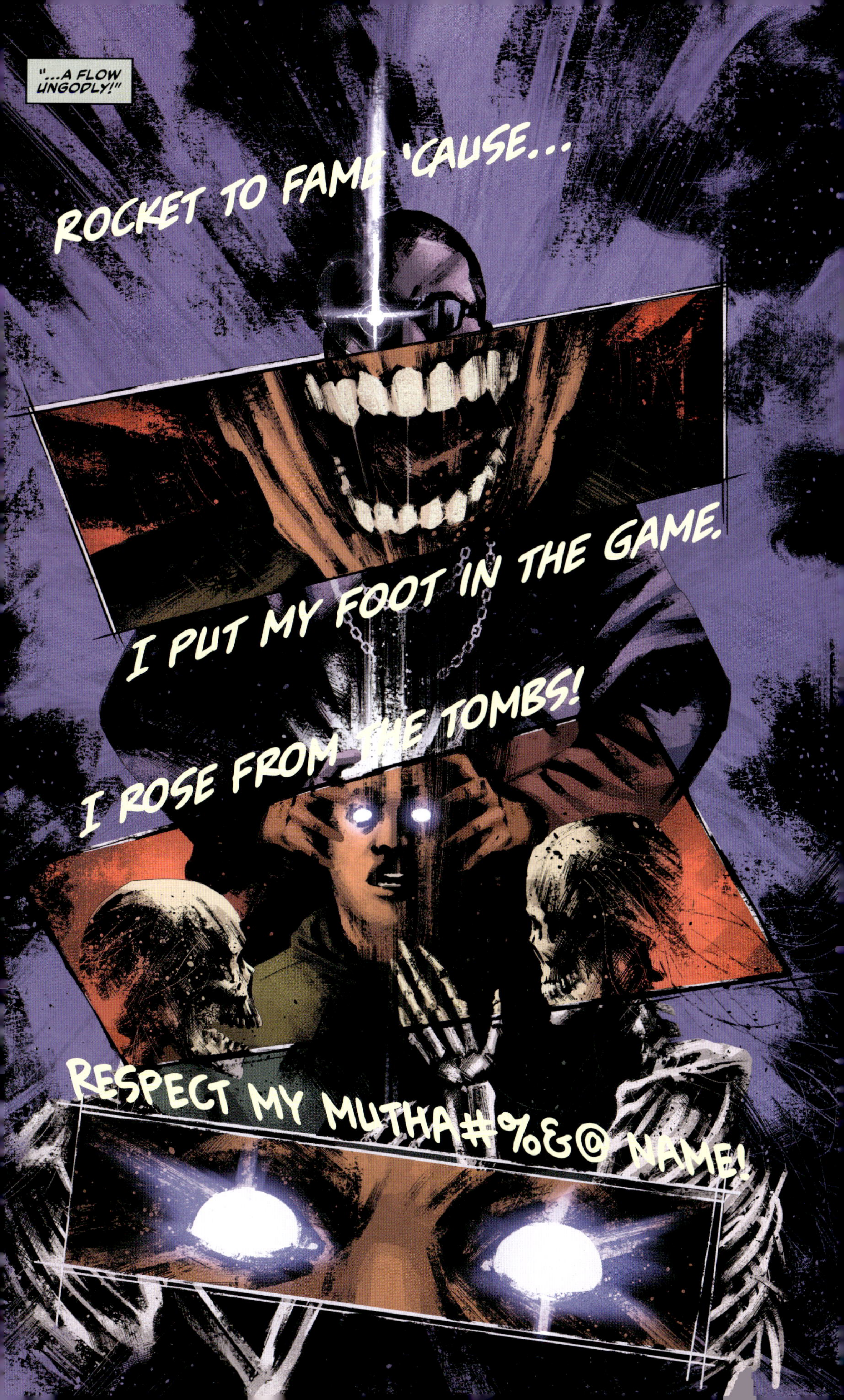
"...A FLOW UNGODLY!"
ROCKET TO FAME 'CAUSE...
I PUT MY FOOT IN THE GAME.
I ROSE FROM THE TOMBS!
RESPECT MY MUTHA#%&@ NAME!

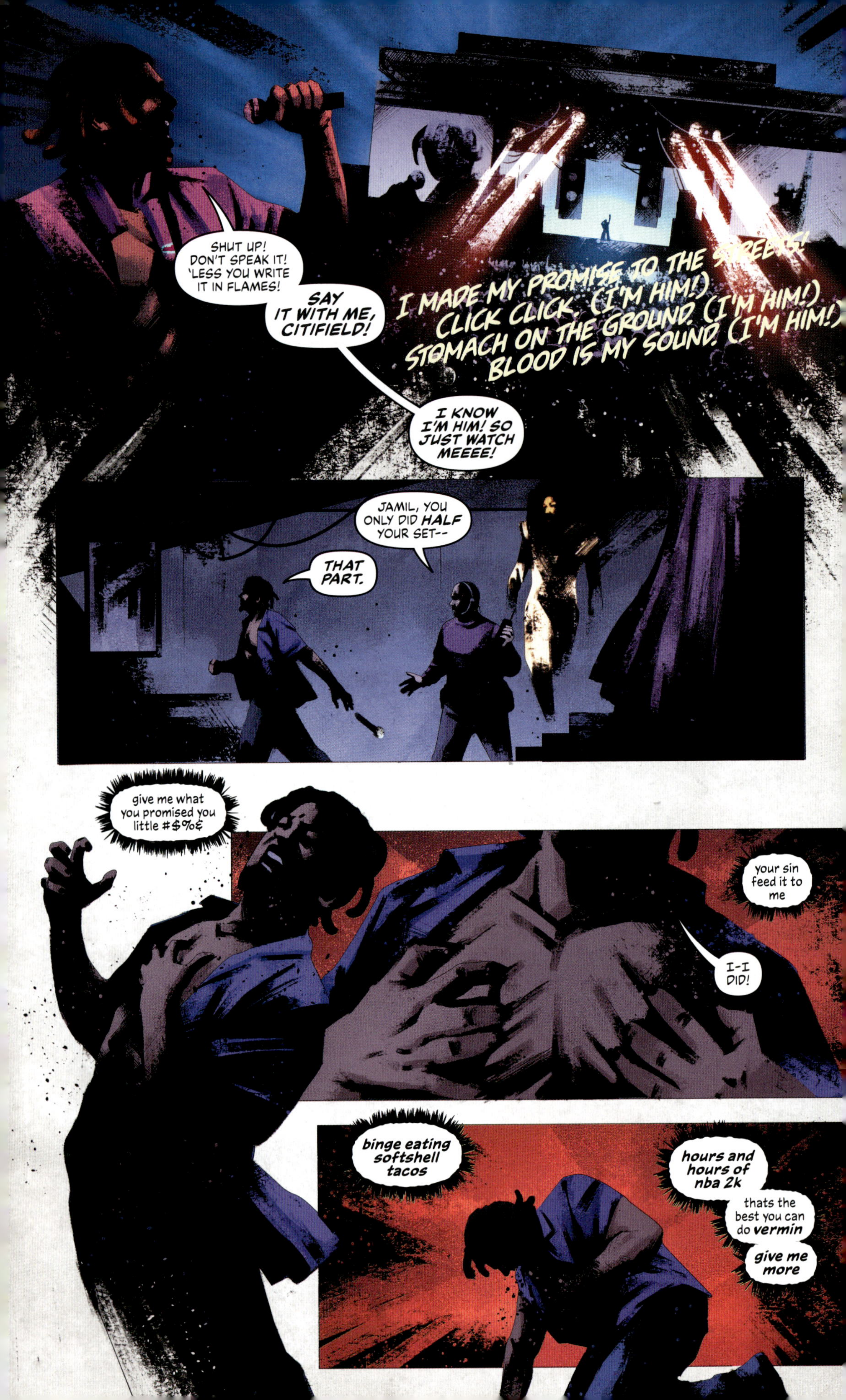
SHUT UP! DON'T SPEAK IT! 'LESS YOU WRITE IT IN FLAMES!
SAY IT WITH ME, CITIFIELD!
I MADE MY PROMISE TO THE STREETS! CLICK CLICK. (I'M HIM!) STOMACH ON THE GROUND. (I'M HIM!) BLOOD IS MY SOUND. (I'M HIM!)
I KNOW I'M HIM! SO JUST WATCH MEEEE!
JAMIL, YOU ONLY DID HALF YOUR SET--
THAT PART.
give me what you promised you little #$%&
your sin feed it to me
I-I DID!
binge eating softshell tacos
hours and hours of nba 2k
thats the best you can do vermin
give me more

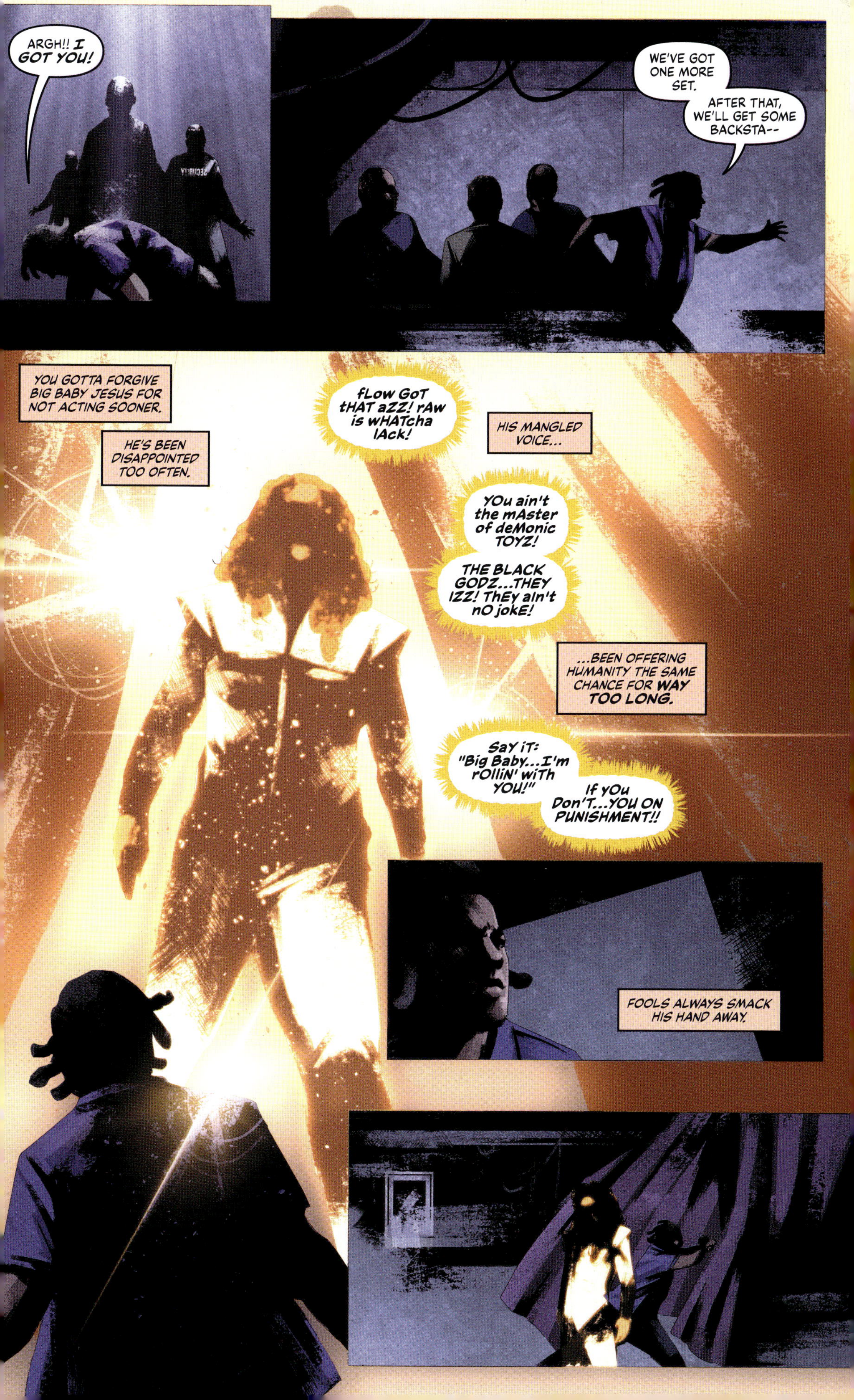
ARGH!! I GOT YOU!
WE'VE GOT ONE MORE SET.
AFTER THAT, WE'LL GET SOME BACKSTA--
YOU GOTTA FORGIVE BIG BABY JESUS FOR NOT ACTING SOONER.
HE'S BEEN DISAPPOINTED TOO OFTEN.
fLow GoT tHAT aZZ! rAw is wHATcha lAck!
HIS MANGLED VOICE...
YOu ain't the mAster of deMonic TOYZ!
THE BLACK GODZ...THEY IZZ! THEy aIn't nO joke!
...BEEN OFFERING HUMANITY THE SAME CHANCE FOR WAY TOO LONG.
Say iT: "Big Baby...I'm rOllin' wiTh YOU!"
If yOu Don'T...YOU ON PUNISHMENT!!
FOOLS ALWAYS SMACK HIS HAND AWAY.

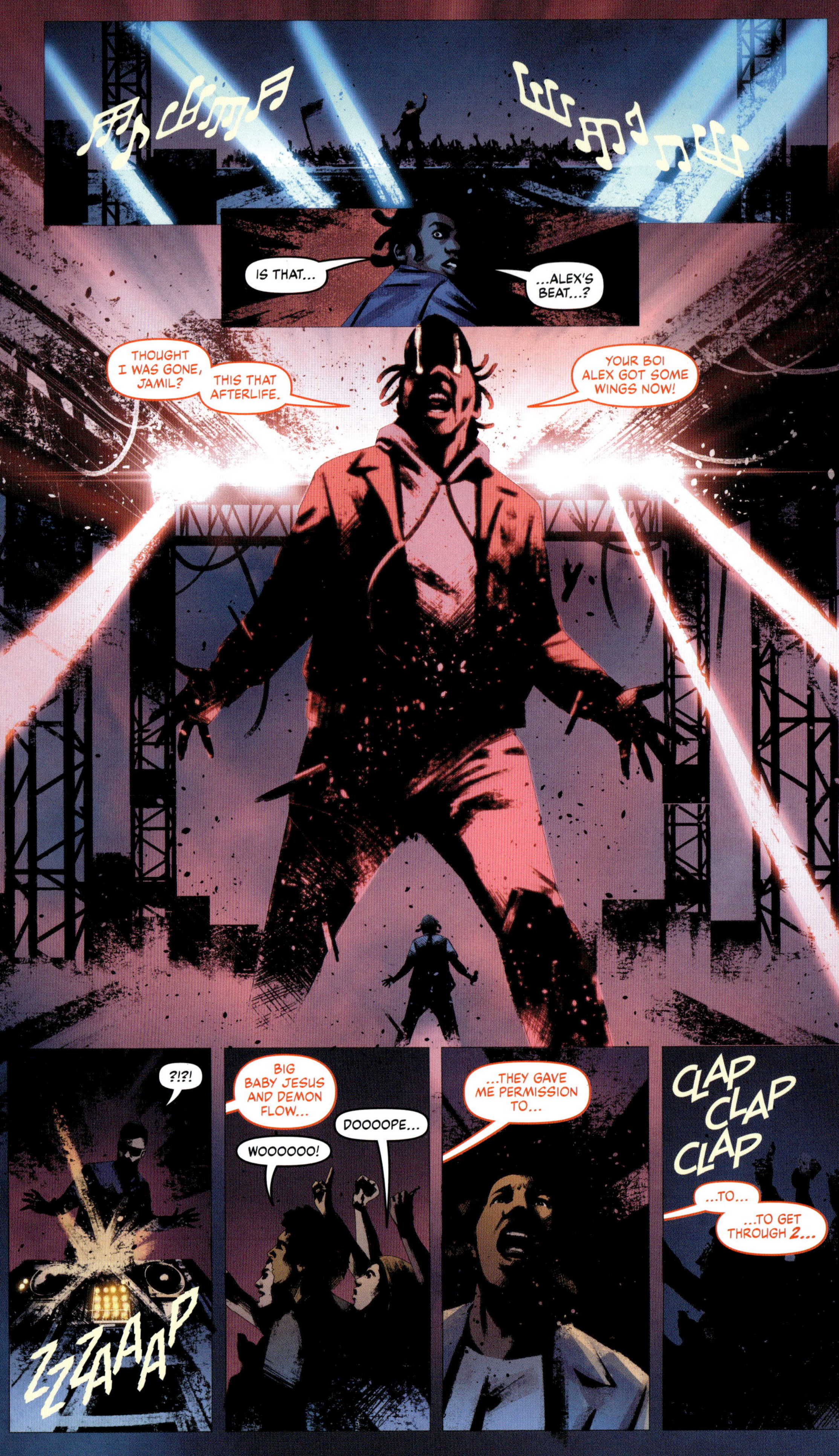
IS THAT...
...ALEX'S BEAT...?
THOUGHT I WAS GONE, JAMIL?
THIS THAT AFTERLIFE.
YOUR BOI ALEX GOT SOME WINGS NOW!
?!?!
ZZZAAAP
BIG BABY JESUS AND DEMON FLOW...
WOOOOOO!
DOOOOPE...
...THEY GAVE ME PERMISSION TO...
CLAP CLAP CLAP
...TO...
...TO GET THROUGH 2...

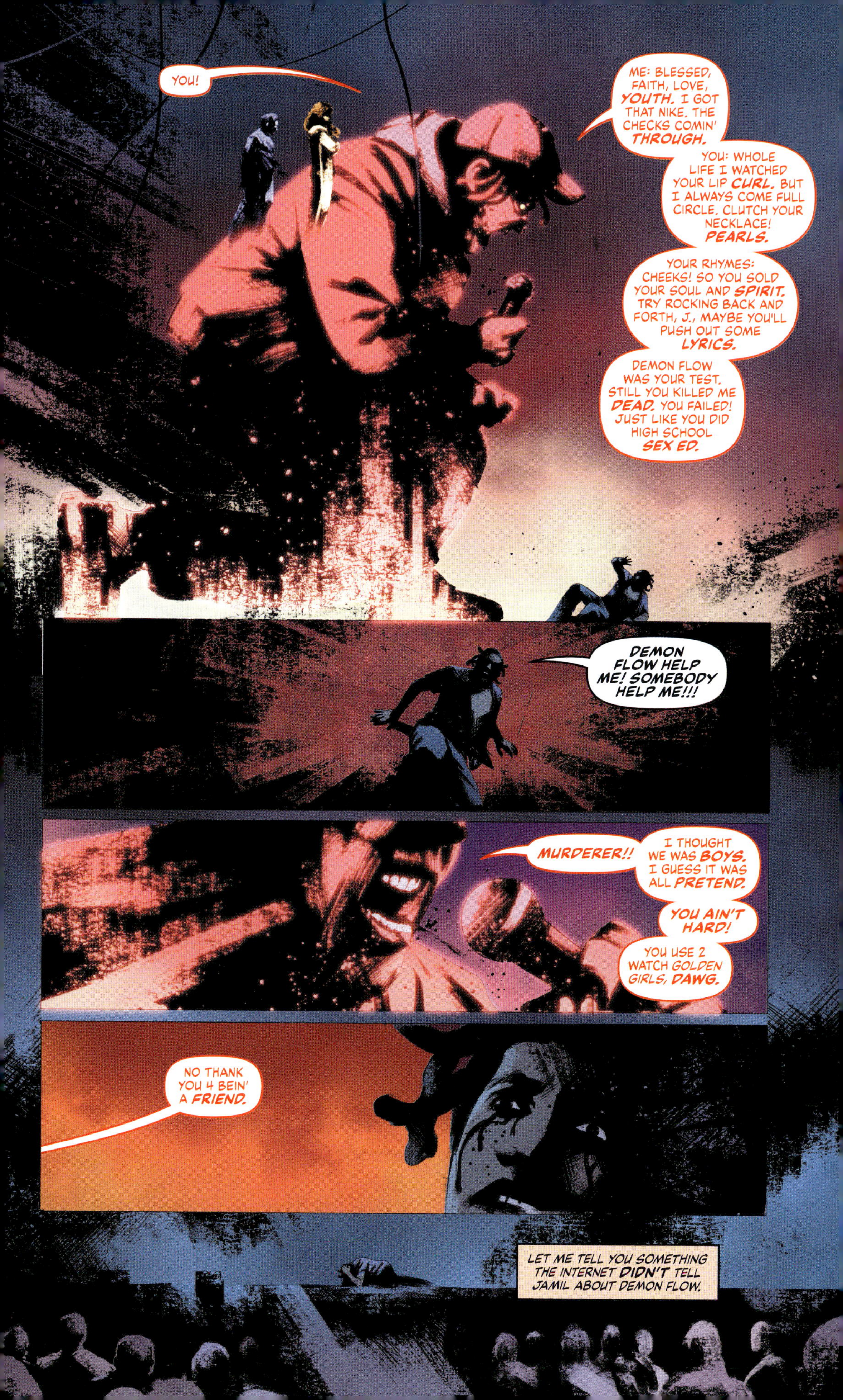
YOU!
ME: BLESSED, FAITH, LOVE, YOUTH. I GOT THAT NIKE. THE CHECKS COMIN' THROUGH.
YOU: WHOLE LIFE I WATCHED YOUR LIP CURL. BUT I ALWAYS COME FULL CIRCLE. CLUTCH YOUR NECKLACE! PEARLS.
YOUR RHYMES: CHEEKS! SO YOU SOLD YOUR SOUL AND SPIRIT. TRY ROCKING BACK AND FORTH, J., MAYBE YOU'LL PUSH OUT SOME LYRICS.
DEMON FLOW WAS YOUR TEST. STILL YOU KILLED ME DEAD. YOU FAILED! JUST LIKE YOU DID HIGH SCHOOL SEX ED.
DEMON FLOW HELP ME! SOMEBODY HELP ME!!!
MURDERER!!
I THOUGHT WE WAS BOYS. I GUESS IT WAS ALL PRETEND.
YOU AIN'T HARD!
YOU USE 2 WATCH GOLDEN GIRLS, DAWG.
NO THANK YOU 4 BEIN' A FRIEND.
LET ME TELL YOU SOMETHING THE INTERNET DIDN'T TELL JAMIL ABOUT DEMON FLOW.

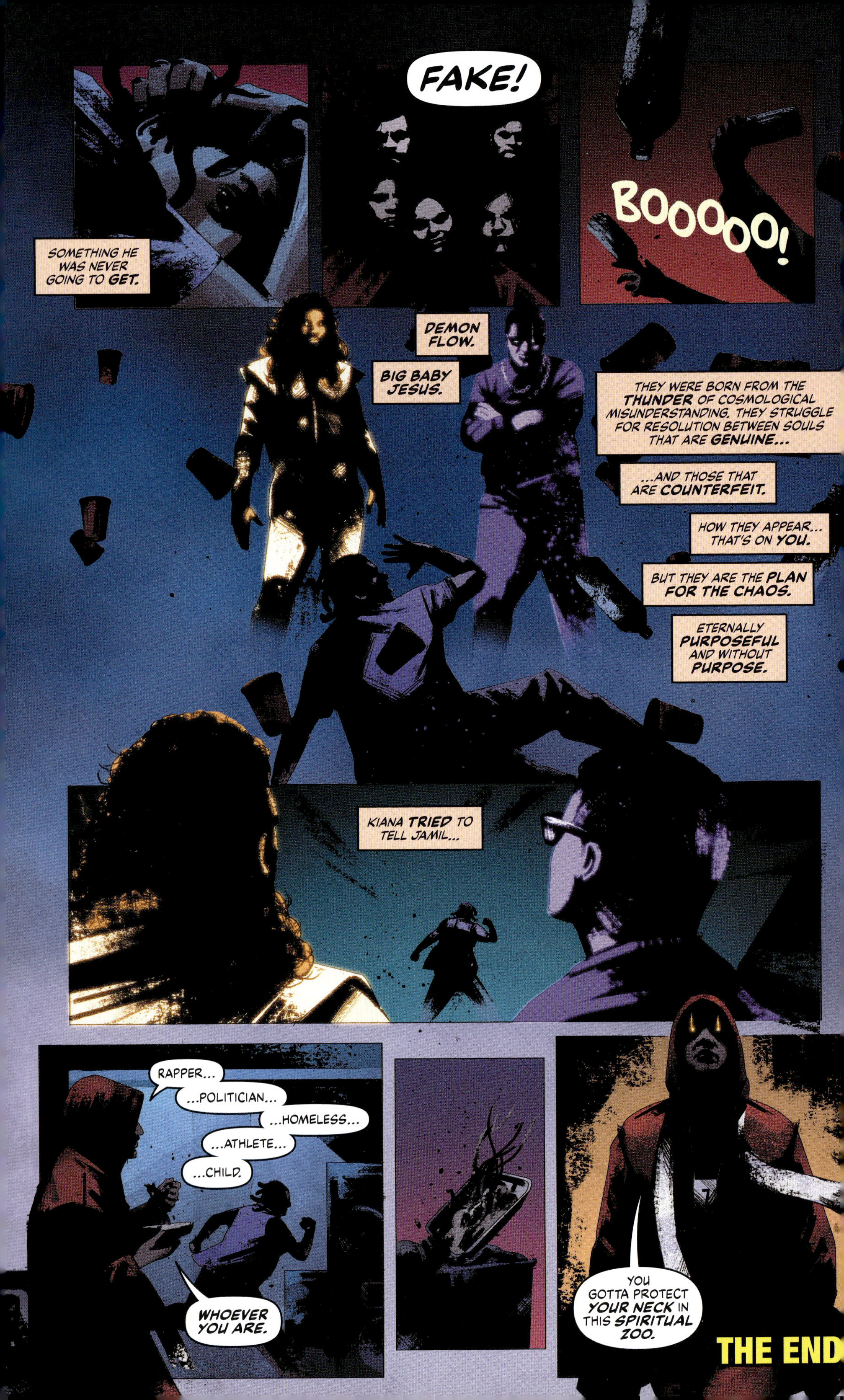
SOMETHING HE WAS NEVER GOING TO GET.
FAKE!
BOOOOO!
DEMON FLOW.
BIG BABY JESUS.
THEY WERE BORN FROM THE THUNDER OF COSMOLOGICAL MISUNDERSTANDING. THEY STRUGGLE FOR RESOLUTION BETWEEN SOULS THAT ARE GENUINE...
...AND THOSE THAT ARE COUNTERFEIT.
HOW THEY APPEAR... THAT'S ON YOU.
BUT THEY ARE THE PLAN FOR THE CHAOS.
ETERNALLY PURPOSEFUL AND WITHOUT PURPOSE.
KIANA TRIED TO TELL JAMIL...
RAPPER...
...POLITICIAN...
...HOMELESS...
...ATHLETE...
...CHILD.
WHOEVER YOU ARE.
YOU GOTTA PROTECT YOUR NECK IN THIS SPIRITUAL ZOO.
THE END

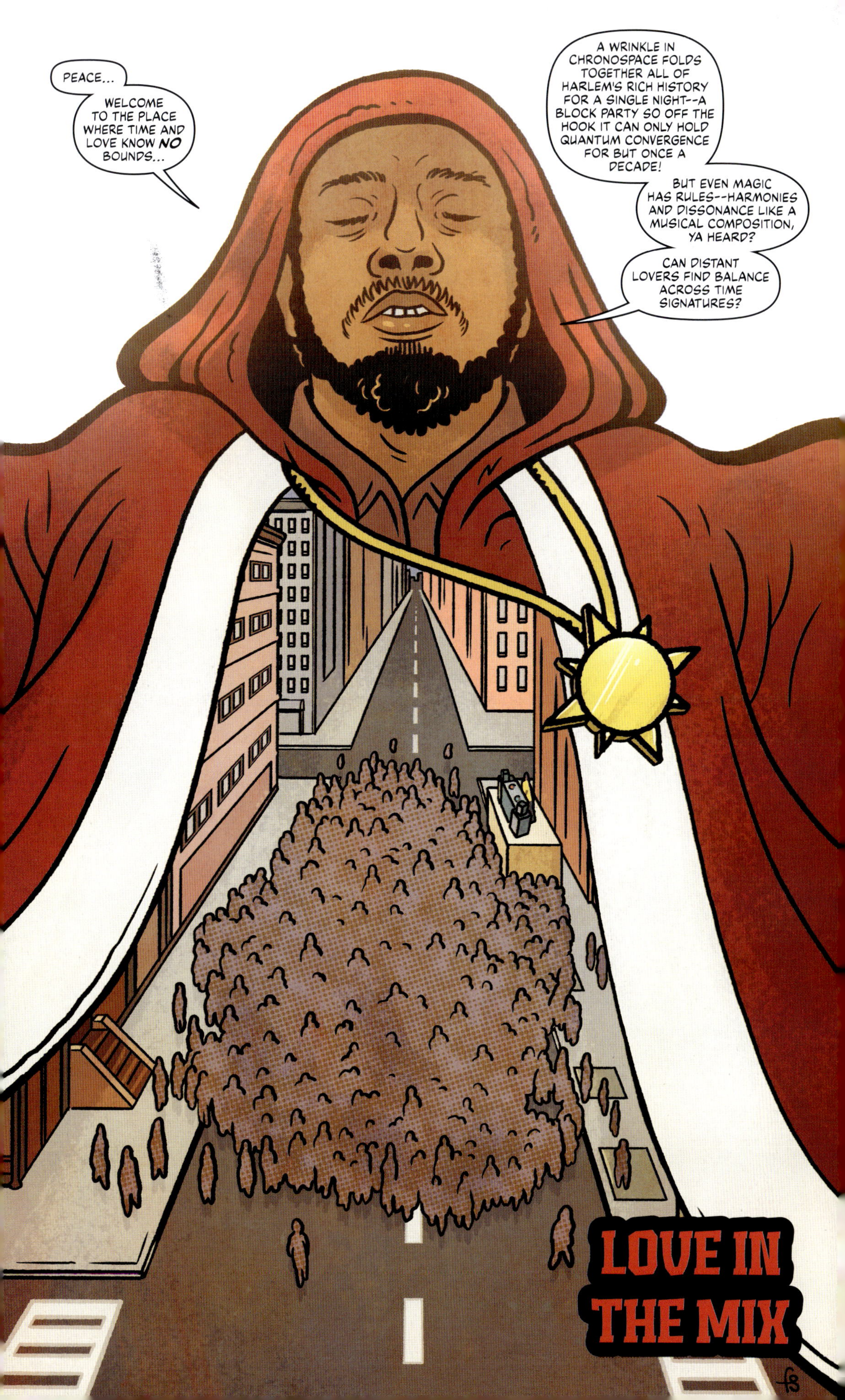
PEACE...
WELCOME TO THE PLACE WHERE TIME AND LOVE KNOW **NO** BOUNDS...
A WRINKLE IN CHRONOSPACE FOLDS TOGETHER ALL OF HARLEM'S RICH HISTORY FOR A SINGLE NIGHT--A BLOCK PARTY SO OFF THE HOOK IT CAN ONLY HOLD QUANTUM CONVERGENCE FOR BUT ONCE A DECADE!
BUT EVEN MAGIC HAS RULES--HARMONIES AND DISSONANCE LIKE A MUSICAL COMPOSITION, YA HEARD?
CAN DISTANT LOVERS FIND BALANCE ACROSS TIME SIGNATURES?
LOVE IN THE MIX

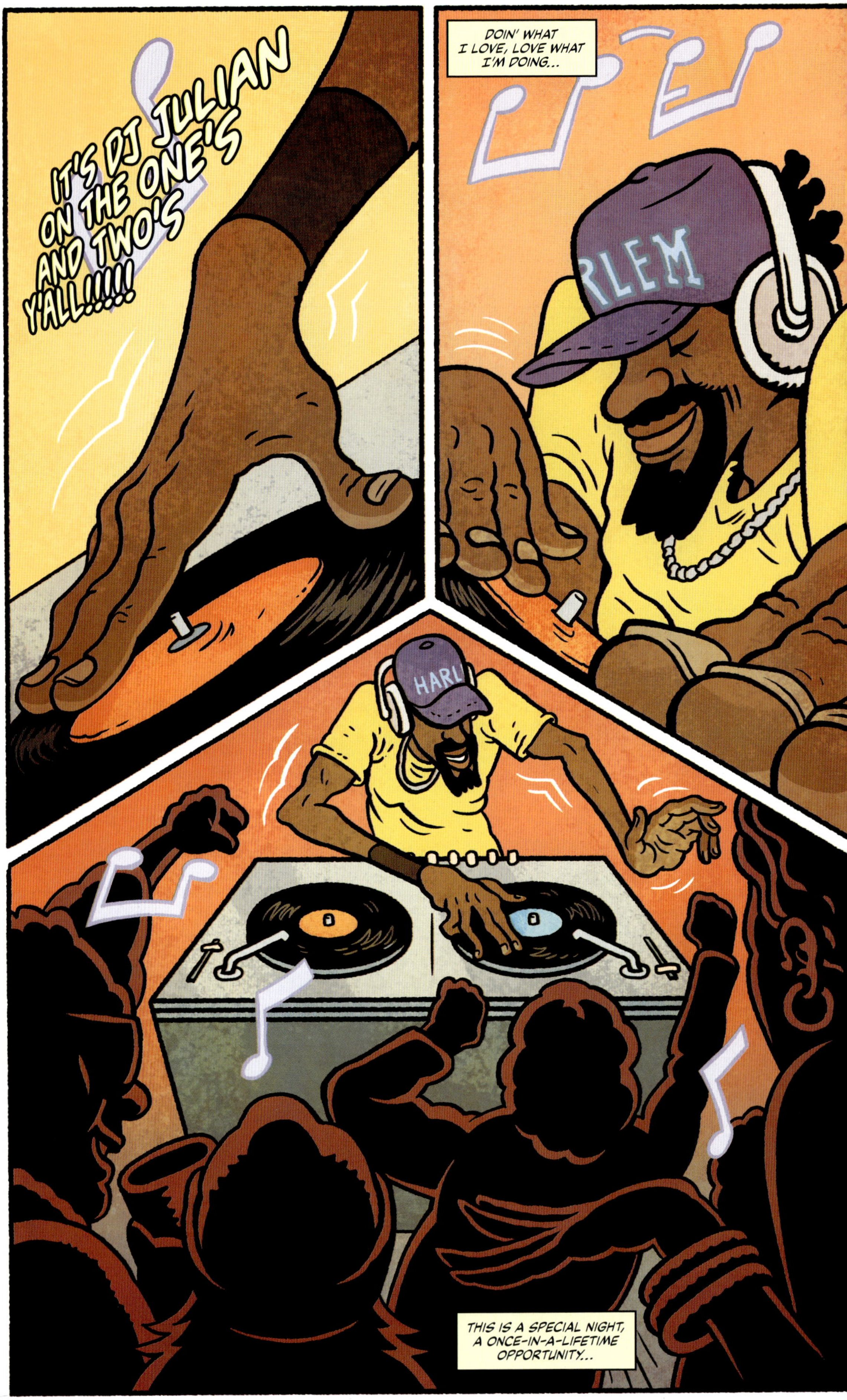
IT'S DJ JULIAN ON THE ONE'S AND TWO'S Y'ALL!!!!!
DOIN' WHAT I LOVE, LOVE WHAT I'M DOING...
RLEM
HARL
THIS IS A SPECIAL NIGHT, A ONCE-IN-A-LIFETIME OPPORTUNITY...

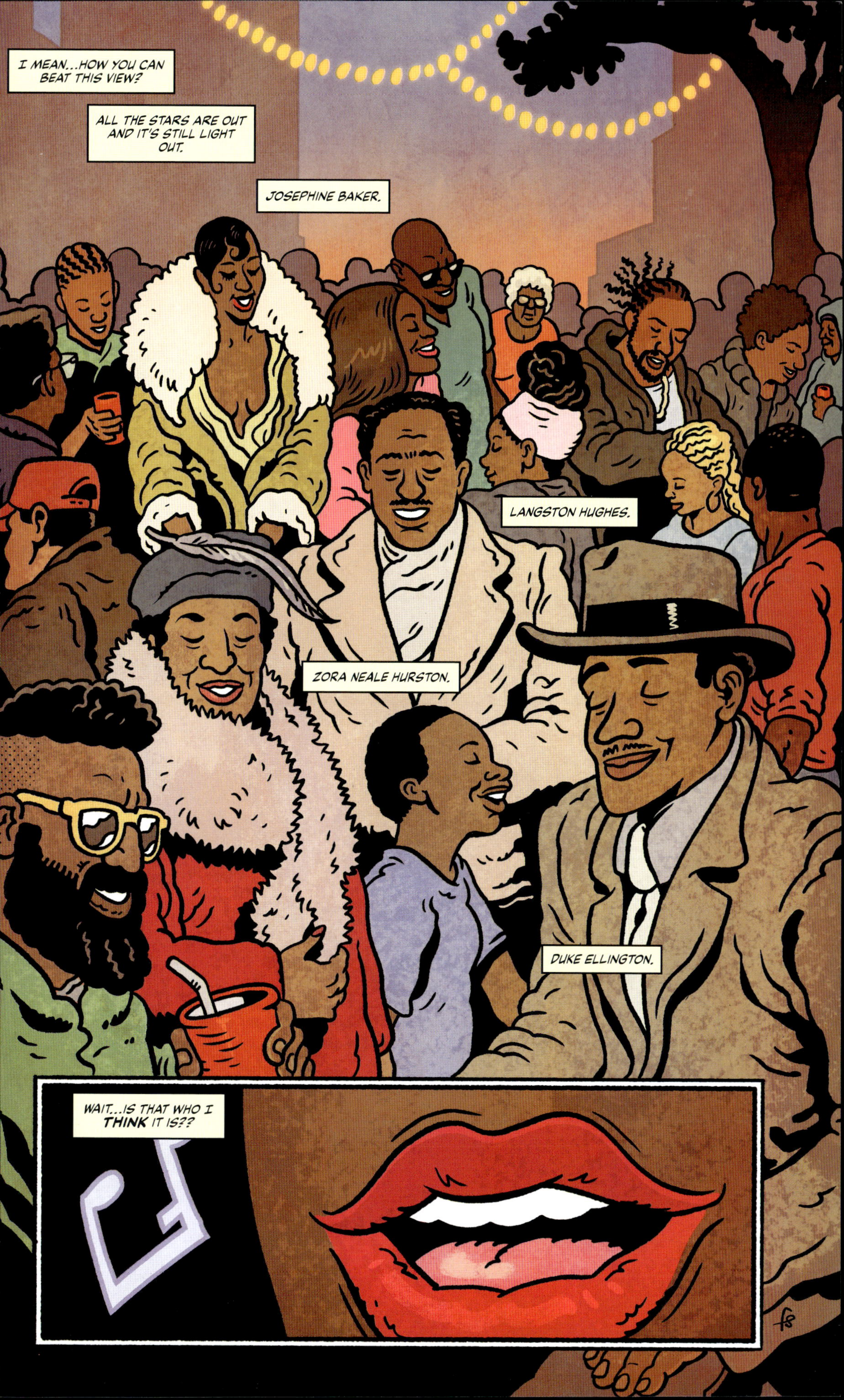
I MEAN...HOW YOU CAN BEAT THIS VIEW?
ALL THE STARS ARE OUT AND IT'S STILL LIGHT OUT.
JOSEPHINE BAKER.
LANGSTON HUGHES.
ZORA NEALE HURSTON.
DUKE ELLINGTON.
WAIT...IS THAT WHO I **THINK** IT IS??

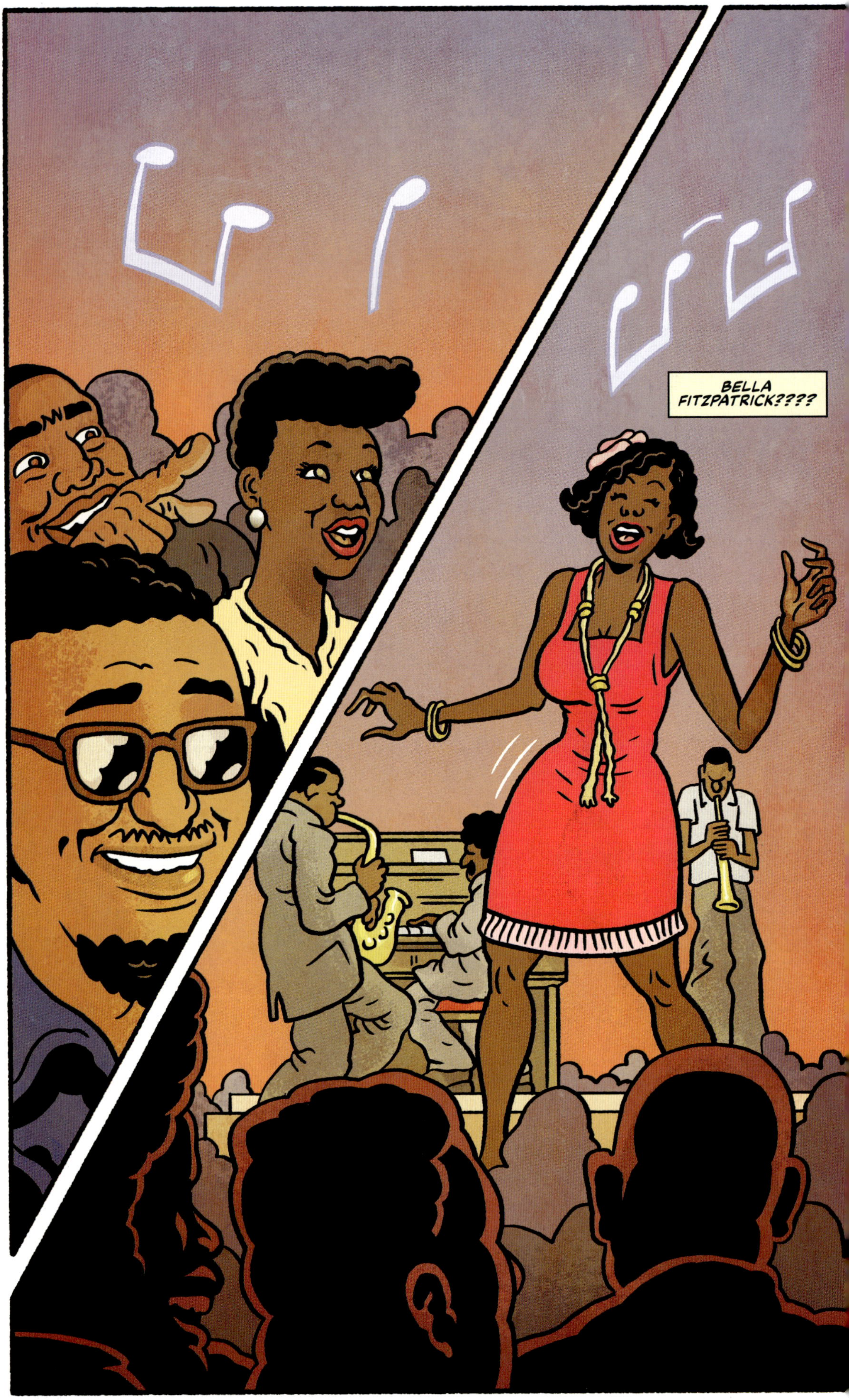
BELLA FITZPATRICK????

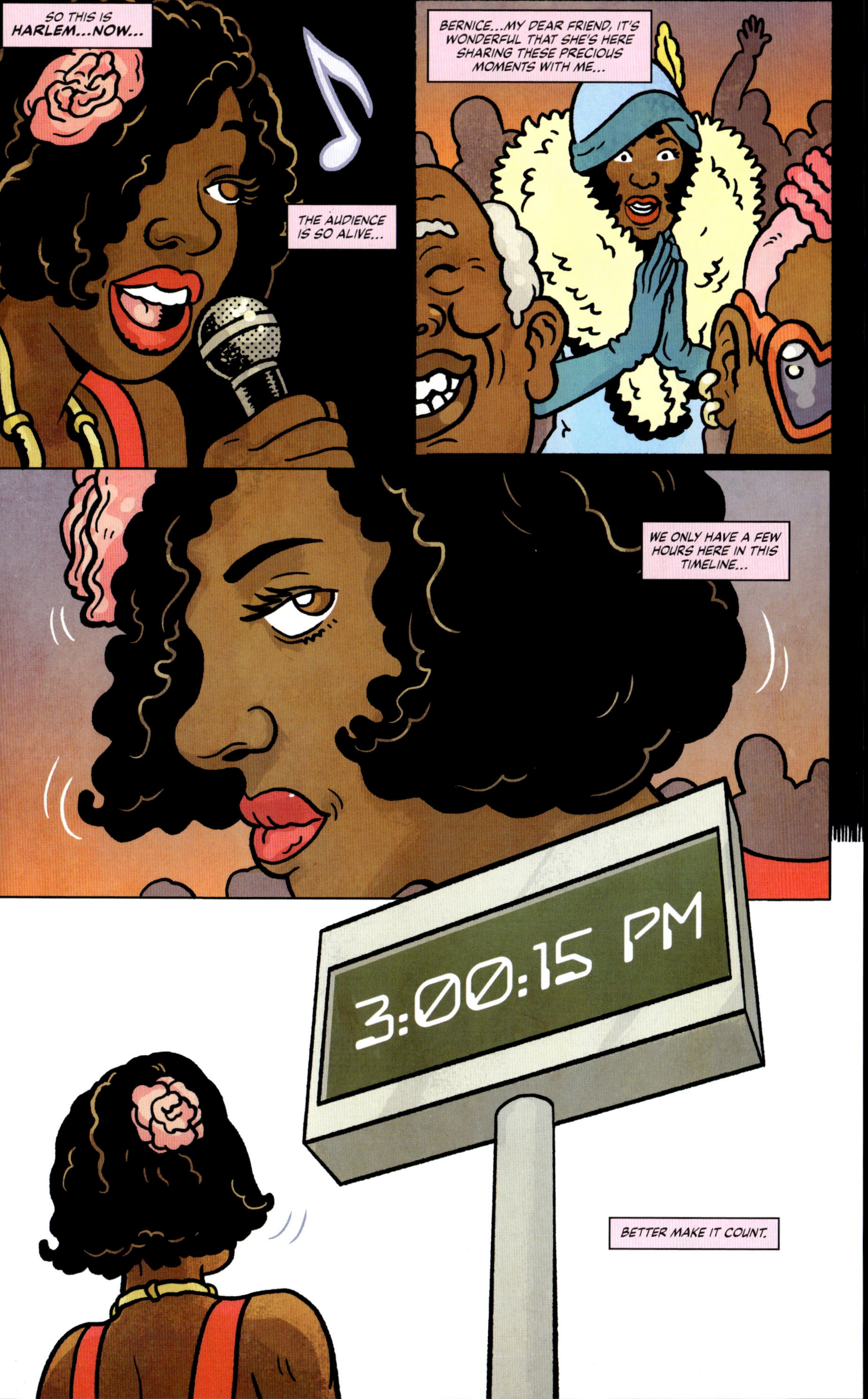
SO THIS IS HARLEM...NOW...
THE AUDIENCE IS SO ALIVE...
BERNICE...MY DEAR FRIEND, IT'S WONDERFUL THAT SHE'S HERE SHARING THESE PRECIOUS MOMENTS WITH ME...
WE ONLY HAVE A FEW HOURS HERE IN THIS TIMELINE...
3:00:15 PM
BETTER MAKE IT COUNT.

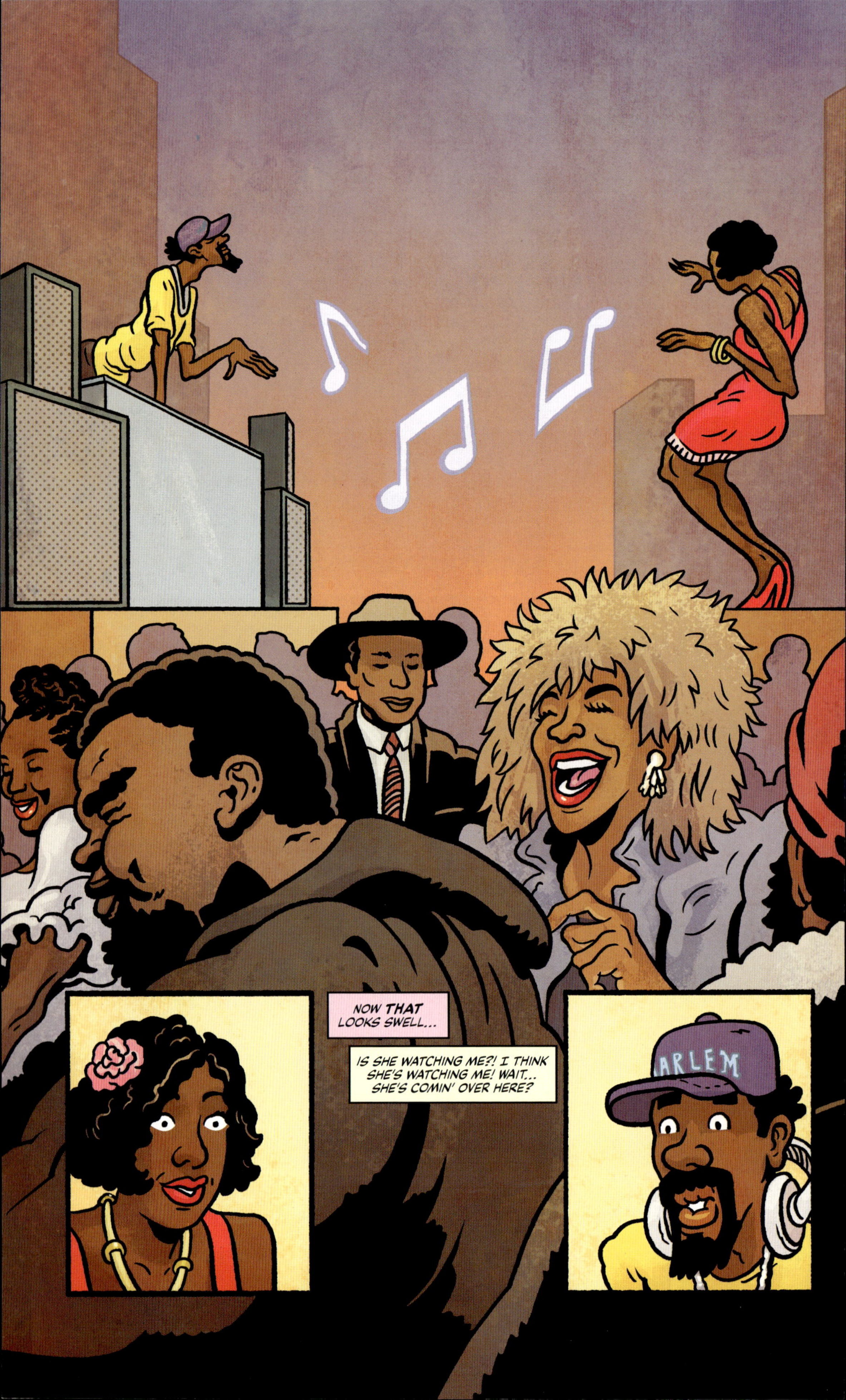
NOW THAT LOOKS SWELL...
IS SHE WATCHING ME?! I THINK SHE'S WATCHING ME! WAIT... SHE'S COMIN' OVER HERE?
HARLEM

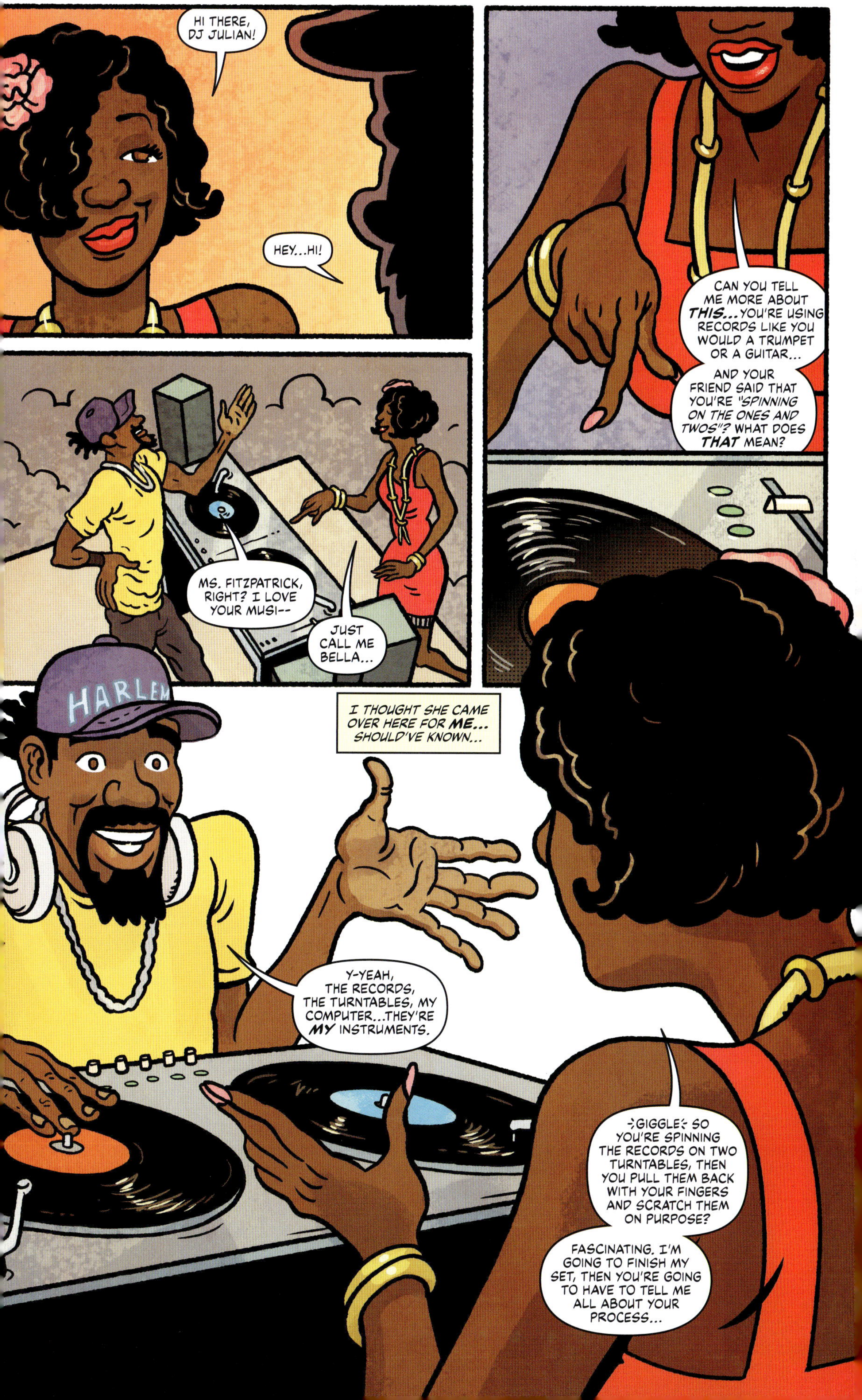
HI THERE, DJ JULIAN!
HEY...HI!
CAN YOU TELL ME MORE ABOUT **THIS...** YOU'RE USING RECORDS LIKE YOU WOULD A TRUMPET OR A GUITAR...
AND YOUR FRIEND SAID THAT YOU'RE *"SPINNING ON THE ONES AND TWOS"*? WHAT DOES **THAT** MEAN?
MS. FITZPATRICK, RIGHT? I LOVE YOUR MUSI--
JUST CALL ME BELLA...
HARLEM
*I THOUGHT SHE CAME OVER HERE FOR **ME...** SHOULD'VE KNOWN...*
Y-YEAH, THE RECORDS, THE TURNTABLES, MY COMPUTER...THEY'RE ***MY*** INSTRUMENTS.
GIGGLE SO YOU'RE SPINNING THE RECORDS ON TWO TURNTABLES, THEN YOU PULL THEM BACK WITH YOUR FINGERS AND SCRATCH THEM ON PURPOSE?
FASCINATING. I'M GOING TO FINISH MY SET, THEN YOU'RE GOING TO HAVE TO TELL ME ALL ABOUT YOUR PROCESS...

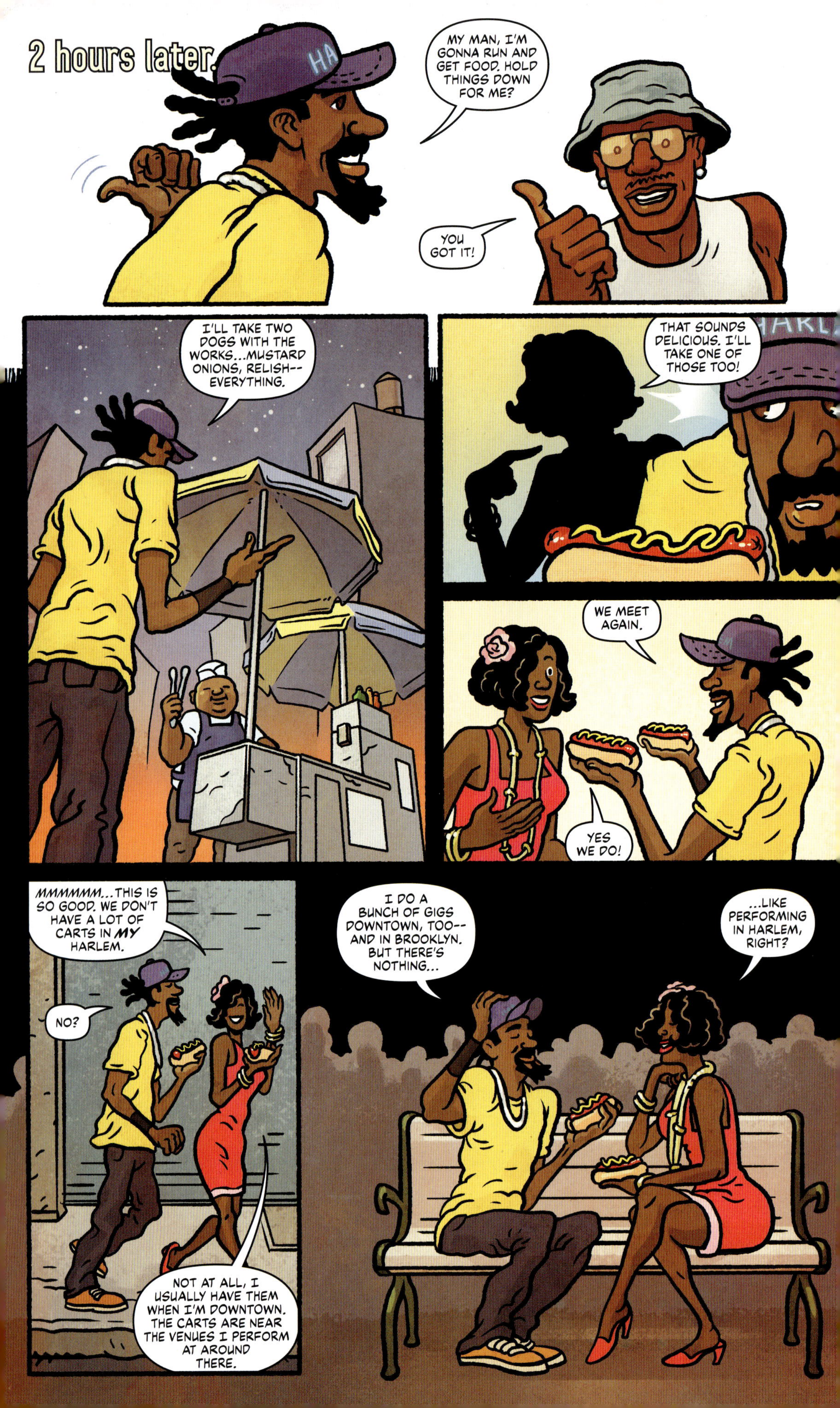
2 hours later.
MY MAN, I'M GONNA RUN AND GET FOOD. HOLD THINGS DOWN FOR ME?
YOU GOT IT!
I'LL TAKE TWO DOGS WITH THE WORKS...MUSTARD ONIONS, RELISH--EVERYTHING.
THAT SOUNDS DELICIOUS. I'LL TAKE ONE OF THOSE TOO!
WE MEET AGAIN.
YES WE DO!
MMMMMM...THIS IS SO GOOD. WE DON'T HAVE A LOT OF CARTS IN *MY* HARLEM.
NO?
NOT AT ALL, I USUALLY HAVE THEM WHEN I'M DOWNTOWN. THE CARTS ARE NEAR THE VENUES I PERFORM AT AROUND THERE.
I DO A BUNCH OF GIGS DOWNTOWN, TOO--AND IN BROOKLYN. BUT THERE'S NOTHING...
...LIKE PERFORMING IN HARLEM, RIGHT?

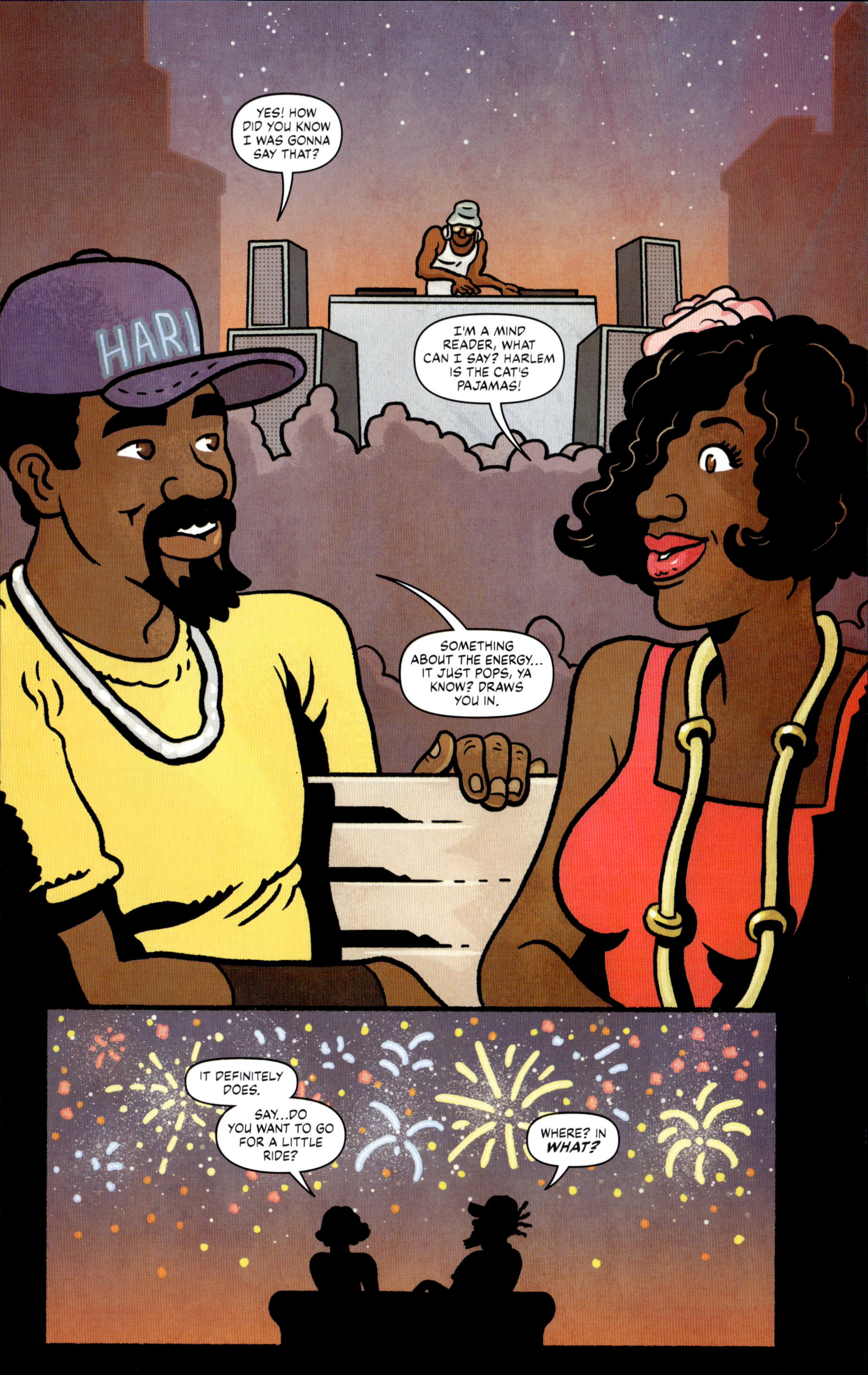

YES! HOW DID YOU KNOW I WAS GONNA SAY THAT?
I'M A MIND READER, WHAT CAN I SAY? HARLEM IS THE CAT'S PAJAMAS!
SOMETHING ABOUT THE ENERGY... IT JUST POPS, YA KNOW? DRAWS YOU IN.
IT DEFINITELY DOES.
SAY...DO YOU WANT TO GO FOR A LITTLE RIDE?
WHERE? IN ***WHAT?***

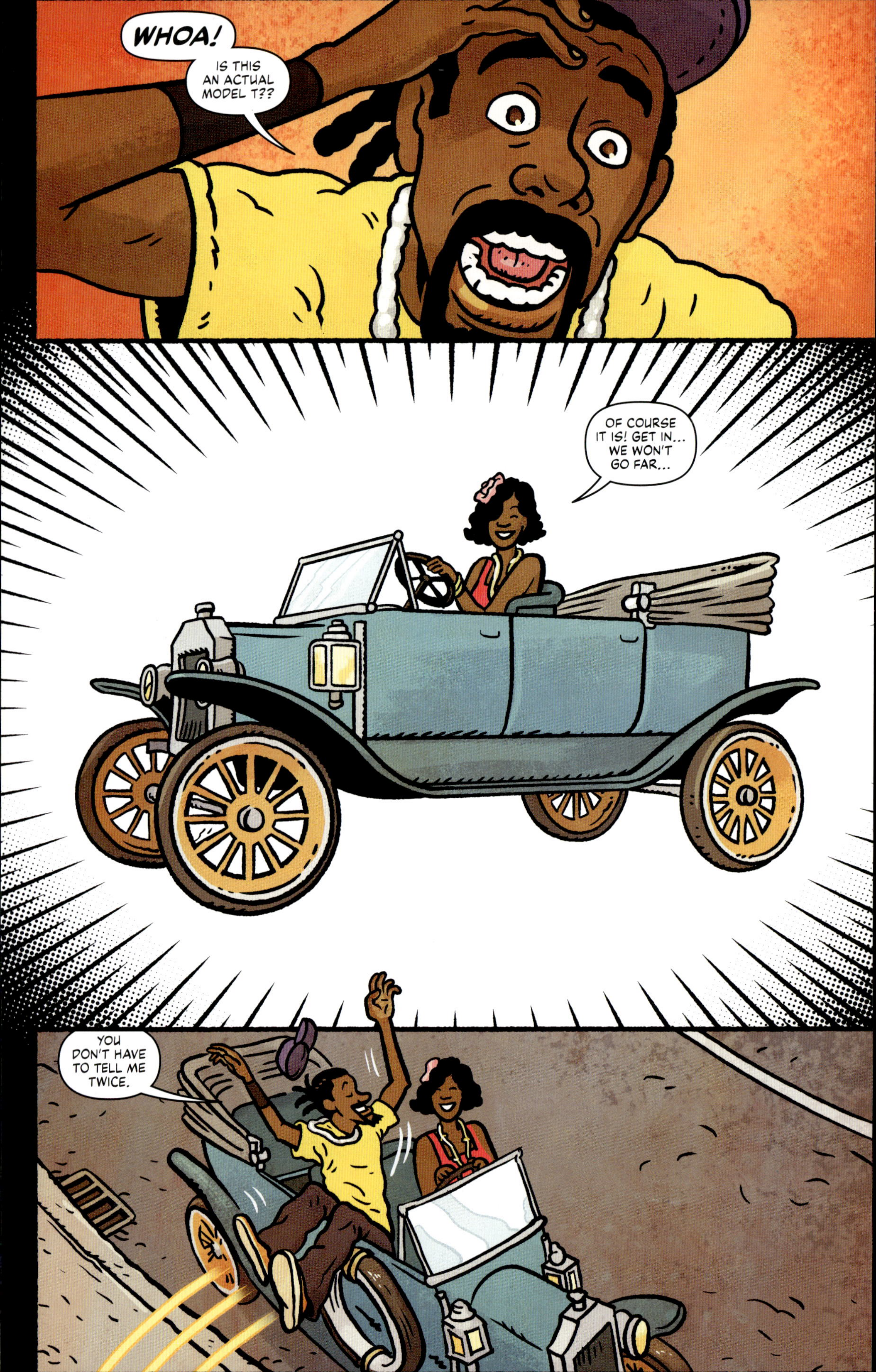
WHOA!
IS THIS AN ACTUAL MODEL T??
OF COURSE IT IS! GET IN... WE WON'T GO FAR...
YOU DON'T HAVE TO TELL ME TWICE.

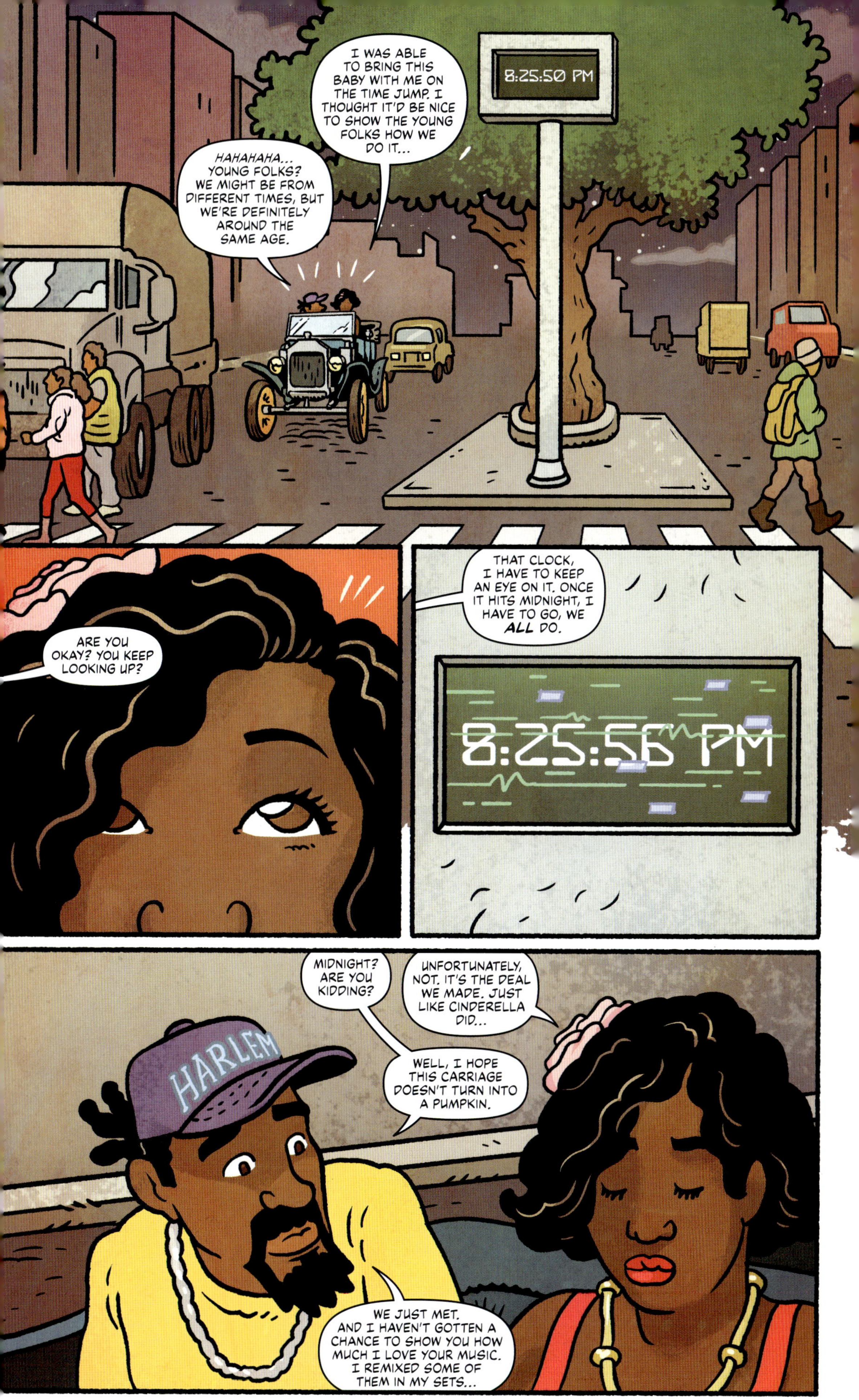
8:25:50 PM
I WAS ABLE TO BRING THIS BABY WITH ME ON THE TIME JUMP. I THOUGHT IT'D BE NICE TO SHOW THE YOUNG FOLKS HOW WE DO IT...
HAHAHAHA... YOUNG FOLKS? WE MIGHT BE FROM DIFFERENT TIMES, BUT WE'RE DEFINITELY AROUND THE SAME AGE.
ARE YOU OKAY? YOU KEEP LOOKING UP?
THAT CLOCK, I HAVE TO KEEP AN EYE ON IT. ONCE IT HITS MIDNIGHT, I HAVE TO GO, WE ***ALL*** DO.
8:25:56 PM
MIDNIGHT? ARE YOU KIDDING?
UNFORTUNATELY, NOT. IT'S THE DEAL WE MADE. JUST LIKE CINDERELLA DID...
WELL, I HOPE THIS CARRIAGE DOESN'T TURN INTO A PUMPKIN.
HARLEM
WE JUST MET. AND I HAVEN'T GOTTEN A CHANCE TO SHOW YOU HOW MUCH I LOVE YOUR MUSIC. I REMIXED SOME OF THEM IN MY SETS...

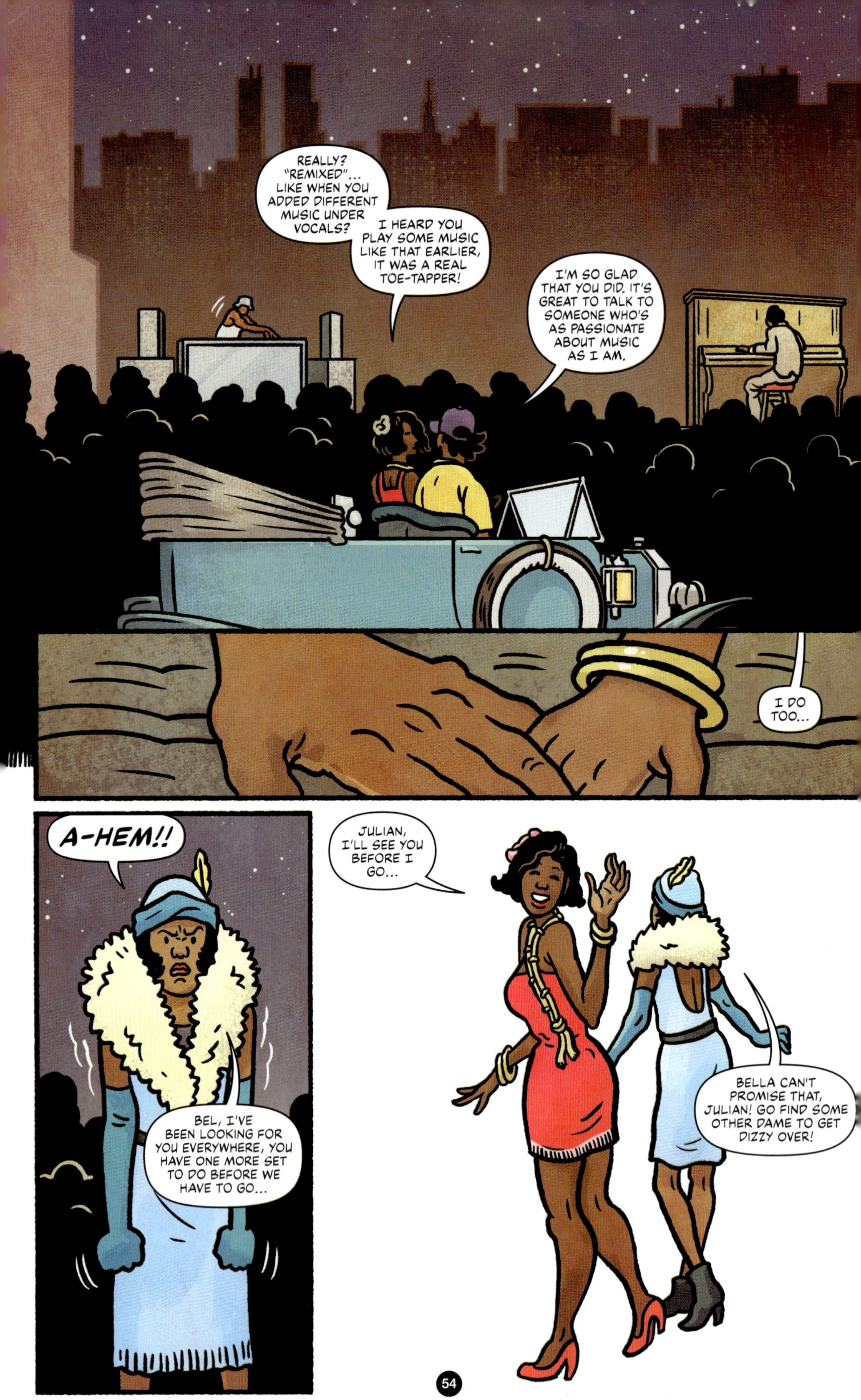
REALLY? "REMIXED"... LIKE WHEN YOU ADDED DIFFERENT MUSIC UNDER VOCALS?
I HEARD YOU PLAY SOME MUSIC LIKE THAT EARLIER, IT WAS A REAL TOE-TAPPER!
I'M SO GLAD THAT YOU DID. IT'S GREAT TO TALK TO SOMEONE WHO'S AS PASSIONATE ABOUT MUSIC AS I AM.
I DO TOO...
A-HEM!!
BEL, I'VE BEEN LOOKING FOR YOU EVERYWHERE, YOU HAVE ONE MORE SET TO DO BEFORE WE HAVE TO GO...
JULIAN, I'LL SEE YOU BEFORE I GO...
BELLA CAN'T PROMISE THAT, JULIAN! GO FIND SOME OTHER DAME TO GET DIZZY OVER!

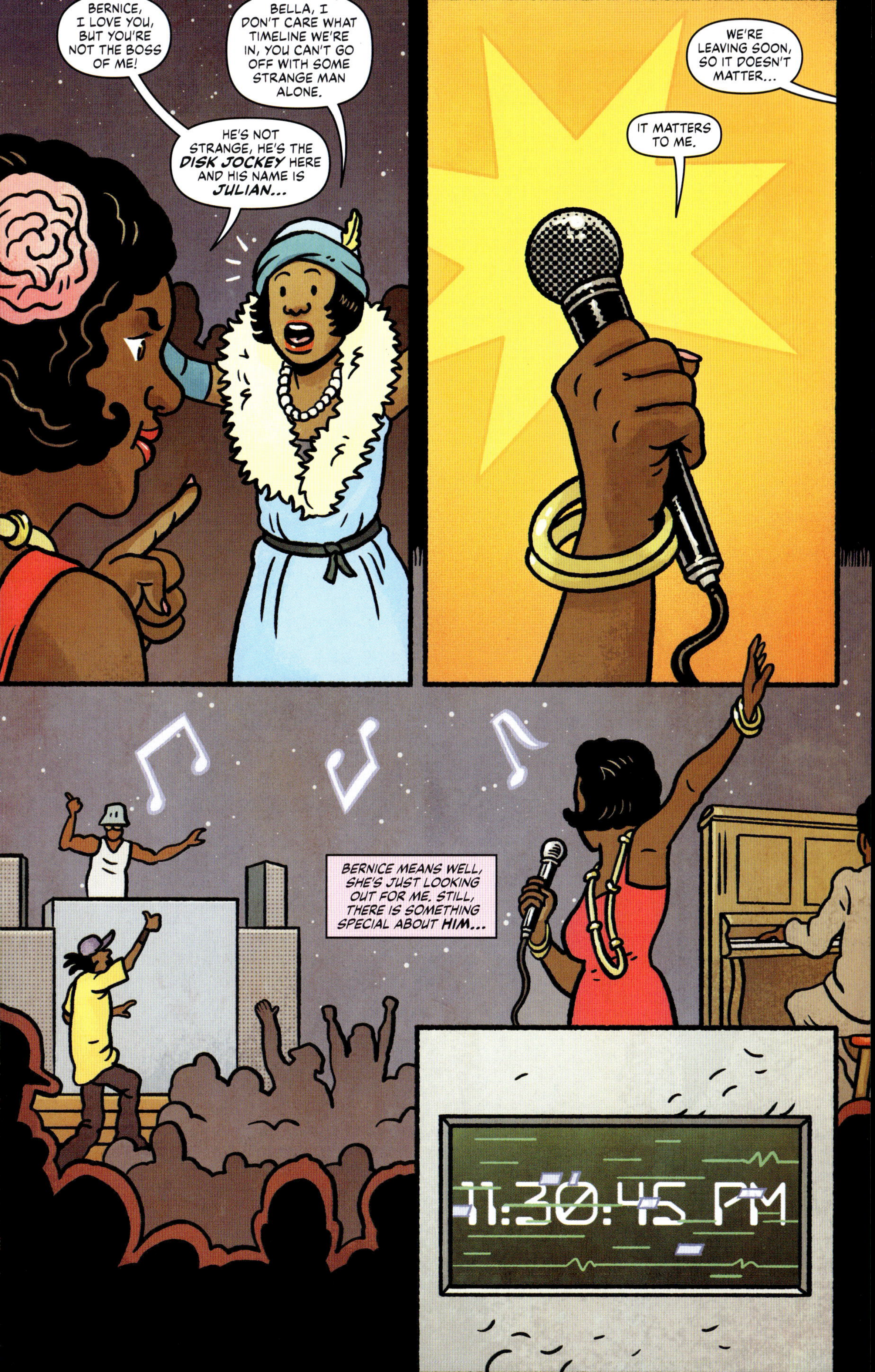
BERNICE, I LOVE YOU, BUT YOU'RE NOT THE BOSS OF ME!
BELLA, I DON'T CARE WHAT TIMELINE WE'RE IN, YOU CAN'T GO OFF WITH SOME STRANGE MAN ALONE.
HE'S NOT STRANGE, HE'S THE *DISK JOCKEY* HERE AND HIS NAME IS *JULIAN...*
WE'RE LEAVING SOON, SO IT DOESN'T MATTER...
IT MATTERS TO ME.
BERNICE MEANS WELL, SHE'S JUST LOOKING OUT FOR ME. STILL, THERE IS SOMETHING SPECIAL ABOUT **HIM...**
11:30:45 PM

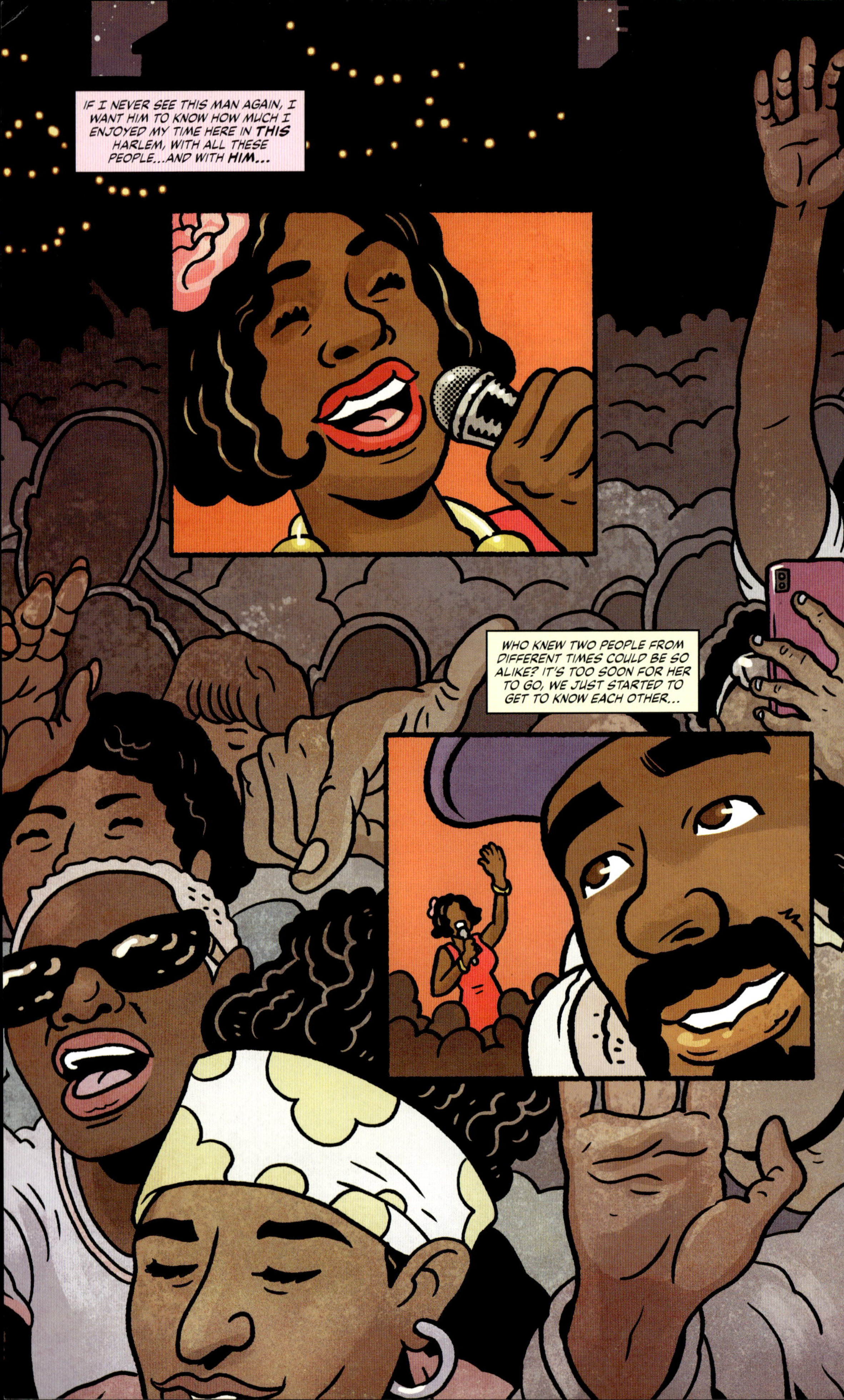
IF I NEVER SEE THIS MAN AGAIN, I WANT HIM TO KNOW HOW MUCH I ENJOYED MY TIME HERE IN **THIS** HARLEM, WITH ALL THESE PEOPLE...AND WITH **HIM**...
WHO KNEW TWO PEOPLE FROM DIFFERENT TIMES COULD BE SO ALIKE? IT'S TOO SOON FOR HER TO GO, WE JUST STARTED TO GET TO KNOW EACH OTHER...

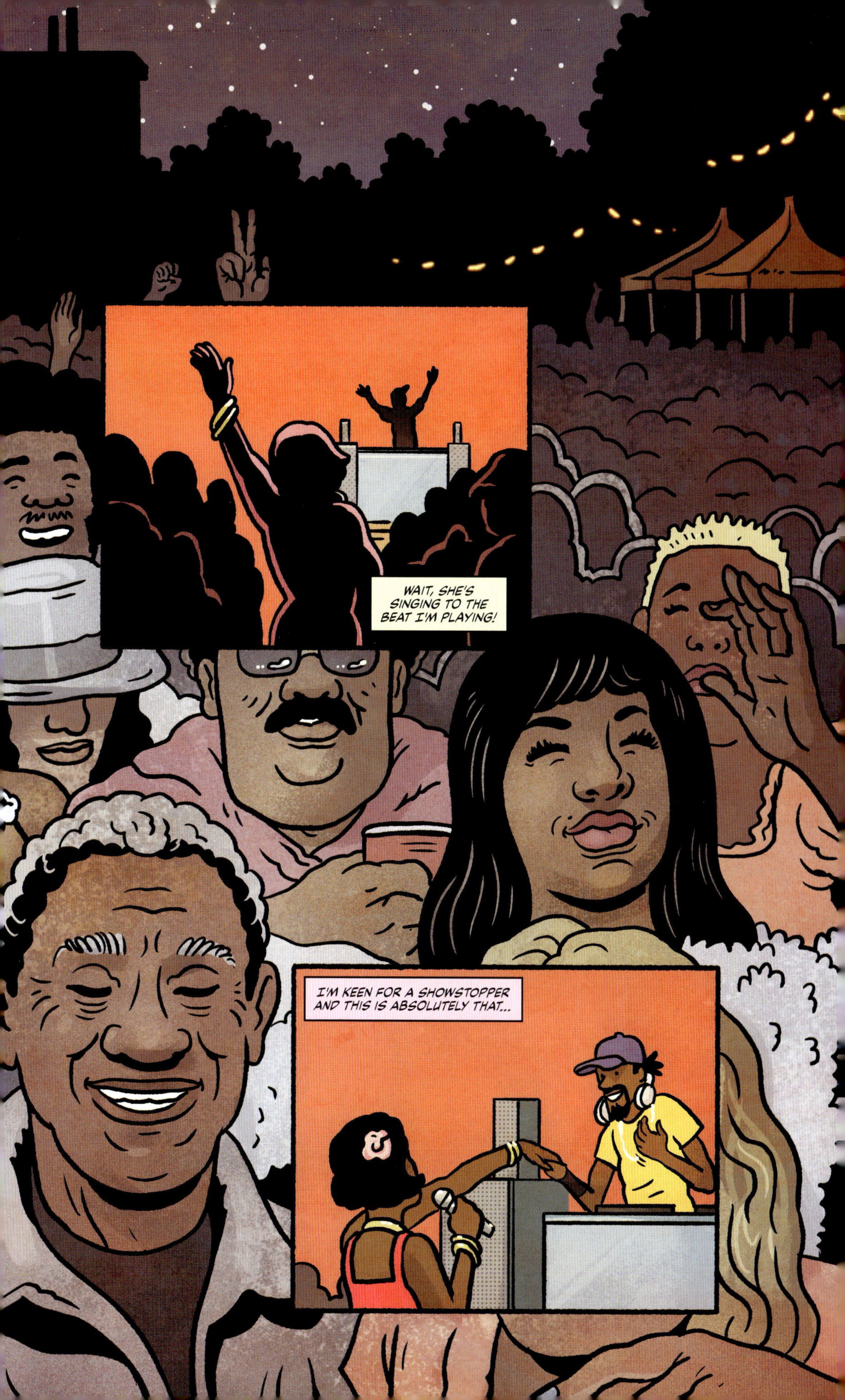
WAIT, SHE'S SINGING TO THE BEAT I'M PLAYING!
I'M KEEN FOR A SHOWSTOPPER AND THIS IS ABSOLUTELY THAT...

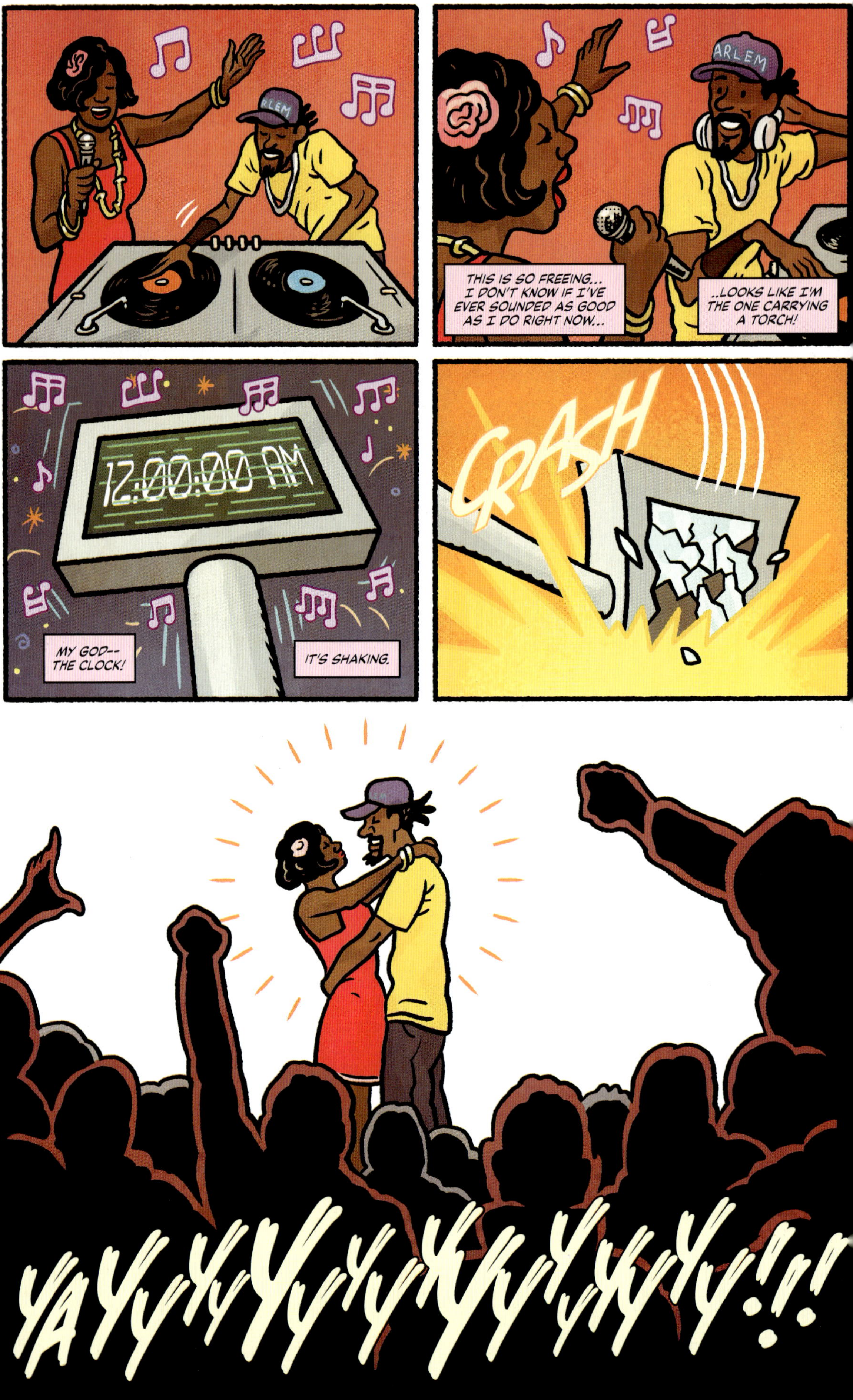
ARLEM
THIS IS SO FREEING... I DON'T KNOW IF I'VE EVER SOUNDED AS GOOD AS I DO RIGHT NOW...
..LOOKS LIKE I'M THE ONE CARRYING A TORCH!
12:00:00 AM
MY GOD-- THE CLOCK!
IT'S SHAKING.
CRASH
YAYYYYYYYYYYYYYYYY!!!

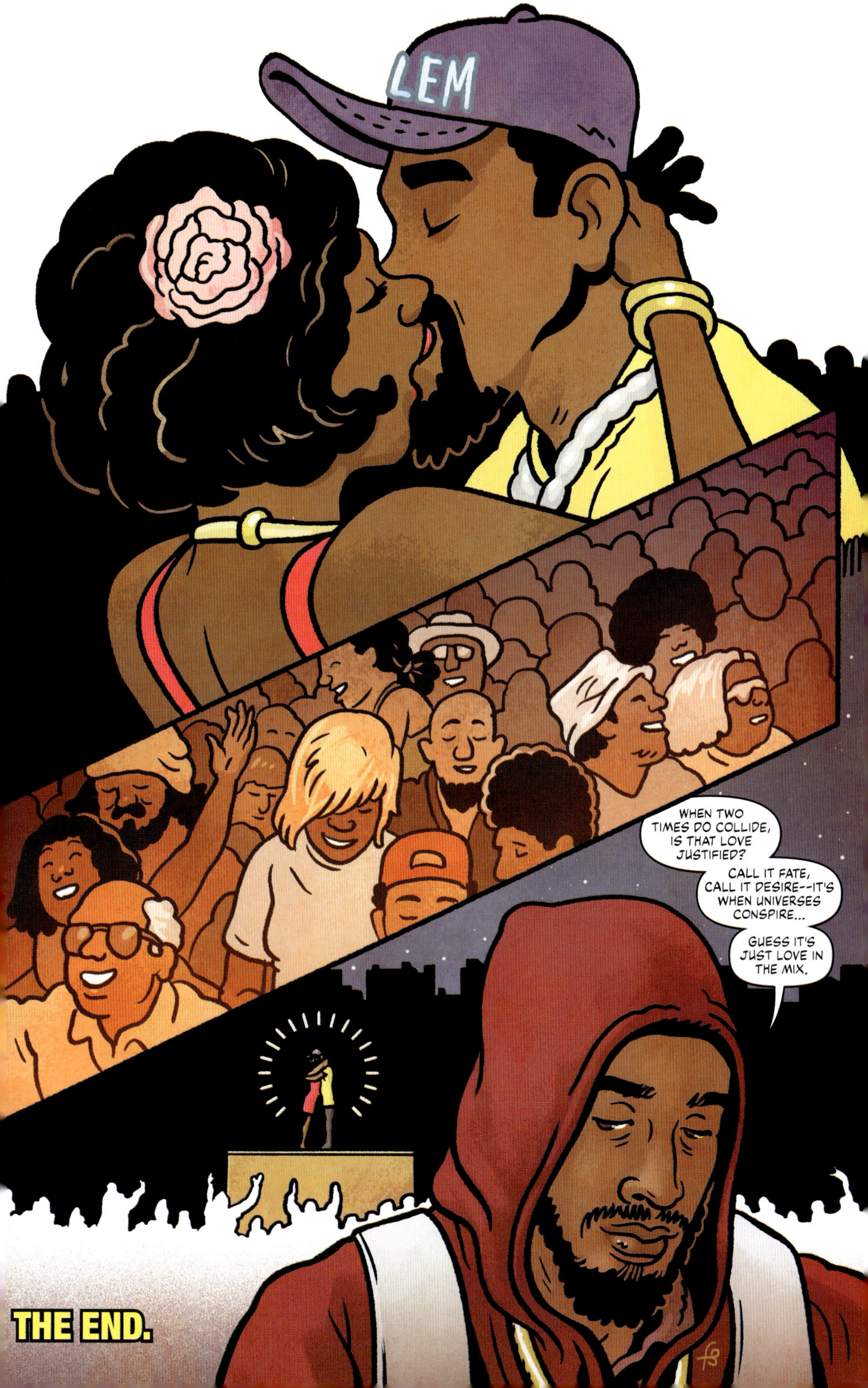
LEM
WHEN TWO TIMES DO COLLIDE, IS THAT LOVE JUSTIFIED?
CALL IT FATE, CALL IT DESIRE--IT'S WHEN UNIVERSES CONSPIRE...
GUESS IT'S JUST LOVE IN THE MIX.
THE END.

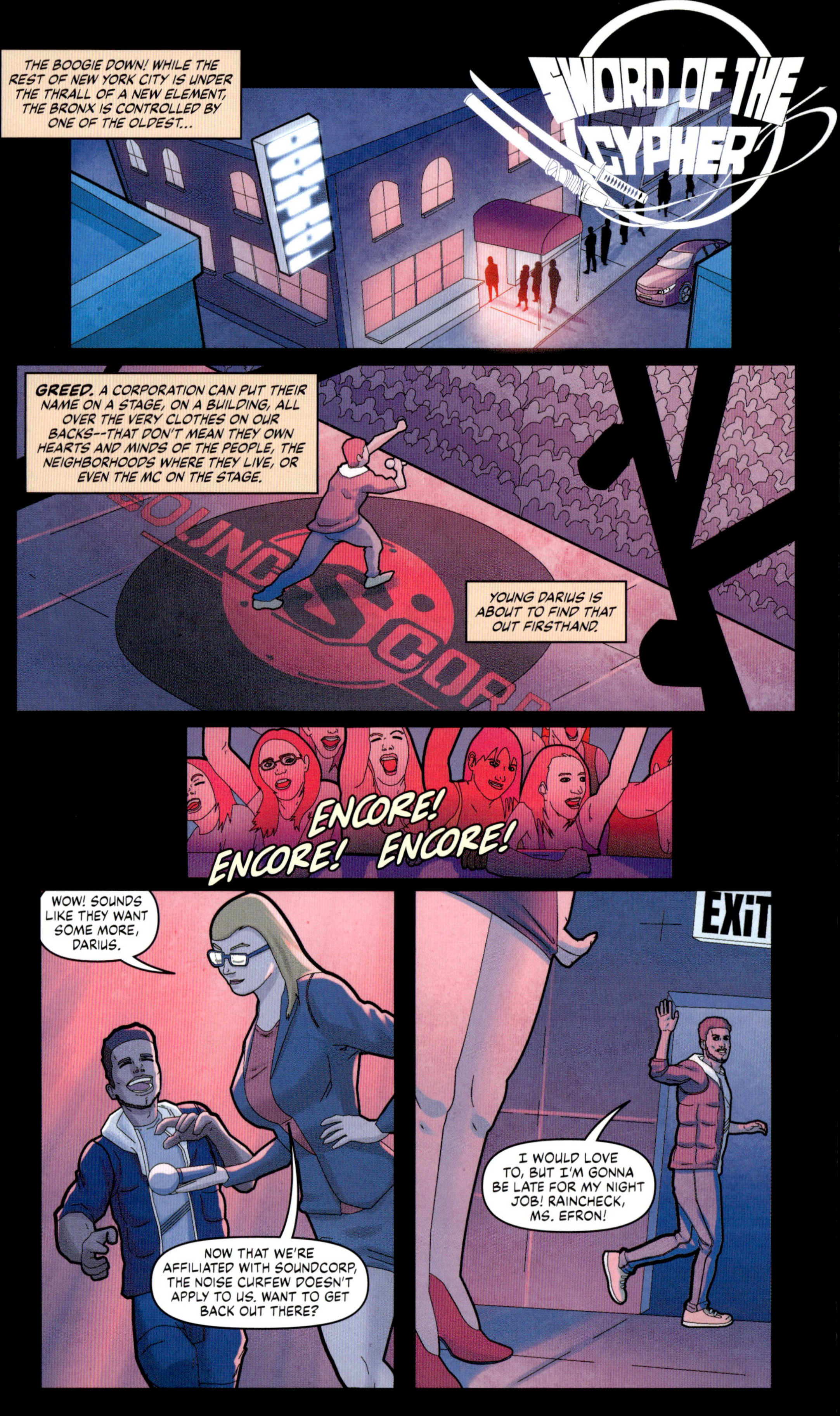
SWORD OF THE CYPHER
THE BOOGIE DOWN! WHILE THE REST OF NEW YORK CITY IS UNDER THE THRALL OF A NEW ELEMENT, THE BRONX IS CONTROLLED BY ONE OF THE OLDEST...
GREED. A CORPORATION CAN PUT THEIR NAME ON A STAGE, ON A BUILDING, ALL OVER THE VERY CLOTHES ON OUR BACKS--THAT DON'T MEAN THEY OWN HEARTS AND MINDS OF THE PEOPLE, THE NEIGHBORHOODS WHERE THEY LIVE, OR EVEN THE MC ON THE STAGE.
YOUNG DARIUS IS ABOUT TO FIND THAT OUT FIRSTHAND.
ENCORE! ENCORE! ENCORE!
WOW! SOUNDS LIKE THEY WANT SOME MORE, DARIUS.
NOW THAT WE'RE AFFILIATED WITH SOUNDCORP, THE NOISE CURFEW DOESN'T APPLY TO US. WANT TO GET BACK OUT THERE?
EXIT
I WOULD LOVE TO, BUT I'M GONNA BE LATE FOR MY NIGHT JOB! RAINCHECK, MS. EFRON!

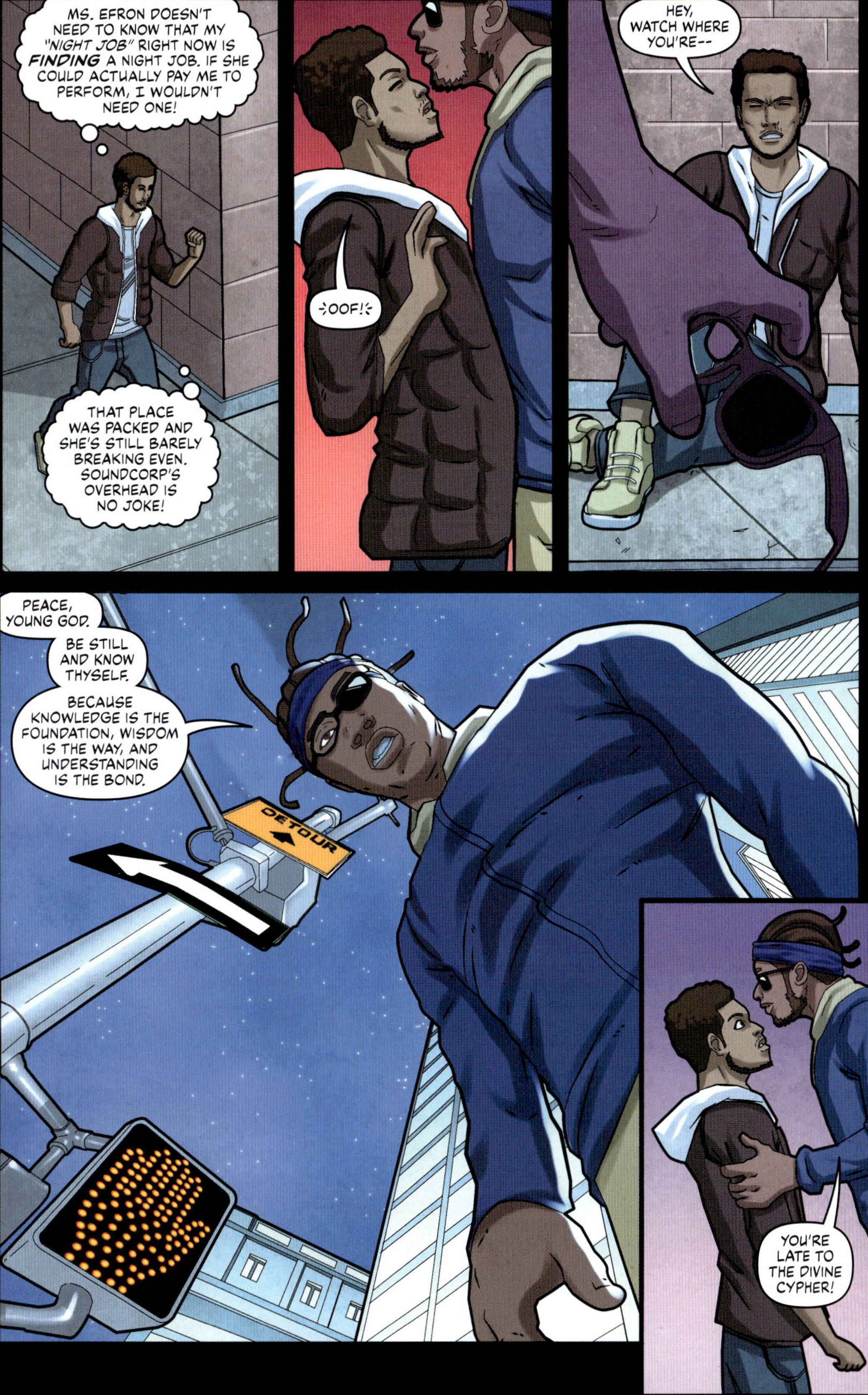
MS. EFRON DOESN'T NEED TO KNOW THAT MY "NIGHT JOB" RIGHT NOW IS FINDING A NIGHT JOB. IF SHE COULD ACTUALLY PAY ME TO PERFORM, I WOULDN'T NEED ONE!
THAT PLACE WAS PACKED AND SHE'S STILL BARELY BREAKING EVEN. SOUNDCORP'S OVERHEAD IS NO JOKE!
OOF!
HEY, WATCH WHERE YOU'RE--
PEACE, YOUNG GOD.
BE STILL AND KNOW THYSELF.
BECAUSE KNOWLEDGE IS THE FOUNDATION, WISDOM IS THE WAY, AND UNDERSTANDING IS THE BOND.
DETOUR
YOU'RE LATE TO THE DIVINE CYPHER!

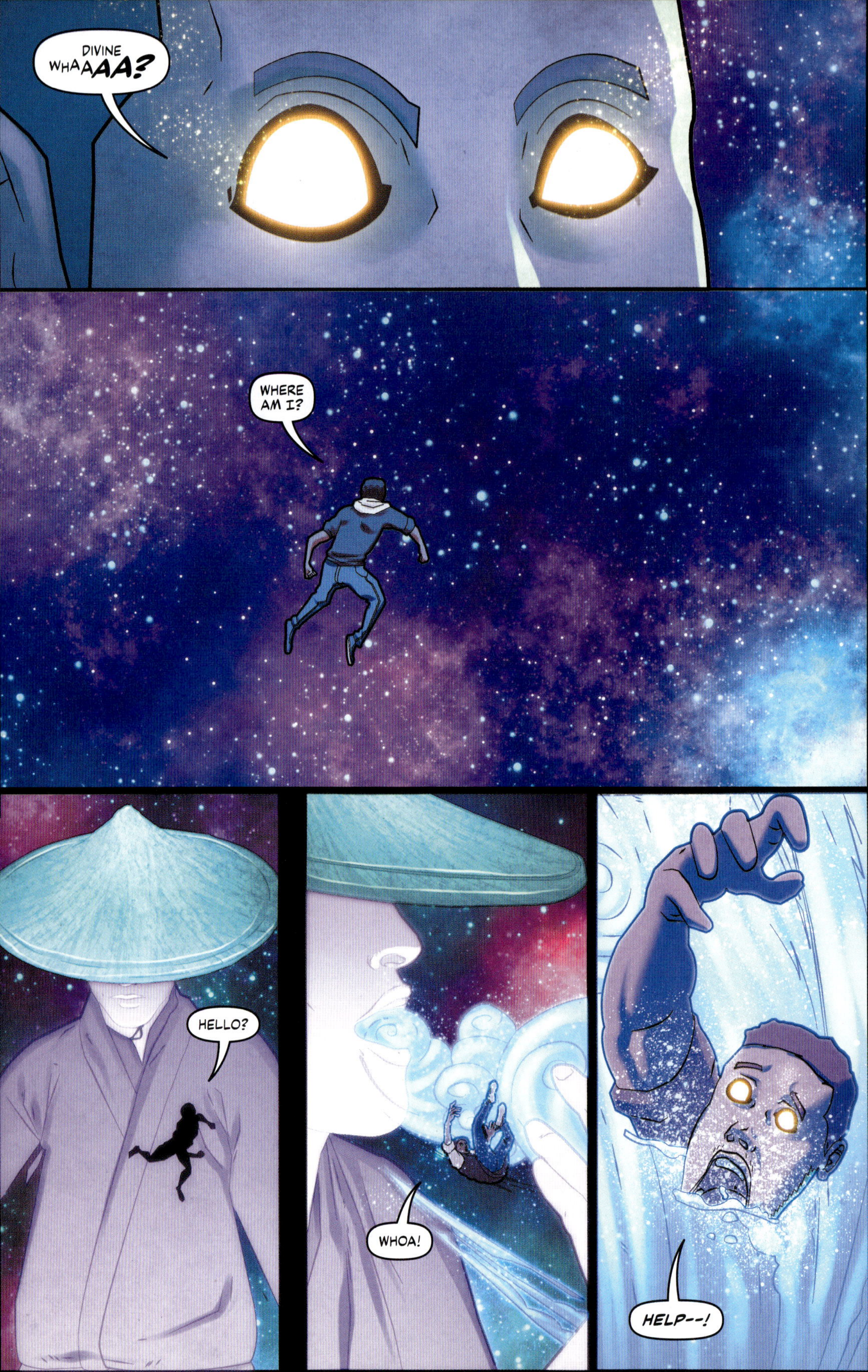
DIVINE WHAAAAA?
WHERE AM I?
HELLO?
WHOA!
HELP--!

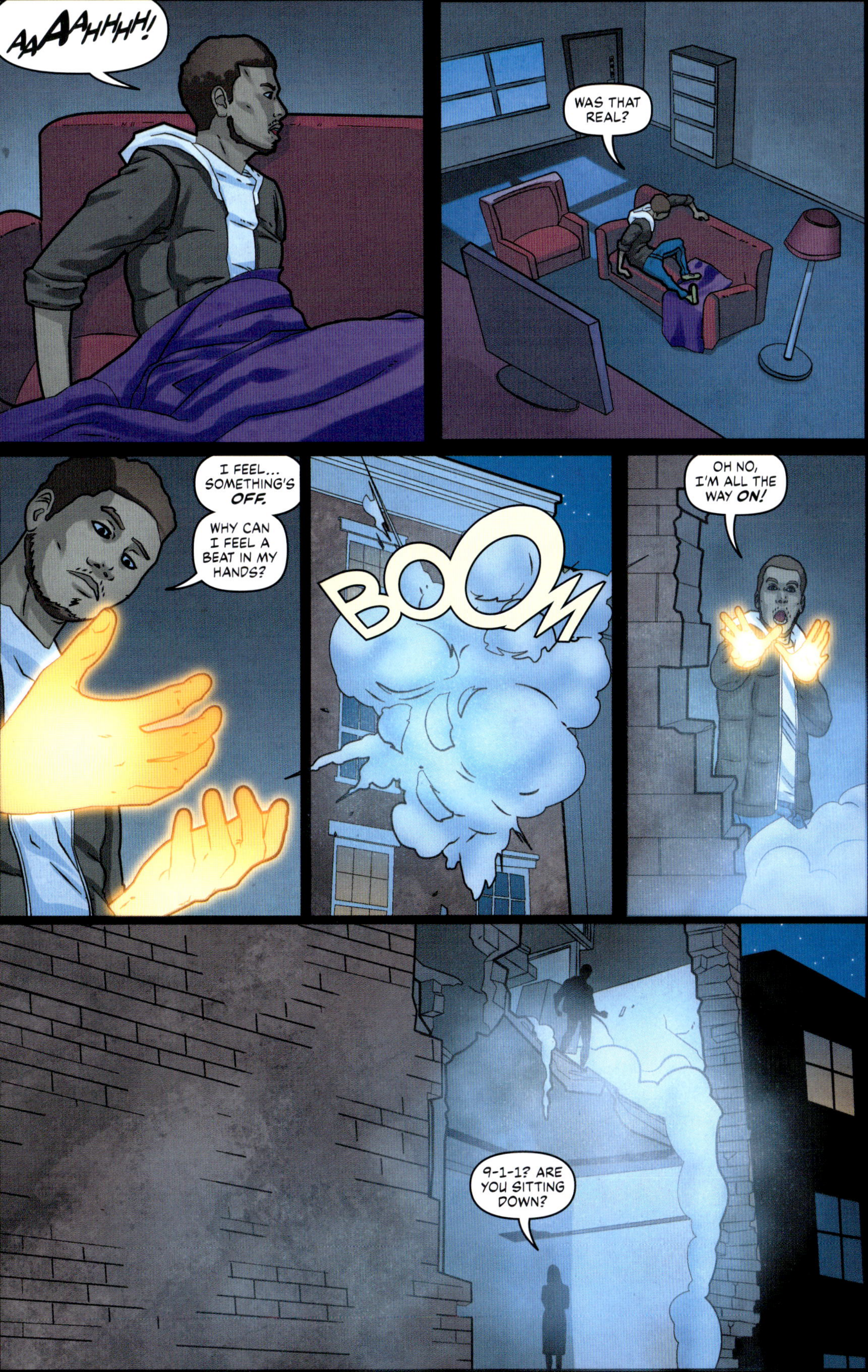
AAAAHHHH!
WAS THAT REAL?
I FEEL... SOMETHING'S OFF.
WHY CAN I FEEL A BEAT IN MY HANDS?
BOOM
OH NO, I'M ALL THE WAY ON!
9-1-1? ARE YOU SITTING DOWN?

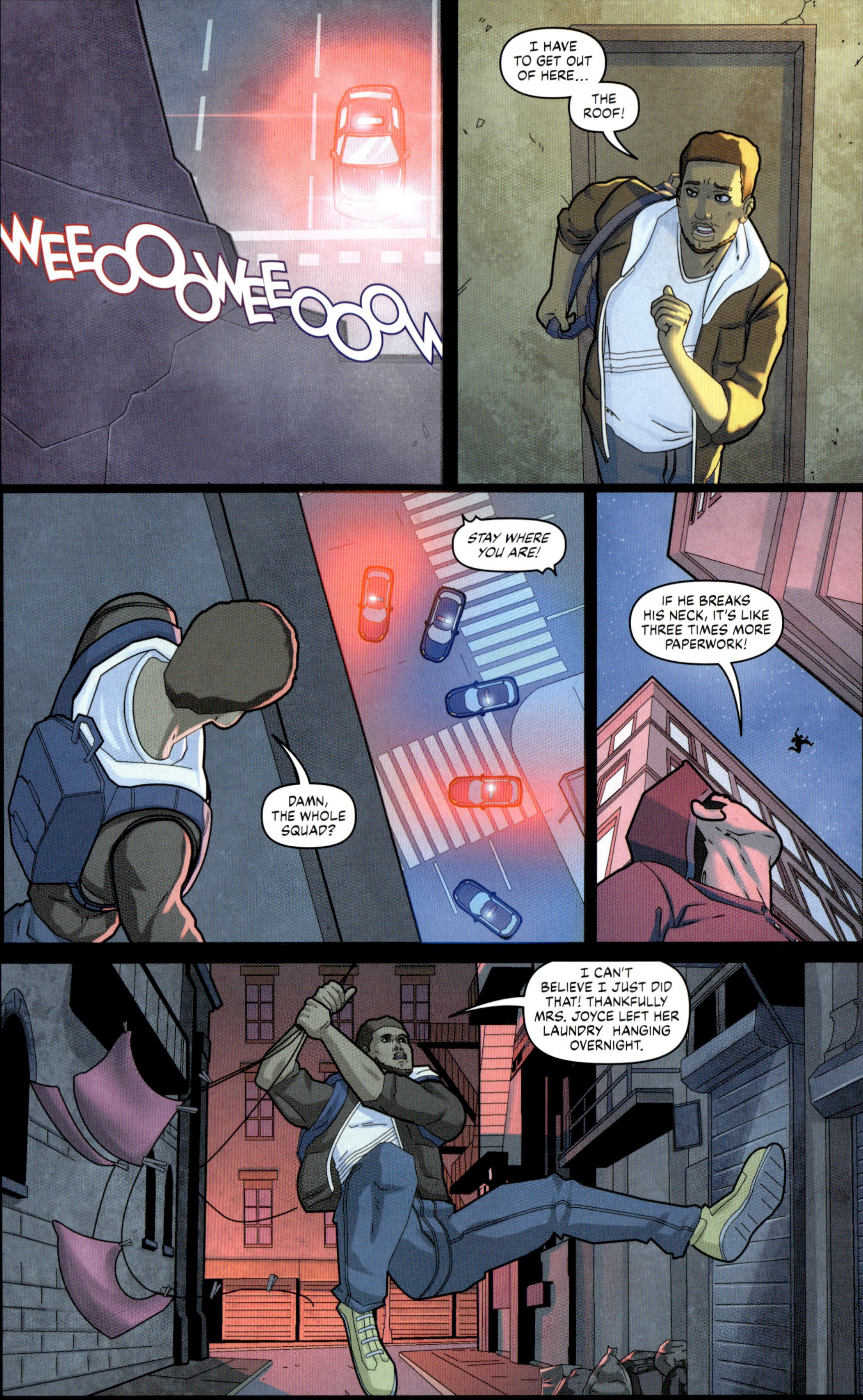
WEEOOOWEEOOOW
I HAVE TO GET OUT OF HERE...
THE ROOF!
STAY WHERE YOU ARE!
DAMN, THE WHOLE SQUAD?
IF HE BREAKS HIS NECK, IT'S LIKE THREE TIMES MORE PAPERWORK!
I CAN'T BELIEVE I JUST DID THAT! THANKFULLY MRS. JOYCE LEFT HER LAUNDRY HANGING OVERNIGHT.

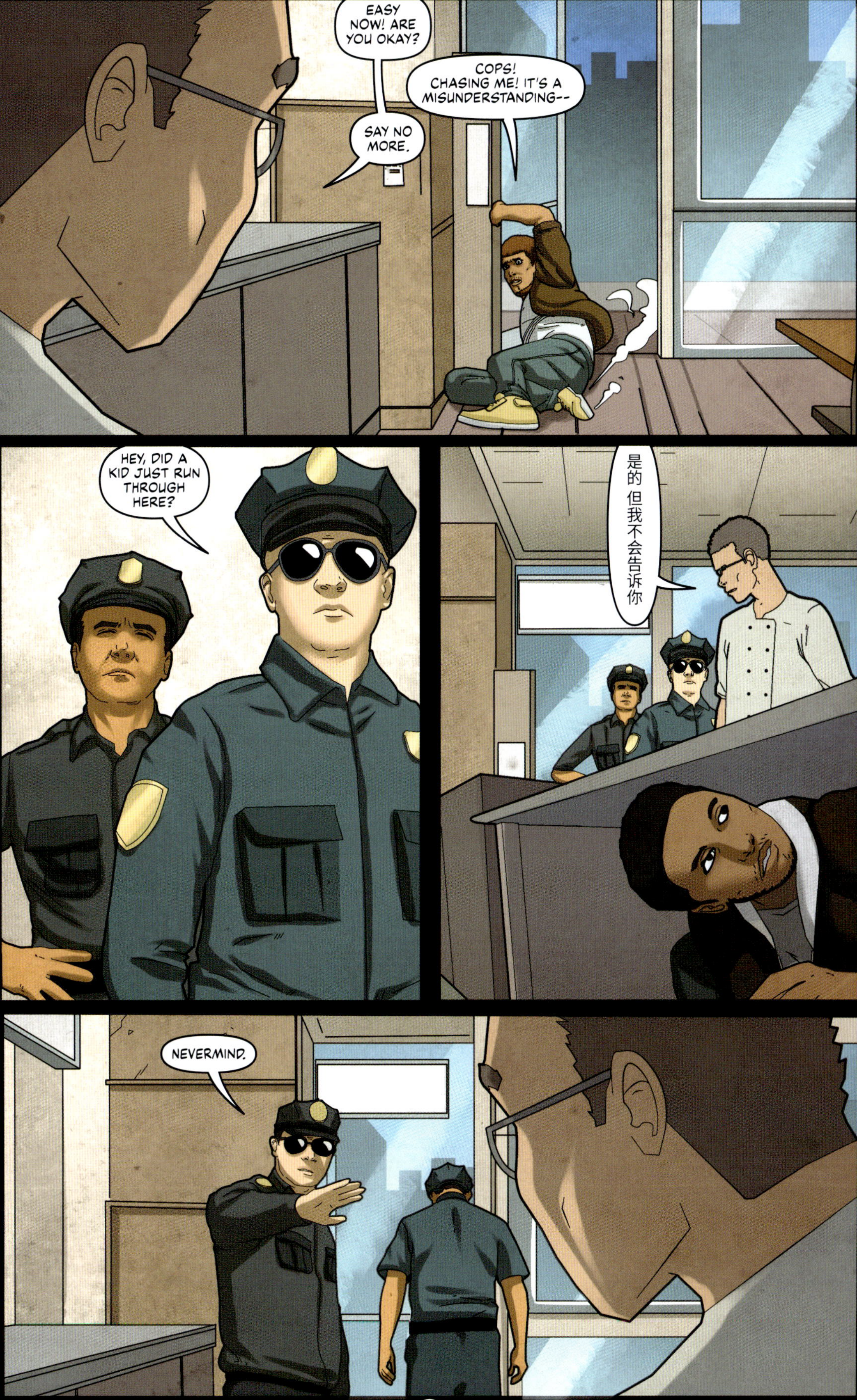

EASY NOW! ARE YOU OKAY?
COPS! CHASING ME! IT'S A MISUNDERSTANDING--
SAY NO MORE.
HEY, DID A KID JUST RUN THROUGH HERE?
是的 但我不会告诉你
NEVERMIND.

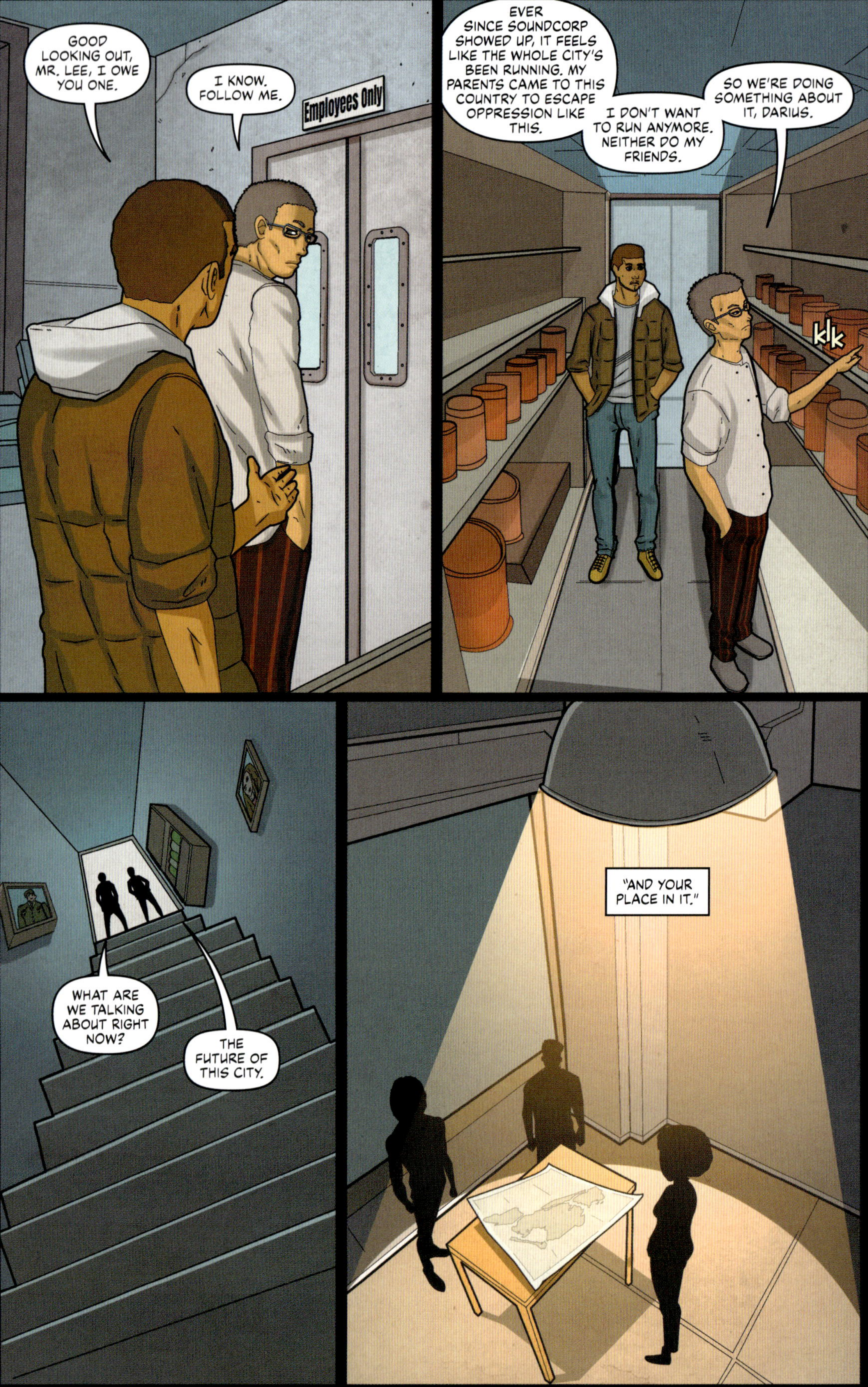
GOOD LOOKING OUT, MR. LEE, I OWE YOU ONE.
I KNOW. FOLLOW ME.
Employees Only
EVER SINCE SOUNDCORP SHOWED UP, IT FEELS LIKE THE WHOLE CITY'S BEEN RUNNING. MY PARENTS CAME TO THIS COUNTRY TO ESCAPE OPPRESSION LIKE THIS.
I DON'T WANT TO RUN ANYMORE. NEITHER DO MY FRIENDS.
SO WE'RE DOING SOMETHING ABOUT IT, DARIUS.
KLK
WHAT ARE WE TALKING ABOUT RIGHT NOW?
THE FUTURE OF THIS CITY.
"AND YOUR PLACE IN IT."

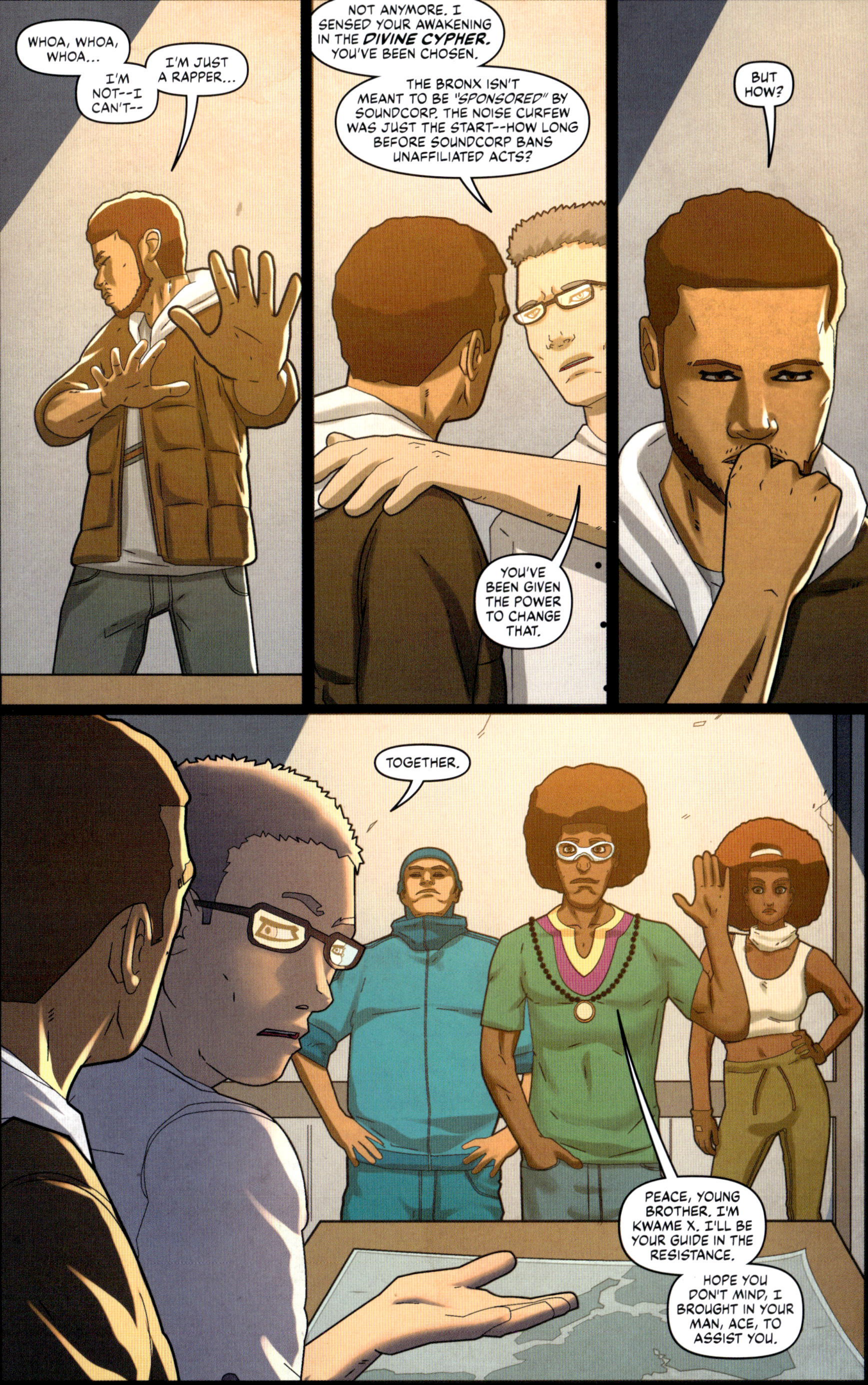
WHOA, WHOA, WHOA...
I'M NOT--I CAN'T--
I'M JUST A RAPPER...
NOT ANYMORE. I SENSED YOUR AWAKENING IN THE ***DIVINE CYPHER.*** YOU'VE BEEN CHOSEN.
THE BRONX ISN'T MEANT TO BE *"SPONSORED"* BY SOUNDCORP. THE NOISE CURFEW WAS JUST THE START--HOW LONG BEFORE SOUNDCORP BANS UNAFFILIATED ACTS?
YOU'VE BEEN GIVEN THE POWER TO CHANGE THAT.
BUT HOW?
TOGETHER.
PEACE, YOUNG BROTHER. I'M KWAME X. I'LL BE YOUR GUIDE IN THE RESISTANCE.
HOPE YOU DON'T MIND, I BROUGHT IN YOUR MAN, ACE, TO ASSIST YOU.

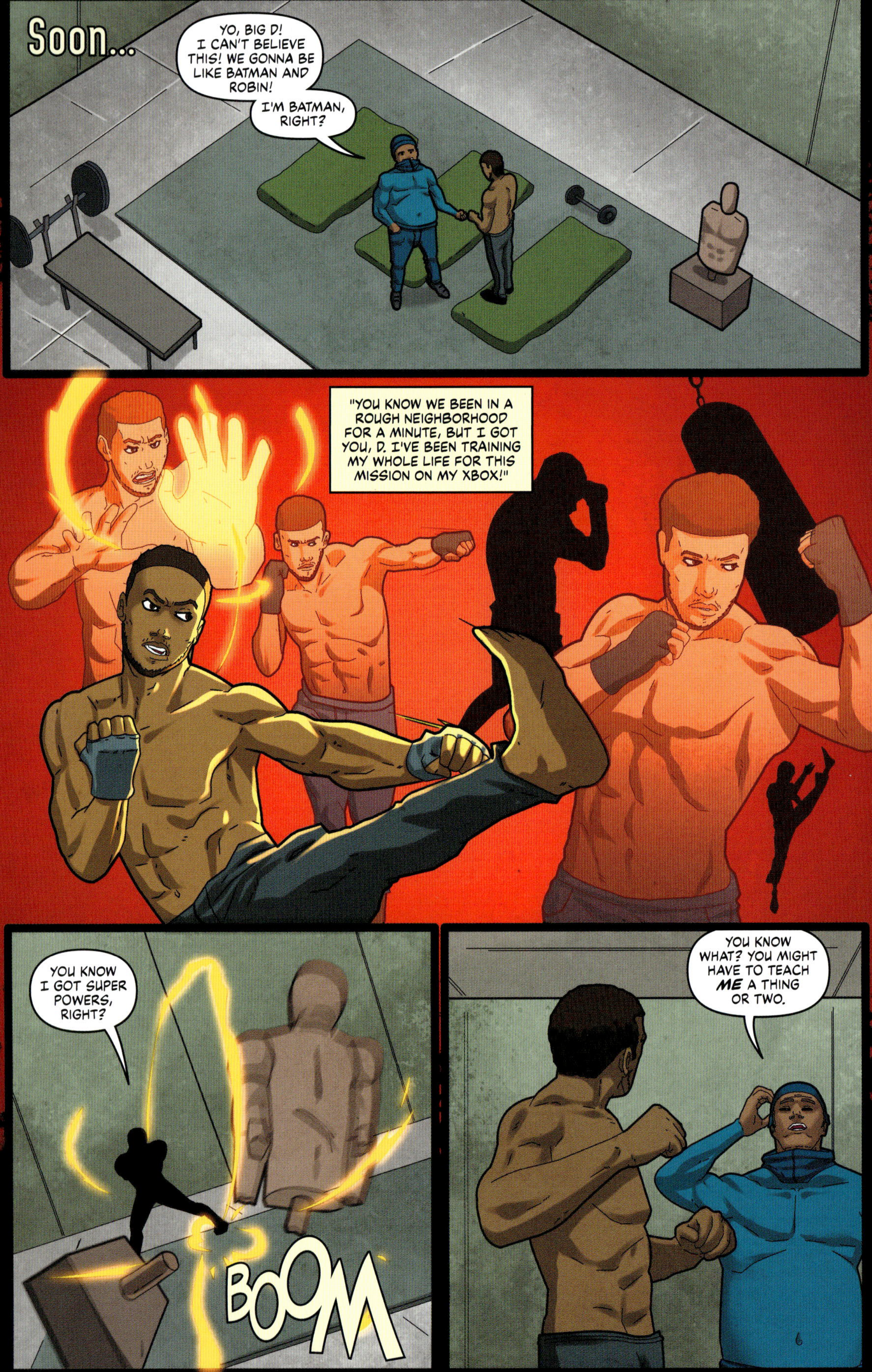
Soon...
YO, BIG D! I CAN'T BELIEVE THIS! WE GONNA BE LIKE BATMAN AND ROBIN!
I'M BATMAN, RIGHT?
"YOU KNOW WE BEEN IN A ROUGH NEIGHBORHOOD FOR A MINUTE, BUT I GOT YOU, D. I'VE BEEN TRAINING MY WHOLE LIFE FOR THIS MISSION ON MY XBOX!"
YOU KNOW I GOT SUPER POWERS, RIGHT?
BOOM
YOU KNOW WHAT? YOU MIGHT HAVE TO TEACH ***ME*** A THING OR TWO.

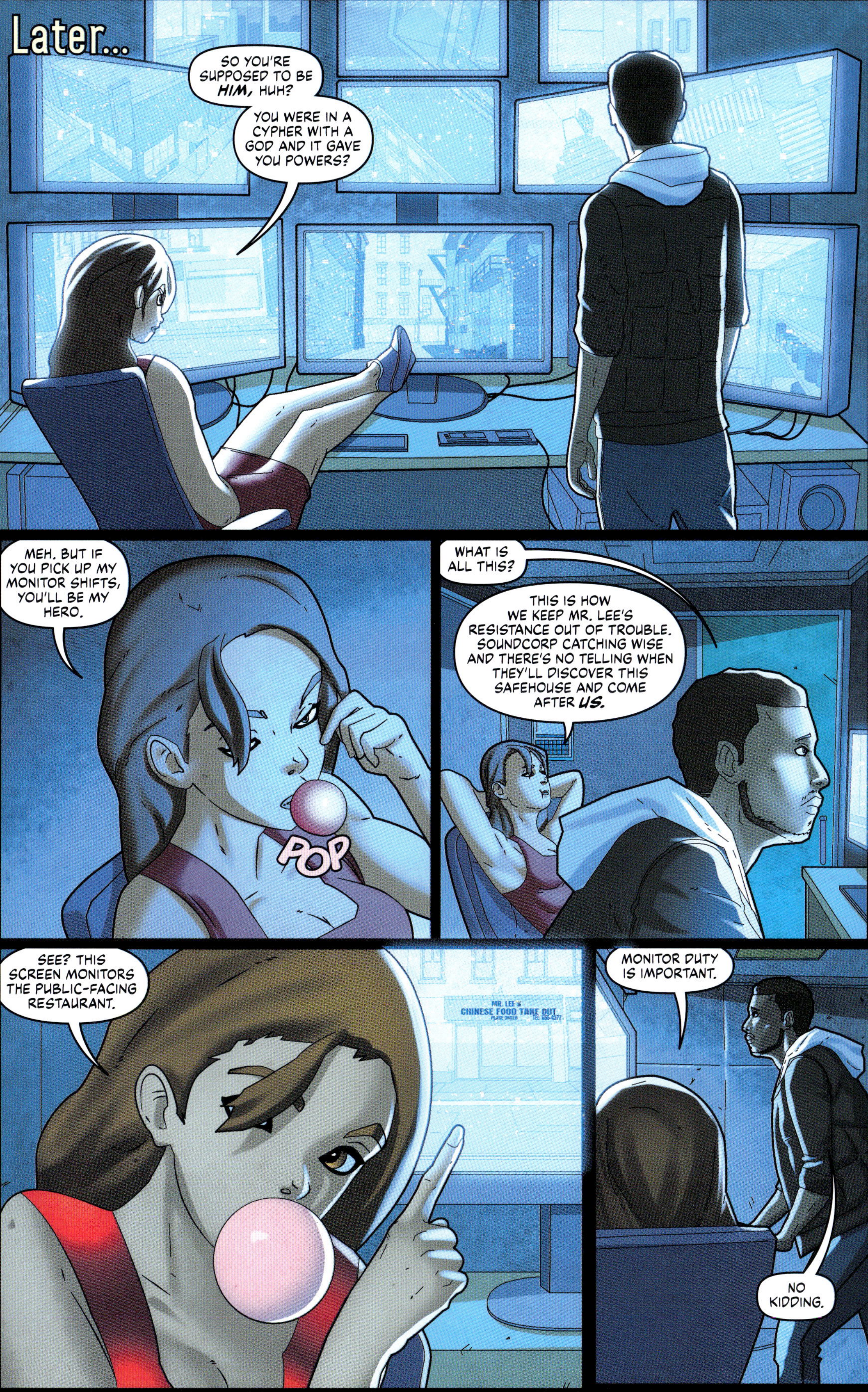
Later...
SO YOU'RE SUPPOSED TO BE *HIM*, HUH?
YOU WERE IN A CYPHER WITH A GOD AND IT GAVE YOU POWERS?
MEH. BUT IF YOU PICK UP MY MONITOR SHIFTS, YOU'LL BE MY HERO.
POP
WHAT IS ALL THIS?
THIS IS HOW WE KEEP MR. LEE'S RESISTANCE OUT OF TROUBLE. SOUNDCORP CATCHING WISE AND THERE'S NO TELLING WHEN THEY'LL DISCOVER THIS SAFEHOUSE AND COME AFTER *US.*
SEE? THIS SCREEN MONITORS THE PUBLIC-FACING RESTAURANT.
MR. LEE'S
CHINESE FOOD TAKE OUT
MONITOR DUTY IS IMPORTANT.
NO KIDDING.

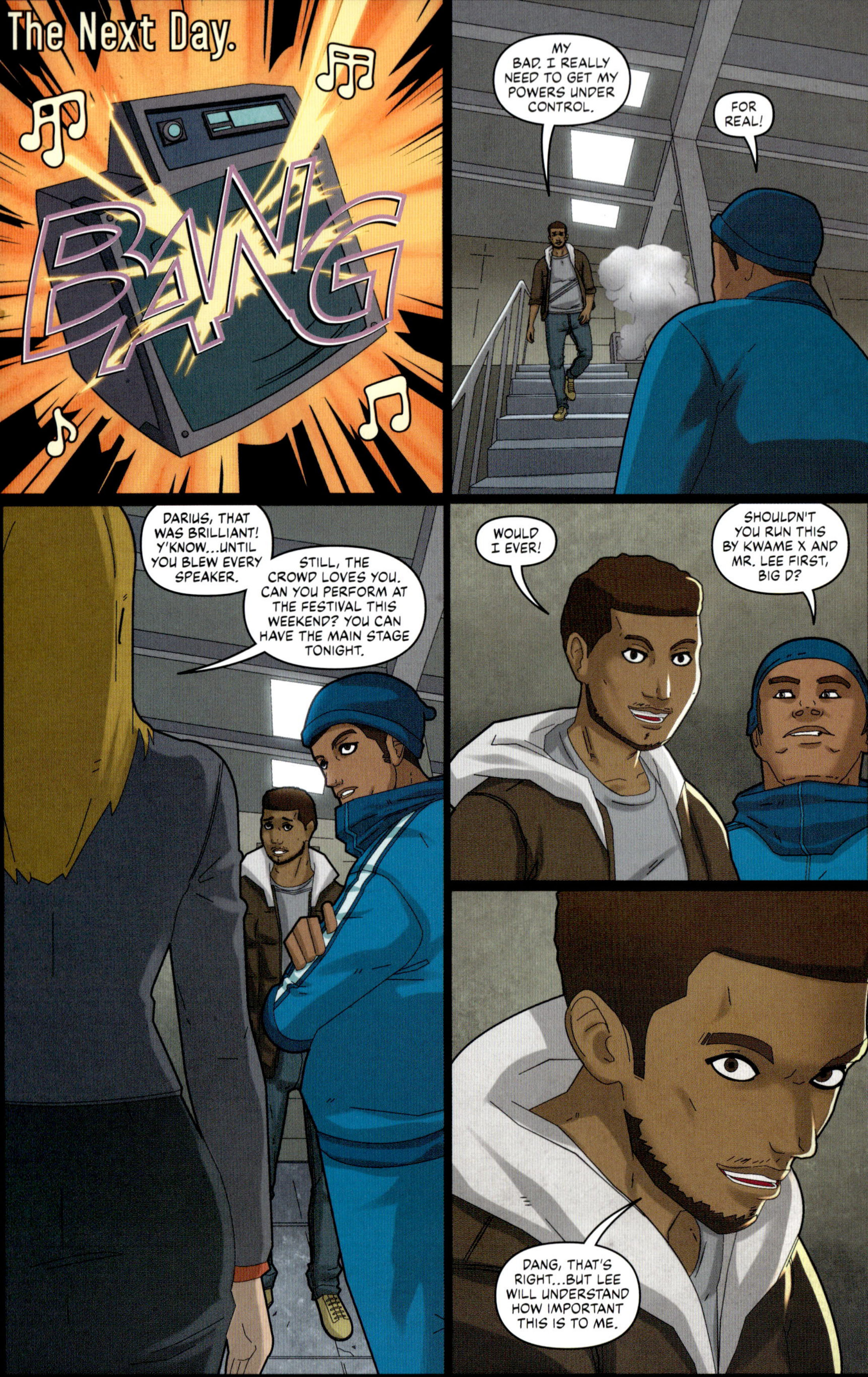
The Next Day.
BANG
MY BAD. I REALLY NEED TO GET MY POWERS UNDER CONTROL.
FOR REAL!
DARIUS, THAT WAS BRILLIANT! Y'KNOW...UNTIL YOU BLEW EVERY SPEAKER.
STILL, THE CROWD LOVES YOU. CAN YOU PERFORM AT THE FESTIVAL THIS WEEKEND? YOU CAN HAVE THE MAIN STAGE TONIGHT.
WOULD I EVER!
SHOULDN'T YOU RUN THIS BY KWAME X AND MR. LEE FIRST, BIG D?
DANG, THAT'S RIGHT...BUT LEE WILL UNDERSTAND HOW IMPORTANT THIS IS TO ME.

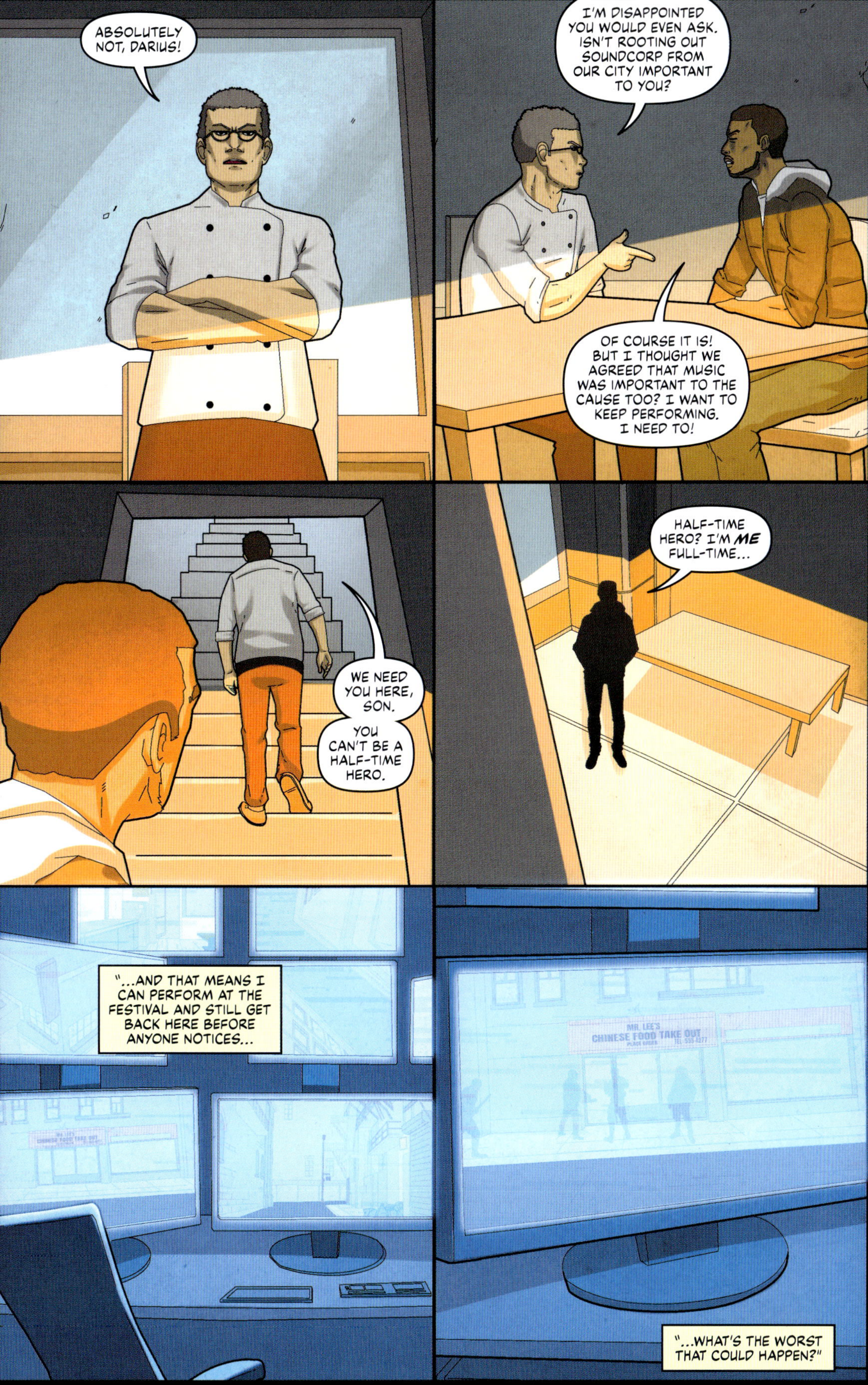
ABSOLUTELY NOT, DARIUS!
I'M DISAPPOINTED YOU WOULD EVEN ASK. ISN'T ROOTING OUT SOUNDCORP FROM OUR CITY IMPORTANT TO YOU?
OF COURSE IT IS! BUT I THOUGHT WE AGREED THAT MUSIC WAS IMPORTANT TO THE CAUSE TOO? I WANT TO KEEP PERFORMING. I NEED TO!
WE NEED YOU HERE, SON.
YOU CAN'T BE A HALF-TIME HERO.
HALF-TIME HERO? I'M **ME** FULL-TIME...
"...AND THAT MEANS I CAN PERFORM AT THE FESTIVAL AND STILL GET BACK HERE BEFORE ANYONE NOTICES...
MR. LEE'S
CHINESE FOOD TAKE OUT
"...WHAT'S THE WORST THAT COULD HAPPEN?"

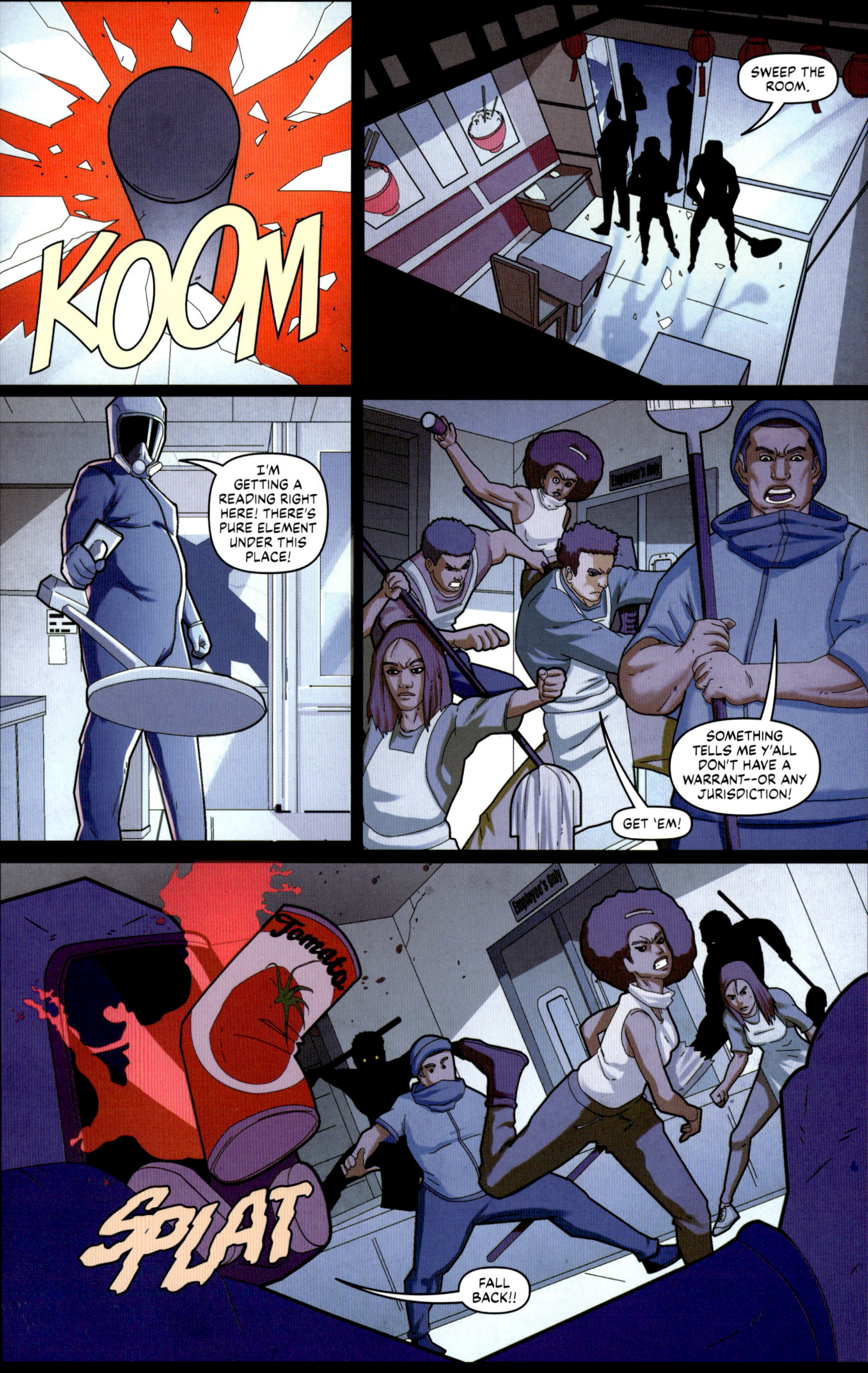
KOOM
SWEEP THE ROOM.
I'M GETTING A READING RIGHT HERE! THERE'S PURE ELEMENT UNDER THIS PLACE!
SOMETHING TELLS ME Y'ALL DON'T HAVE A WARRANT--OR ANY JURISDICTION!
GET 'EM!
Employee's Only
Tomato
SPLAT
FALL BACK!!

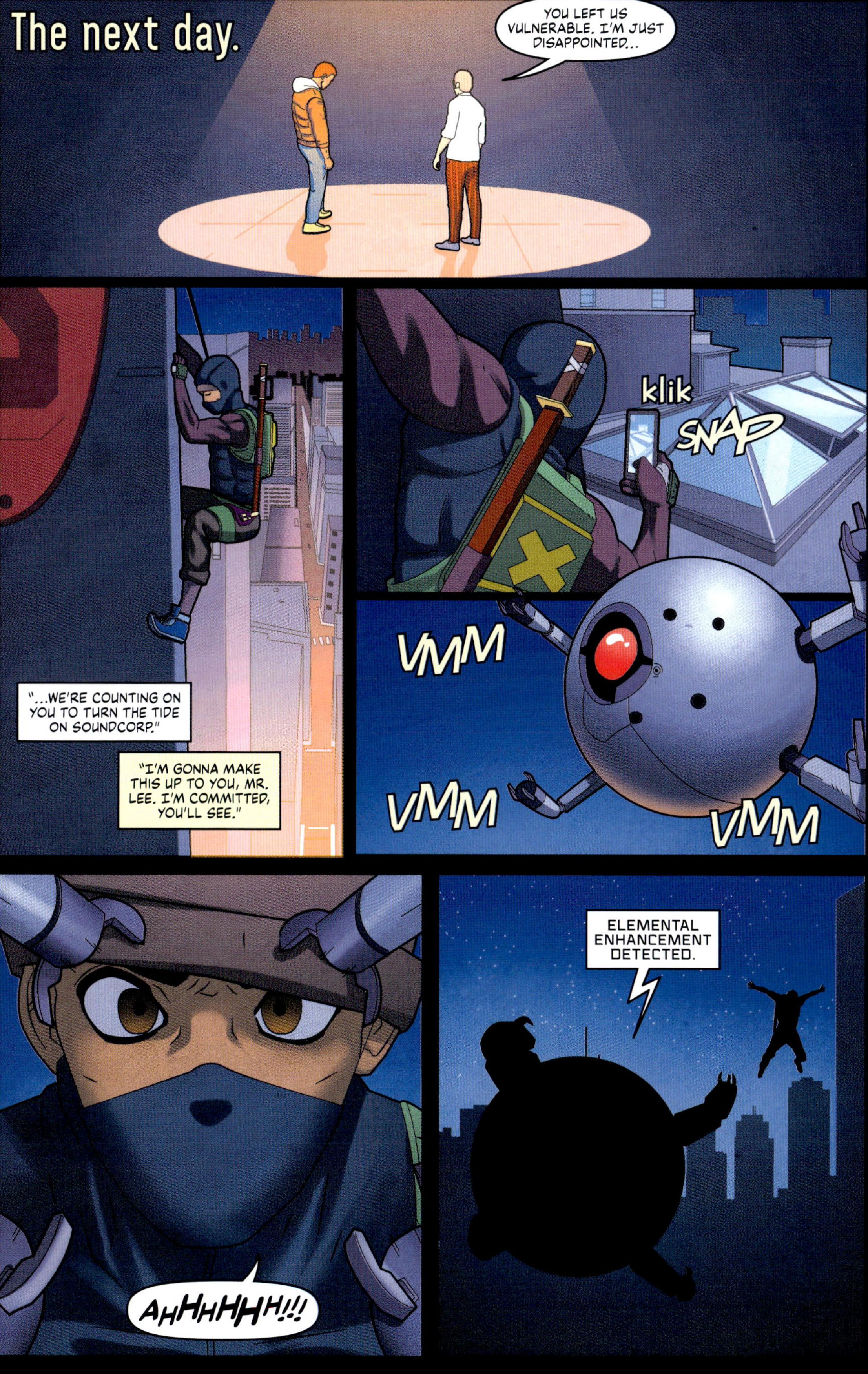
The next day.
YOU LEFT US VULNERABLE. I'M JUST DISAPPOINTED...
"...WE'RE COUNTING ON YOU TO TURN THE TIDE ON SOUNDCORP."
"I'M GONNA MAKE THIS UP TO YOU, MR. LEE. I'M COMMITTED, YOU'LL SEE."
klik
SNAP
VMM
VMM
VMM
AHHHHHH!!!
ELEMENTAL ENHANCEMENT DETECTED.

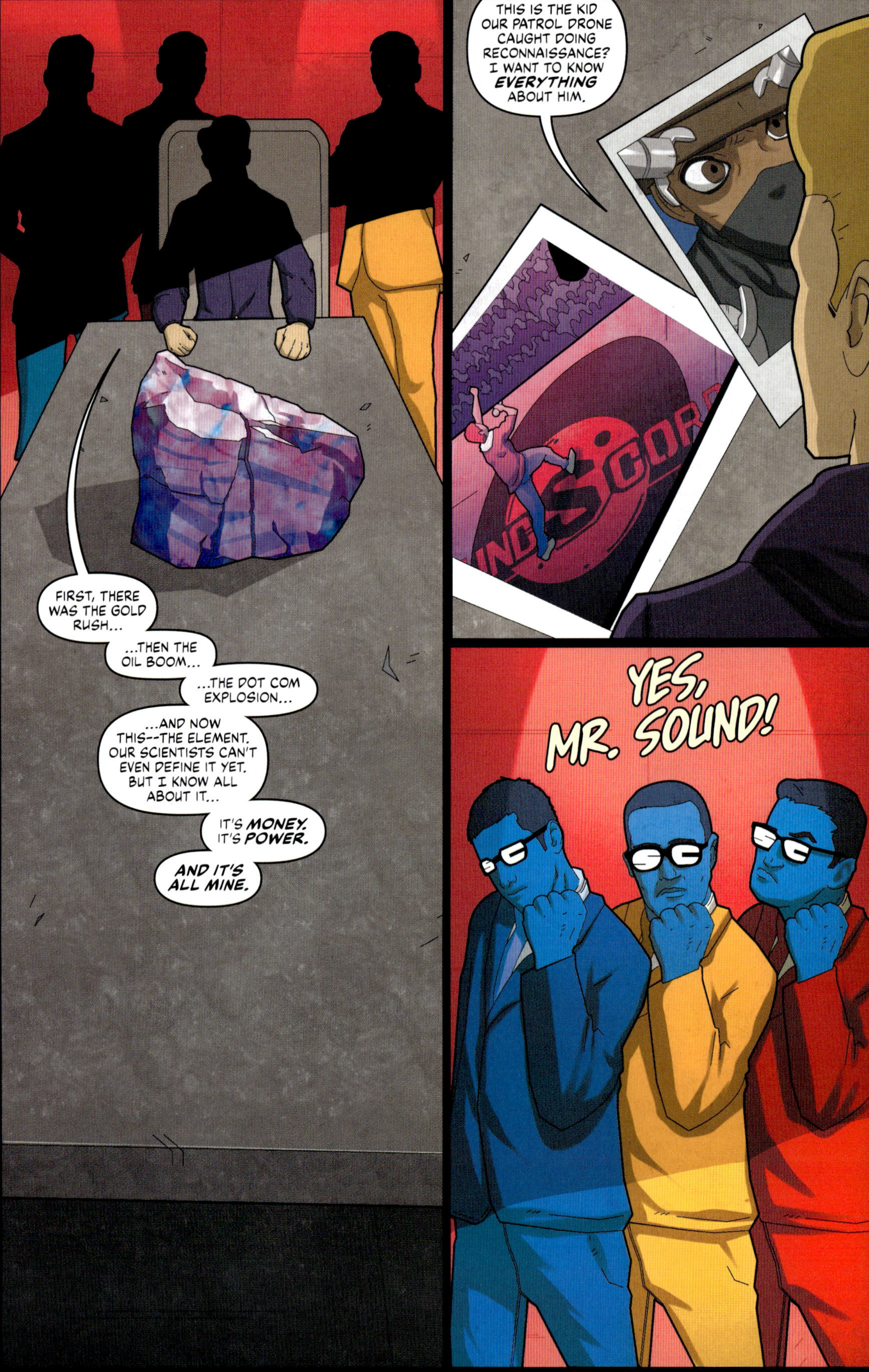
FIRST, THERE WAS THE GOLD RUSH...
...THEN THE OIL BOOM...
...THE DOT COM EXPLOSION...
...AND NOW THIS--THE ELEMENT. OUR SCIENTISTS CAN'T EVEN DEFINE IT YET. BUT I KNOW ALL ABOUT IT...
IT'S MONEY. IT'S POWER.
AND IT'S ALL MINE.
THIS IS THE KID OUR PATROL DRONE CAUGHT DOING RECONNAISSANCE? I WANT TO KNOW EVERYTHING ABOUT HIM.
YES, MR. SOUND!

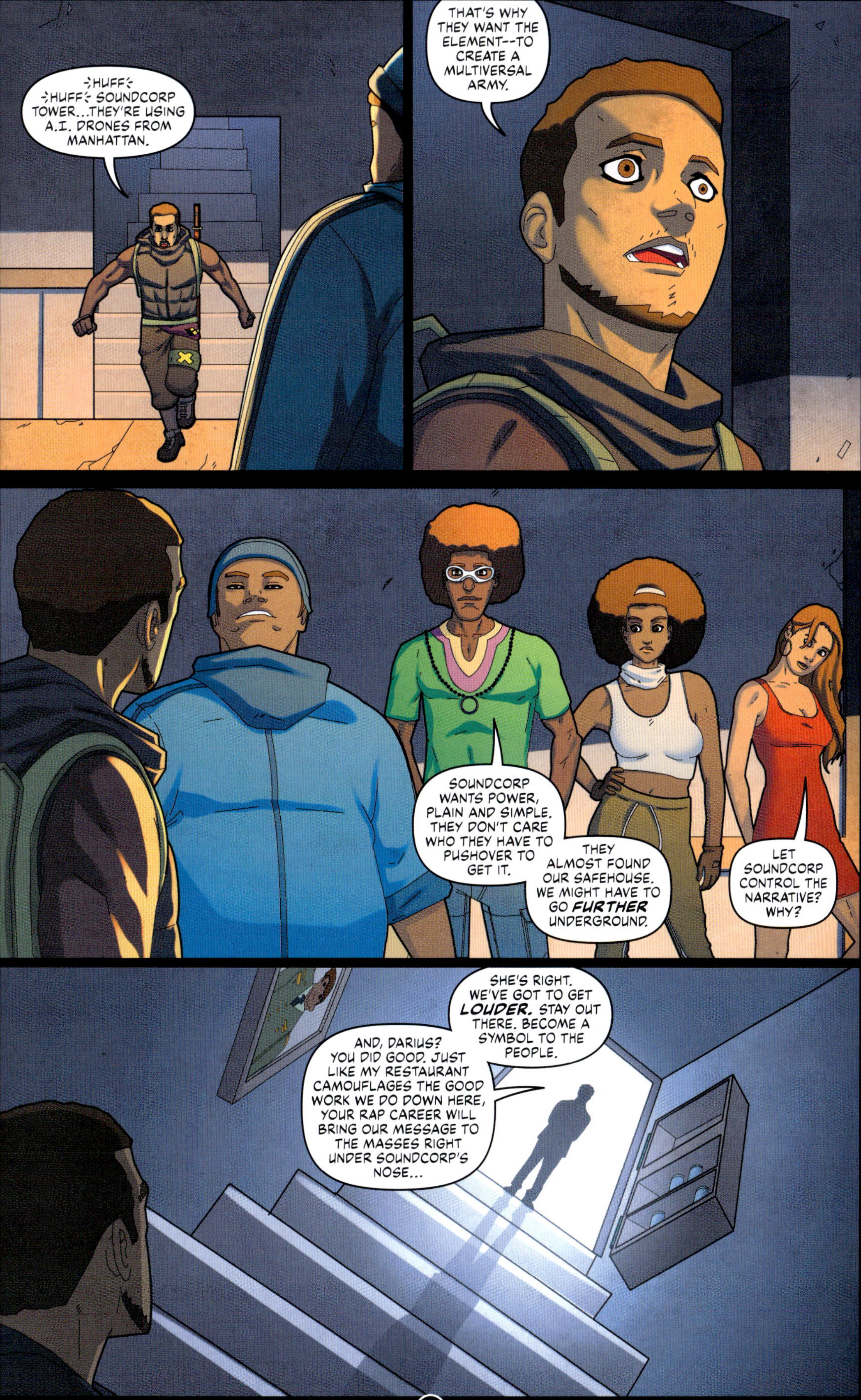

-HUFF- -HUFF- SOUNDCORP TOWER...THEY'RE USING A.I. DRONES FROM MANHATTAN.
THAT'S WHY THEY WANT THE ELEMENT--TO CREATE A MULTIVERSAL ARMY.
SOUNDCORP WANTS POWER, PLAIN AND SIMPLE. THEY DON'T CARE WHO THEY HAVE TO PUSHOVER TO GET IT.
THEY ALMOST FOUND OUR SAFEHOUSE. WE MIGHT HAVE TO GO FURTHER UNDERGROUND.
LET SOUNDCORP CONTROL THE NARRATIVE? WHY?
SHE'S RIGHT. WE'VE GOT TO GET LOUDER. STAY OUT THERE. BECOME A SYMBOL TO THE PEOPLE.
AND, DARIUS? YOU DID GOOD. JUST LIKE MY RESTAURANT CAMOUFLAGES THE GOOD WORK WE DO DOWN HERE, YOUR RAP CAREER WILL BRING OUR MESSAGE TO THE MASSES RIGHT UNDER SOUNDCORP'S NOSE...

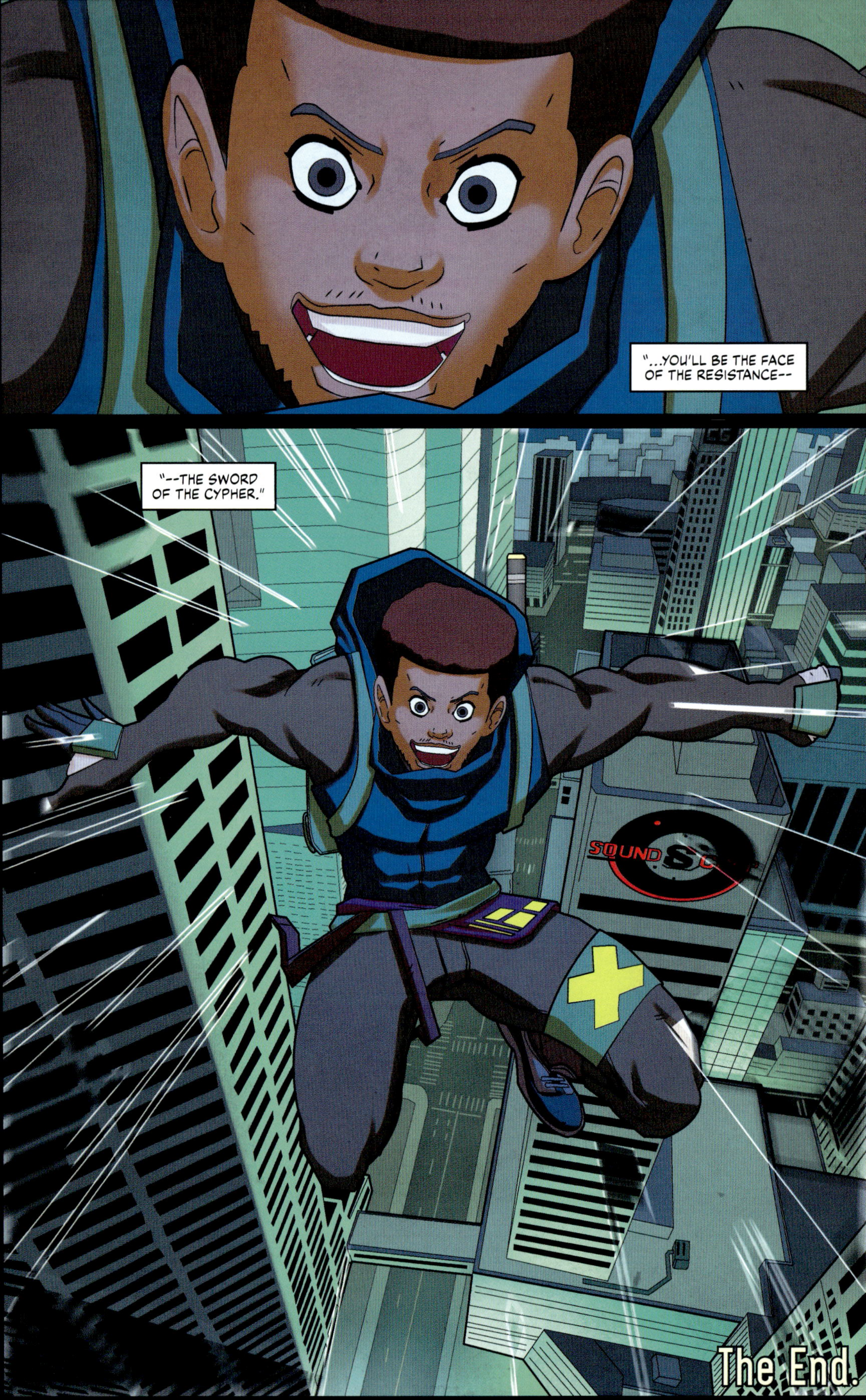
"...YOU'LL BE THE FACE OF THE RESISTANCE--
"--THE SWORD OF THE CYPHER."
SOUND
The End.

MARCUS AND THE DRUNKEN FIST

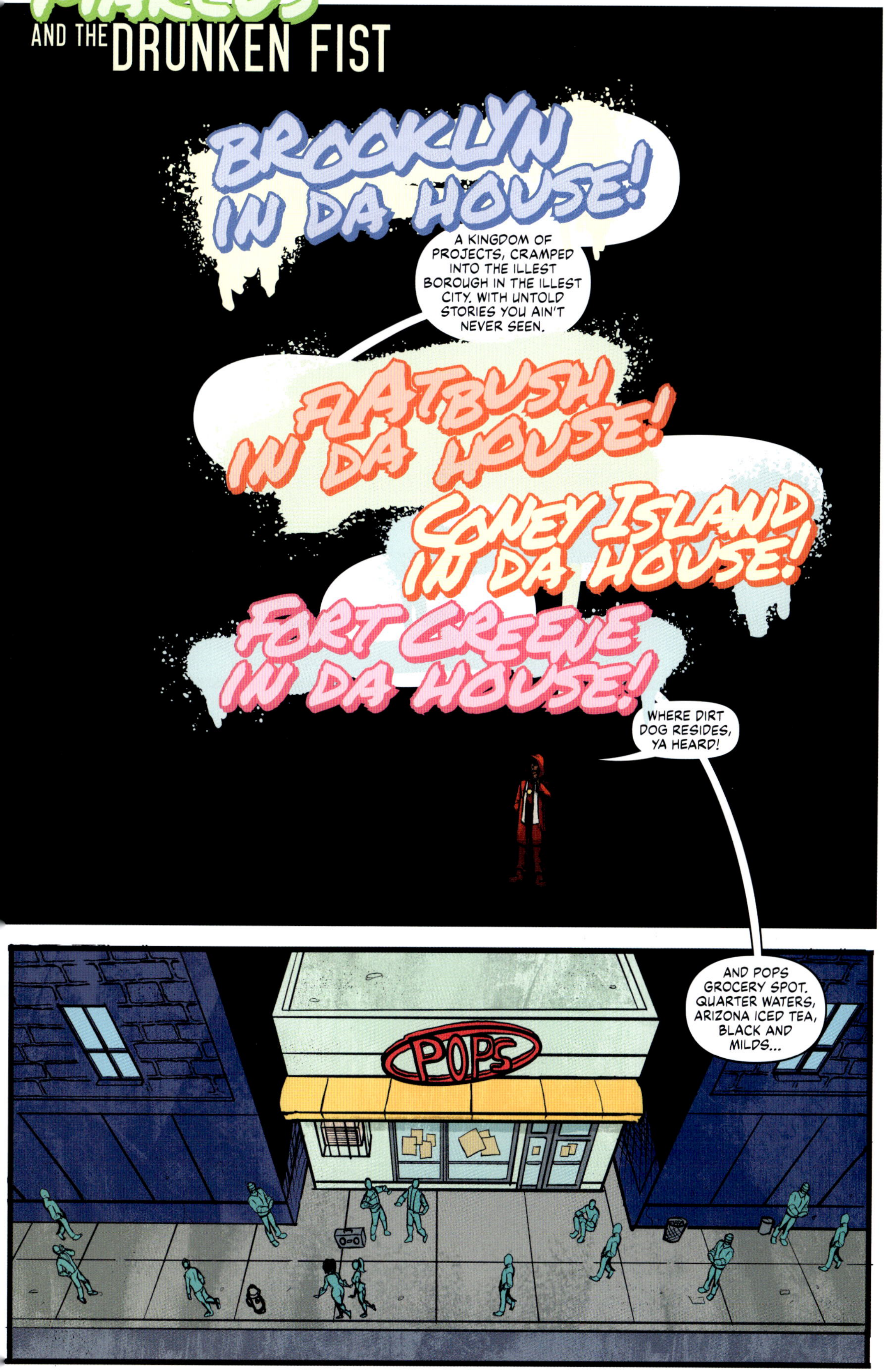
BROOKLYN IN DA HOUSE!
A KINGDOM OF PROJECTS, CRAMPED INTO THE ILLEST BOROUGH IN THE ILLEST CITY. WITH UNTOLD STORIES YOU AIN'T NEVER SEEN.
FLATBUSH IN DA HOUSE!
CONEY ISLAND IN DA HOUSE!
FORT GREENE IN DA HOUSE!
WHERE DIRT DOG RESIDES, YA HEARD!
AND POPS GROCERY SPOT. QUARTER WATERS, ARIZONA ICED TEA, BLACK AND MILDS...
POPS

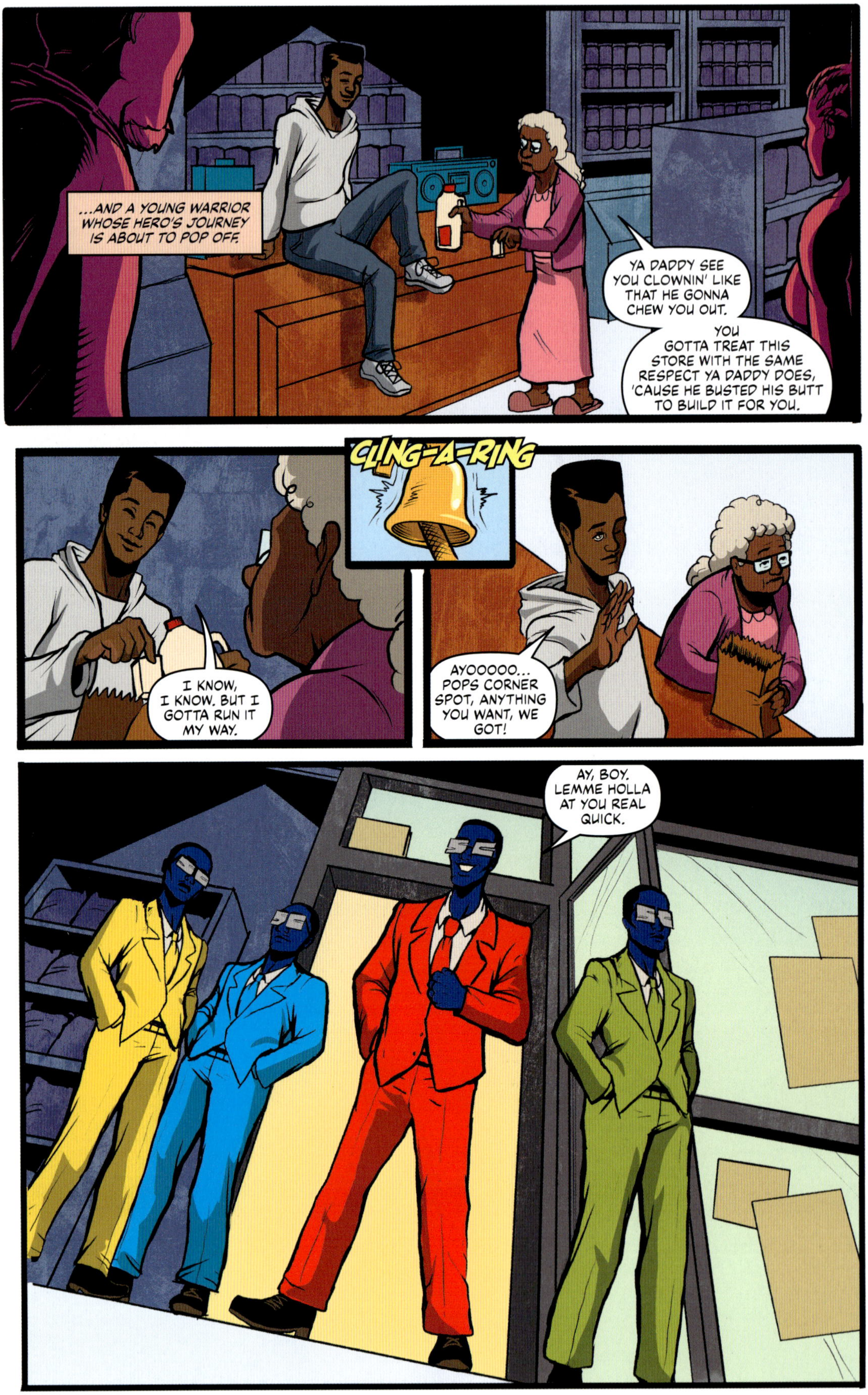
...AND A YOUNG WARRIOR WHOSE HERO'S JOURNEY IS ABOUT TO POP OFF.
YA DADDY SEE YOU CLOWNIN' LIKE THAT HE GONNA CHEW YOU OUT.
YOU GOTTA TREAT THIS STORE WITH THE SAME RESPECT YA DADDY DOES, 'CAUSE HE BUSTED HIS BUTT TO BUILD IT FOR YOU.
I KNOW, I KNOW. BUT I GOTTA RUN IT MY WAY.
CLING-A-RING
AYOOOOO... POPS CORNER SPOT, ANYTHING YOU WANT, WE GOT!
AY, BOY. LEMME HOLLA AT YOU REAL QUICK.

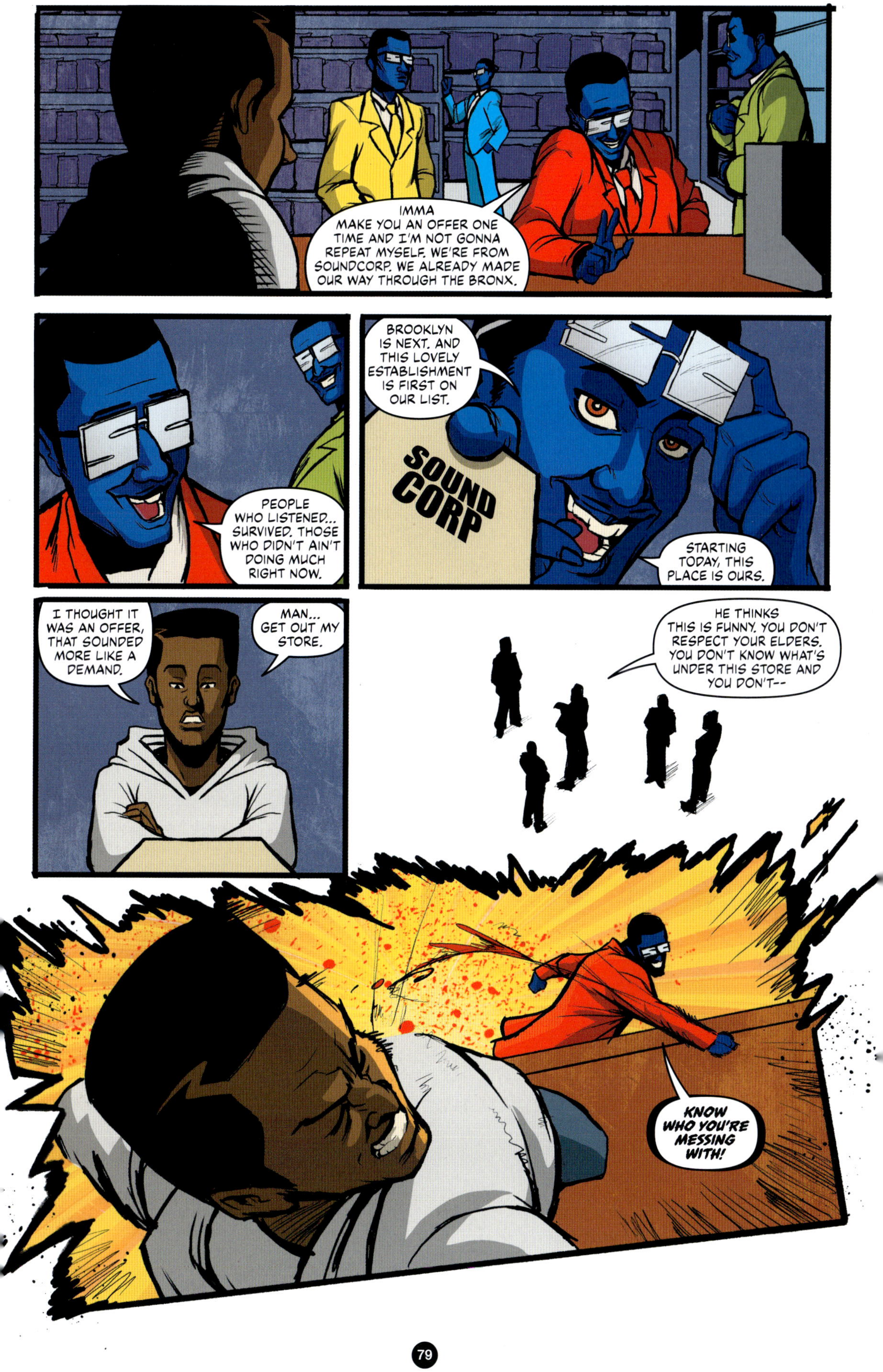
IMMA MAKE YOU AN OFFER ONE TIME AND I'M NOT GONNA REPEAT MYSELF. WE'RE FROM SOUNDCORP. WE ALREADY MADE OUR WAY THROUGH THE BRONX.
PEOPLE WHO LISTENED... SURVIVED. THOSE WHO DIDN'T AIN'T DOING MUCH RIGHT NOW.
BROOKLYN IS NEXT. AND THIS LOVELY ESTABLISHMENT IS FIRST ON OUR LIST.
SOUND CORP
STARTING TODAY, THIS PLACE IS OURS.
I THOUGHT IT WAS AN OFFER, THAT SOUNDED MORE LIKE A DEMAND.
MAN... GET OUT MY STORE.
HE THINKS THIS IS FUNNY. YOU DON'T RESPECT YOUR ELDERS. YOU DON'T KNOW WHAT'S UNDER THIS STORE AND YOU DON'T--
KNOW WHO YOU'RE MESSING WITH!

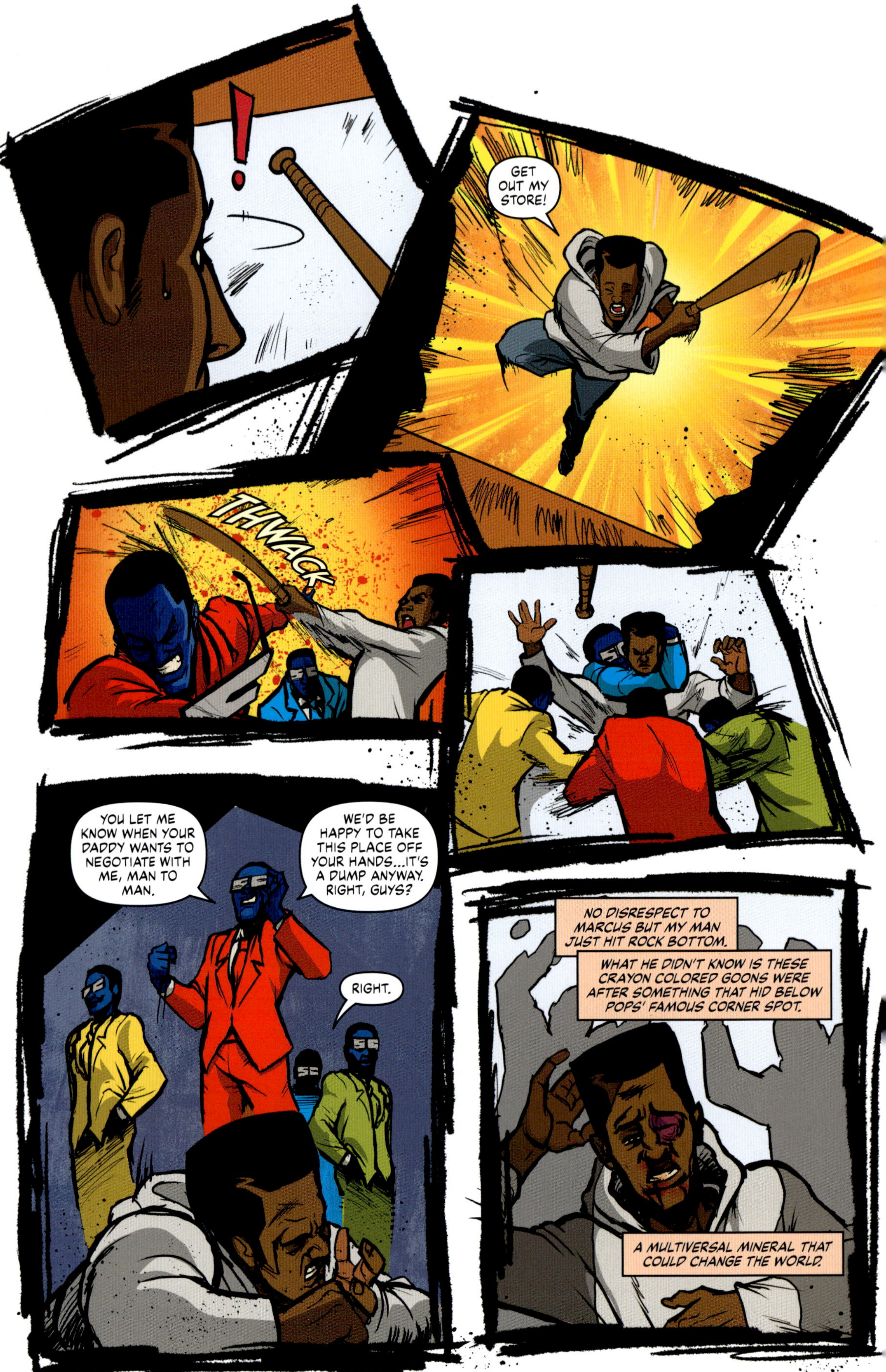
!
GET OUT MY STORE!
THWACK
YOU LET ME KNOW WHEN YOUR DADDY WANTS TO NEGOTIATE WITH ME, MAN TO MAN.
WE'D BE HAPPY TO TAKE THIS PLACE OFF YOUR HANDS...IT'S A DUMP ANYWAY. RIGHT, GUYS?
RIGHT.
NO DISRESPECT TO MARCUS BUT MY MAN JUST HIT ROCK BOTTOM.
WHAT HE DIDN'T KNOW IS THESE CRAYON COLORED GOONS WERE AFTER SOMETHING THAT HID BELOW POPS' FAMOUS CORNER SPOT.
A MULTIVERSAL MINERAL THAT COULD CHANGE THE WORLD.

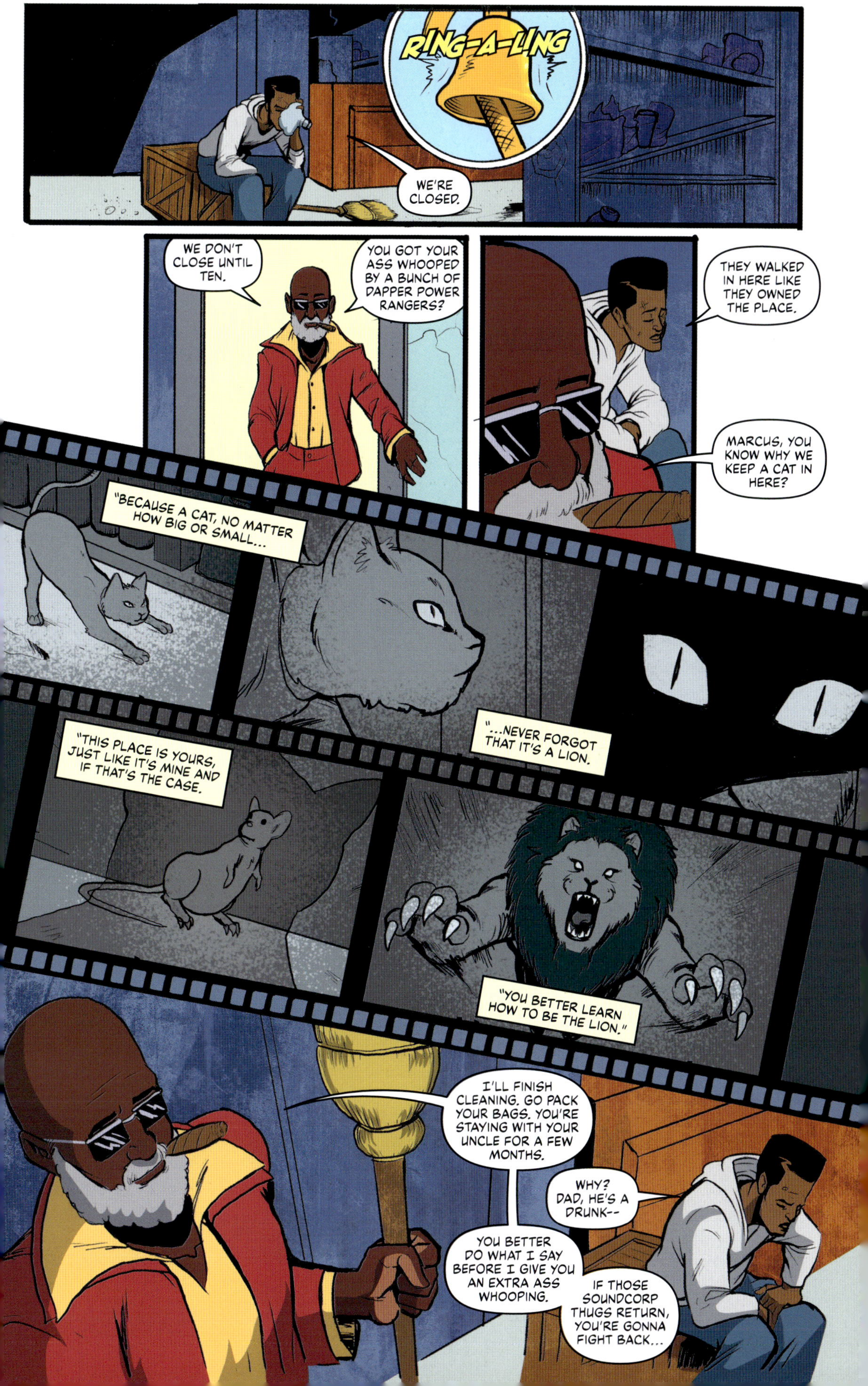
RING-A-LING
WE'RE CLOSED.
WE DON'T CLOSE UNTIL TEN.
YOU GOT YOUR ASS WHOOPED BY A BUNCH OF DAPPER POWER RANGERS?
THEY WALKED IN HERE LIKE THEY OWNED THE PLACE.
MARCUS, YOU KNOW WHY WE KEEP A CAT IN HERE?
"BECAUSE A CAT, NO MATTER HOW BIG OR SMALL...
"...NEVER FORGOT THAT IT'S A LION.
"THIS PLACE IS YOURS, JUST LIKE IT'S MINE AND IF THAT'S THE CASE.
"YOU BETTER LEARN HOW TO BE THE LION."
I'LL FINISH CLEANING. GO PACK YOUR BAGS. YOU'RE STAYING WITH YOUR UNCLE FOR A FEW MONTHS.
WHY? DAD, HE'S A DRUNK--
YOU BETTER DO WHAT I SAY BEFORE I GIVE YOU AN EXTRA ASS WHOOPING.
IF THOSE SOUNDCORP THUGS RETURN, YOU'RE GONNA FIGHT BACK...

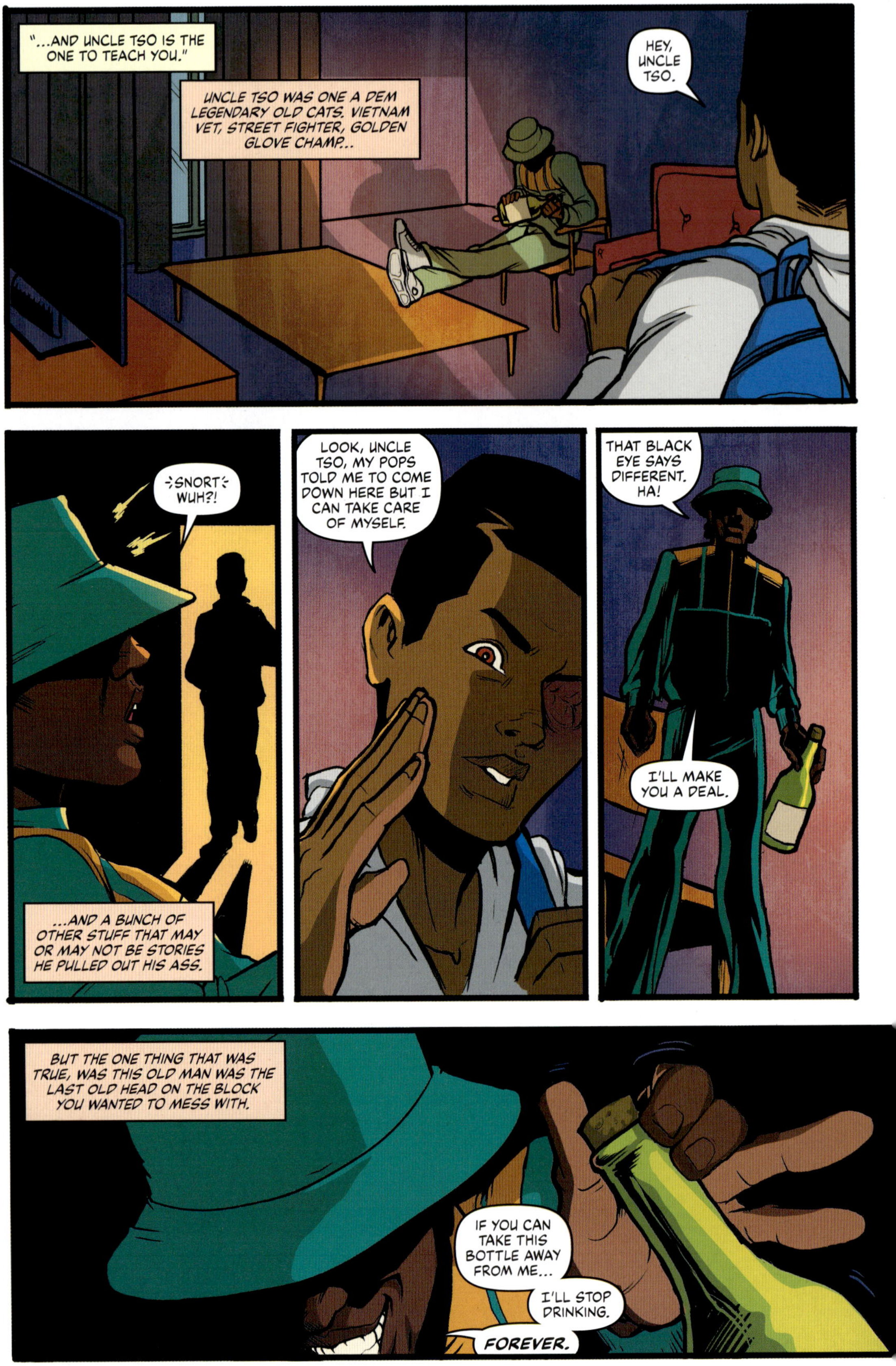
"...AND UNCLE TSO IS THE ONE TO TEACH YOU."
UNCLE TSO WAS ONE A DEM LEGENDARY OLD CATS. VIETNAM VET, STREET FIGHTER, GOLDEN GLOVE CHAMP...
HEY, UNCLE TSO.
SNORT WUH?!
...AND A BUNCH OF OTHER STUFF THAT MAY OR MAY NOT BE STORIES HE PULLED OUT HIS ASS.
LOOK, UNCLE TSO, MY POPS TOLD ME TO COME DOWN HERE BUT I CAN TAKE CARE OF MYSELF.
THAT BLACK EYE SAYS DIFFERENT. HA!
I'LL MAKE YOU A DEAL.
BUT THE ONE THING THAT WAS TRUE, WAS THIS OLD MAN WAS THE LAST OLD HEAD ON THE BLOCK YOU WANTED TO MESS WITH.
IF YOU CAN TAKE THIS BOTTLE AWAY FROM ME...
I'LL STOP DRINKING.
FOREVER.

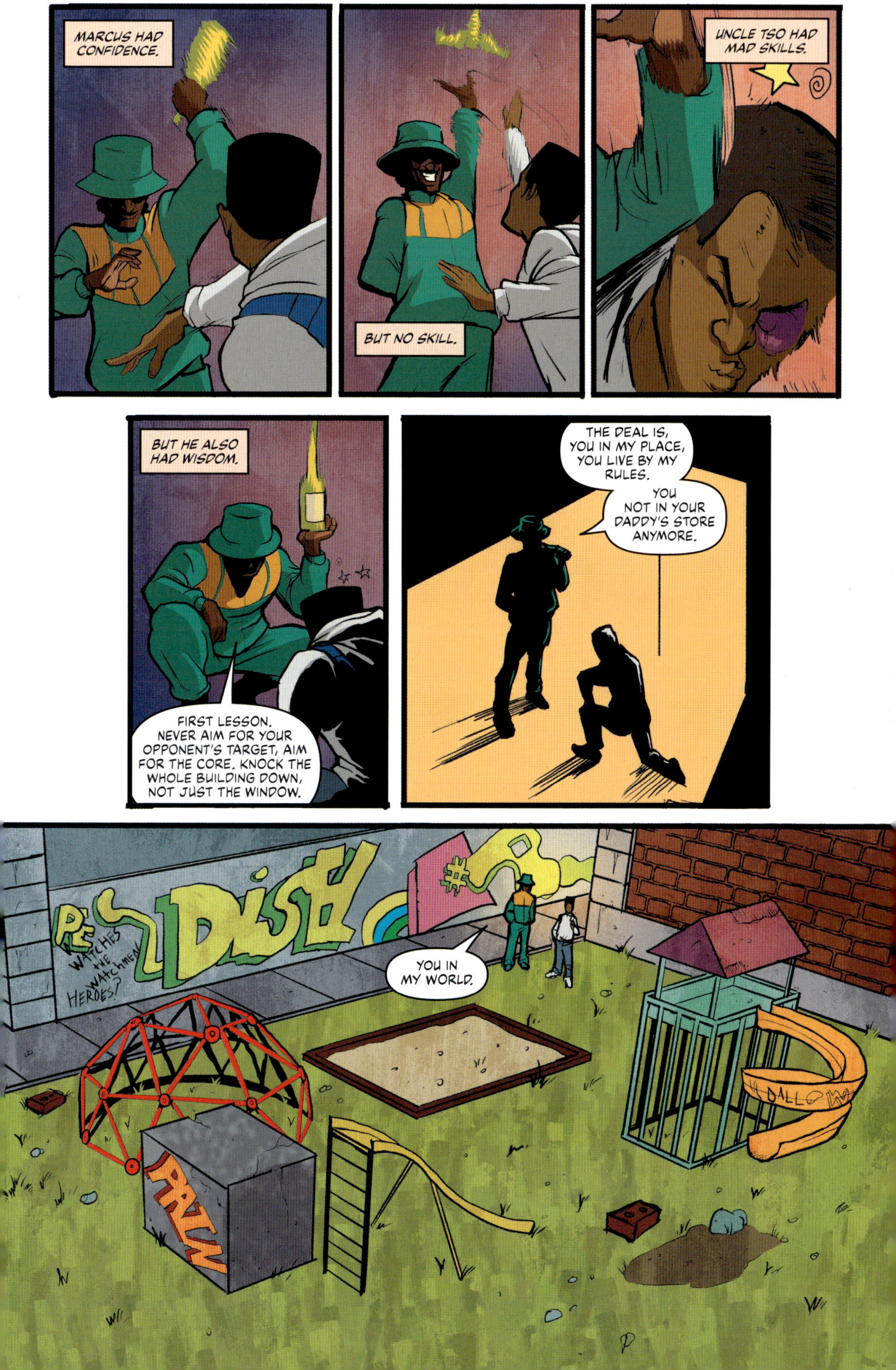
MARCUS HAD CONFIDENCE.
BUT NO SKILL.
UNCLE TSO HAD MAD SKILLS.
BUT HE ALSO HAD WISDOM.
FIRST LESSON. NEVER AIM FOR YOUR OPPONENT'S TARGET, AIM FOR THE CORE. KNOCK THE WHOLE BUILDING DOWN, NOT JUST THE WINDOW.
THE DEAL IS, YOU IN MY PLACE, YOU LIVE BY MY RULES.
YOU NOT IN YOUR DADDY'S STORE ANYMORE.
WATCHES THE WATCHMEN HEROES?
YOU IN MY WORLD.

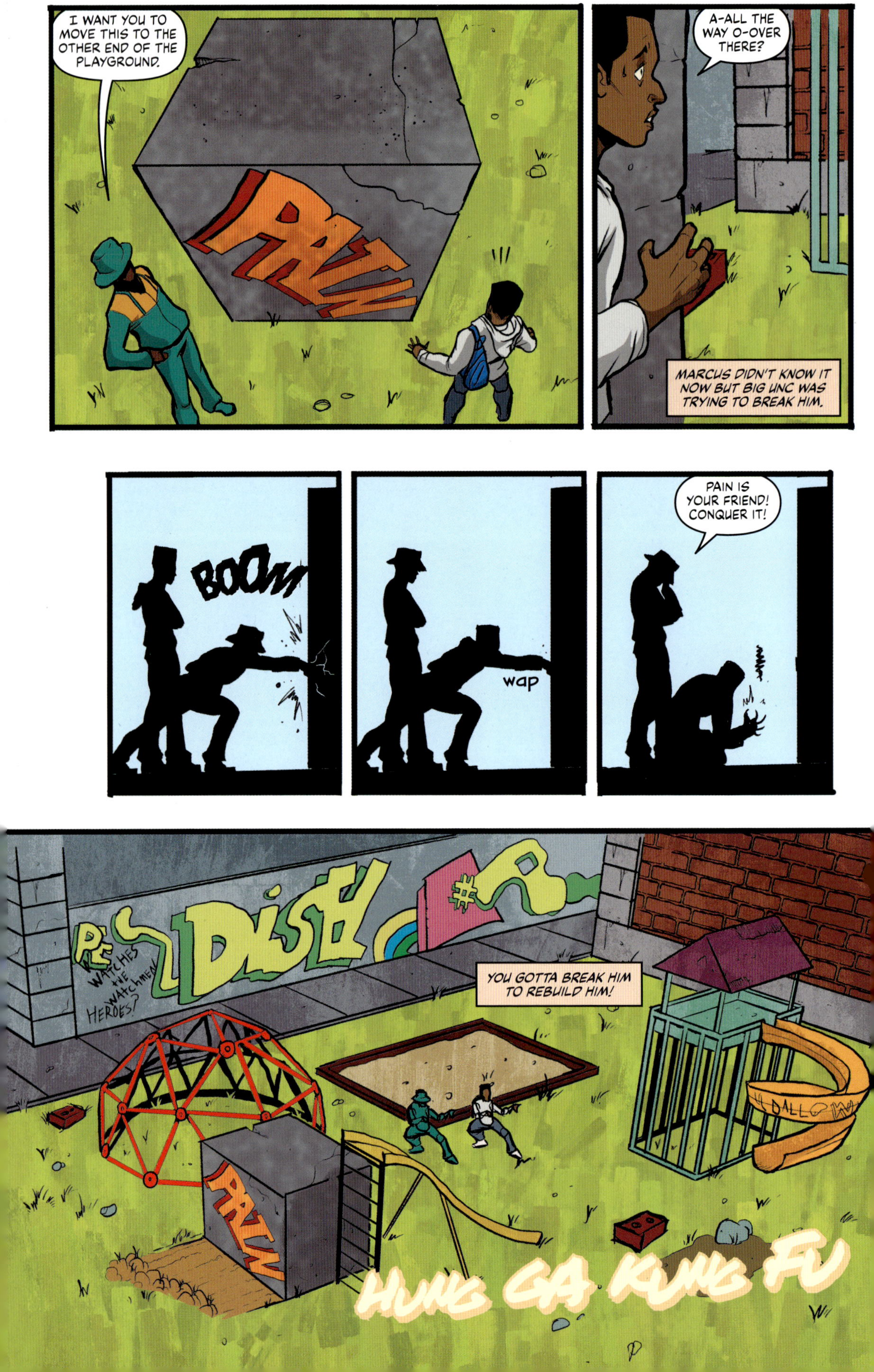
I WANT YOU TO MOVE THIS TO THE OTHER END OF THE PLAYGROUND.
PAIN
A-ALL THE WAY O-OVER THERE?
MARCUS DIDN'T KNOW IT NOW BUT BIG UNC WAS TRYING TO BREAK HIM.
BOOM
wap
PAIN IS YOUR FRIEND! CONQUER IT!
YOU GOTTA BREAK HIM TO REBUILD HIM!
PAIN
HUNG GA KUNG FU

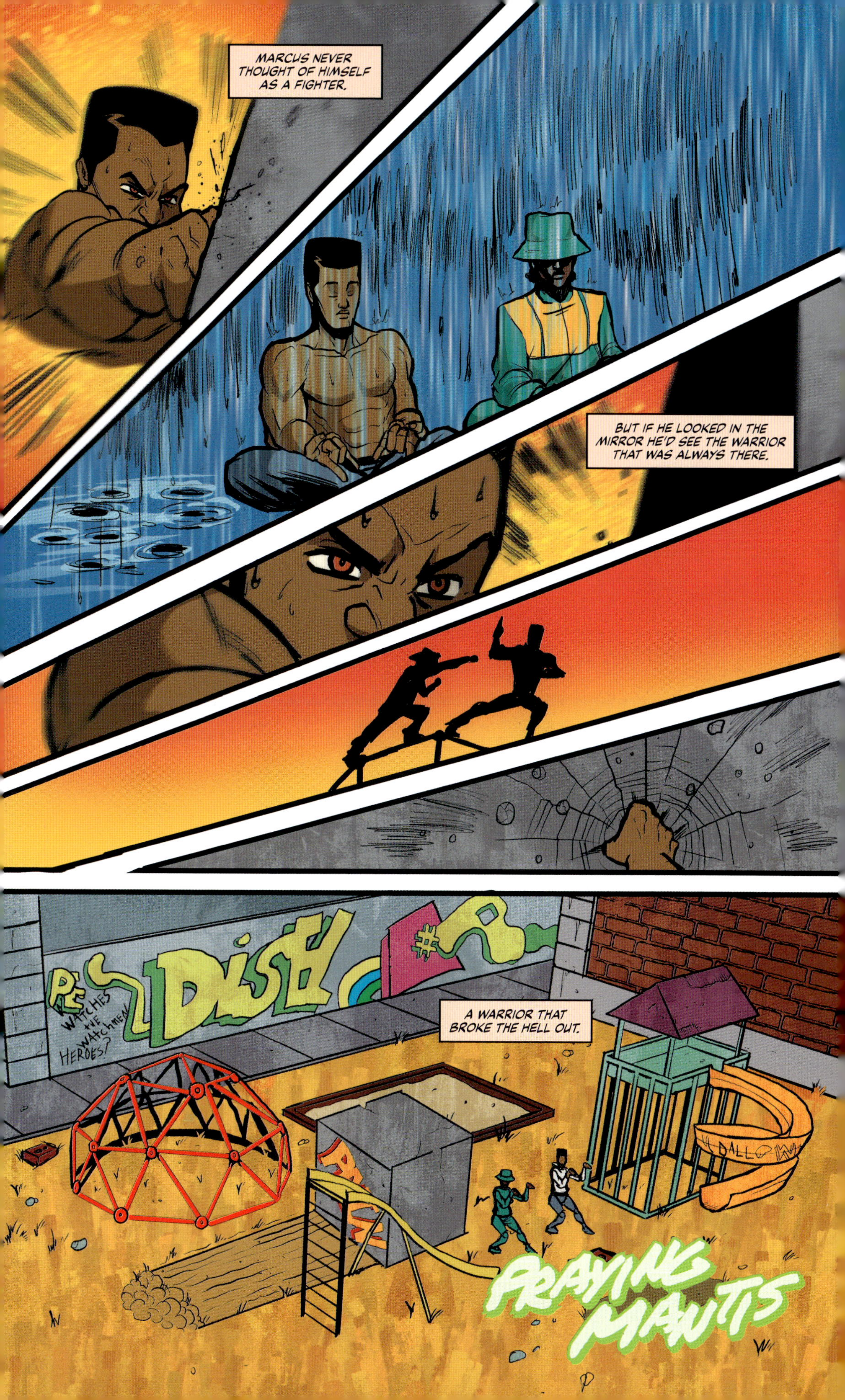
MARCUS NEVER THOUGHT OF HIMSELF AS A FIGHTER.
BUT IF HE LOOKED IN THE MIRROR HE'D SEE THE WARRIOR THAT WAS ALWAYS THERE.
A WARRIOR THAT BROKE THE HELL OUT.
PRAYING MANTIS

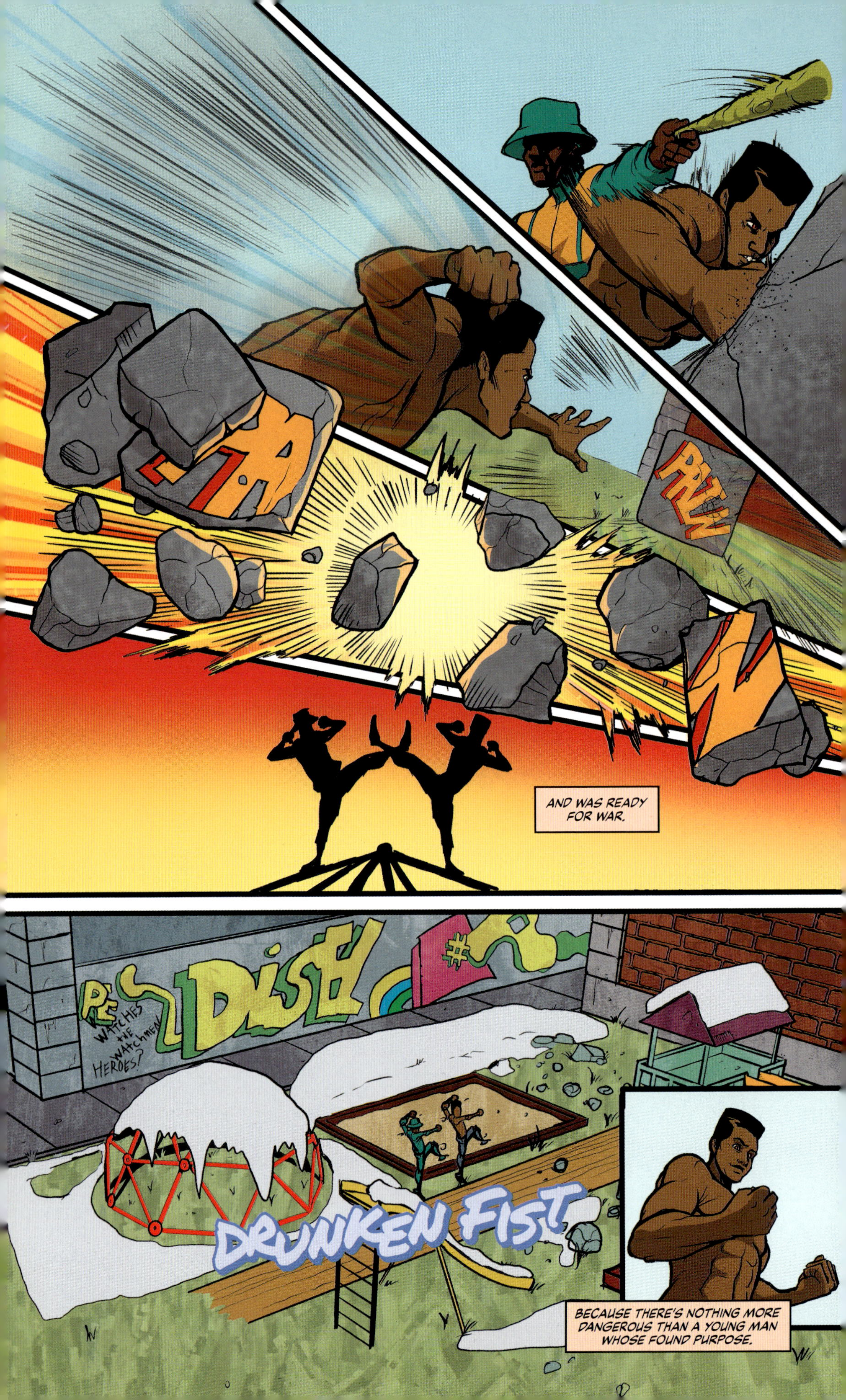
AND WAS READY FOR WAR.
WATCHES the watchmen! HEROES?
DRUNKEN FIST
BECAUSE THERE'S NOTHING MORE DANGEROUS THAN A YOUNG MAN WHOSE FOUND PURPOSE.

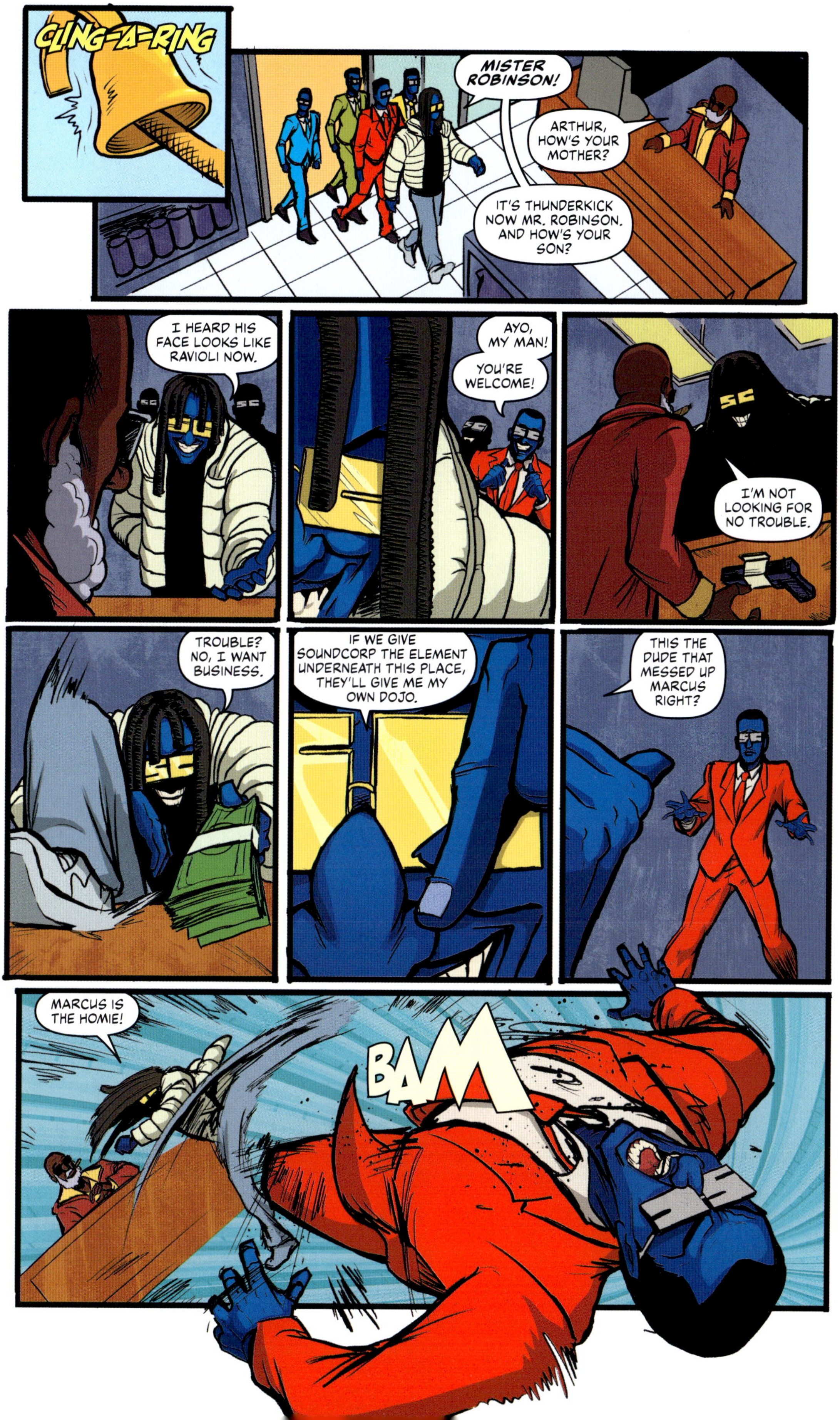
CLING-A-RING
MISTER ROBINSON!
ARTHUR, HOW'S YOUR MOTHER?
IT'S THUNDERKICK NOW MR. ROBINSON. AND HOW'S YOUR SON?
I HEARD HIS FACE LOOKS LIKE RAVIOLI NOW.
AYO, MY MAN!
YOU'RE WELCOME!
I'M NOT LOOKING FOR NO TROUBLE.
TROUBLE? NO, I WANT BUSINESS.
IF WE GIVE SOUNDCORP THE ELEMENT UNDERNEATH THIS PLACE, THEY'LL GIVE ME MY OWN DOJO.
THIS THE DUDE THAT MESSED UP MARCUS RIGHT?
MARCUS IS THE HOMIE!
BAM

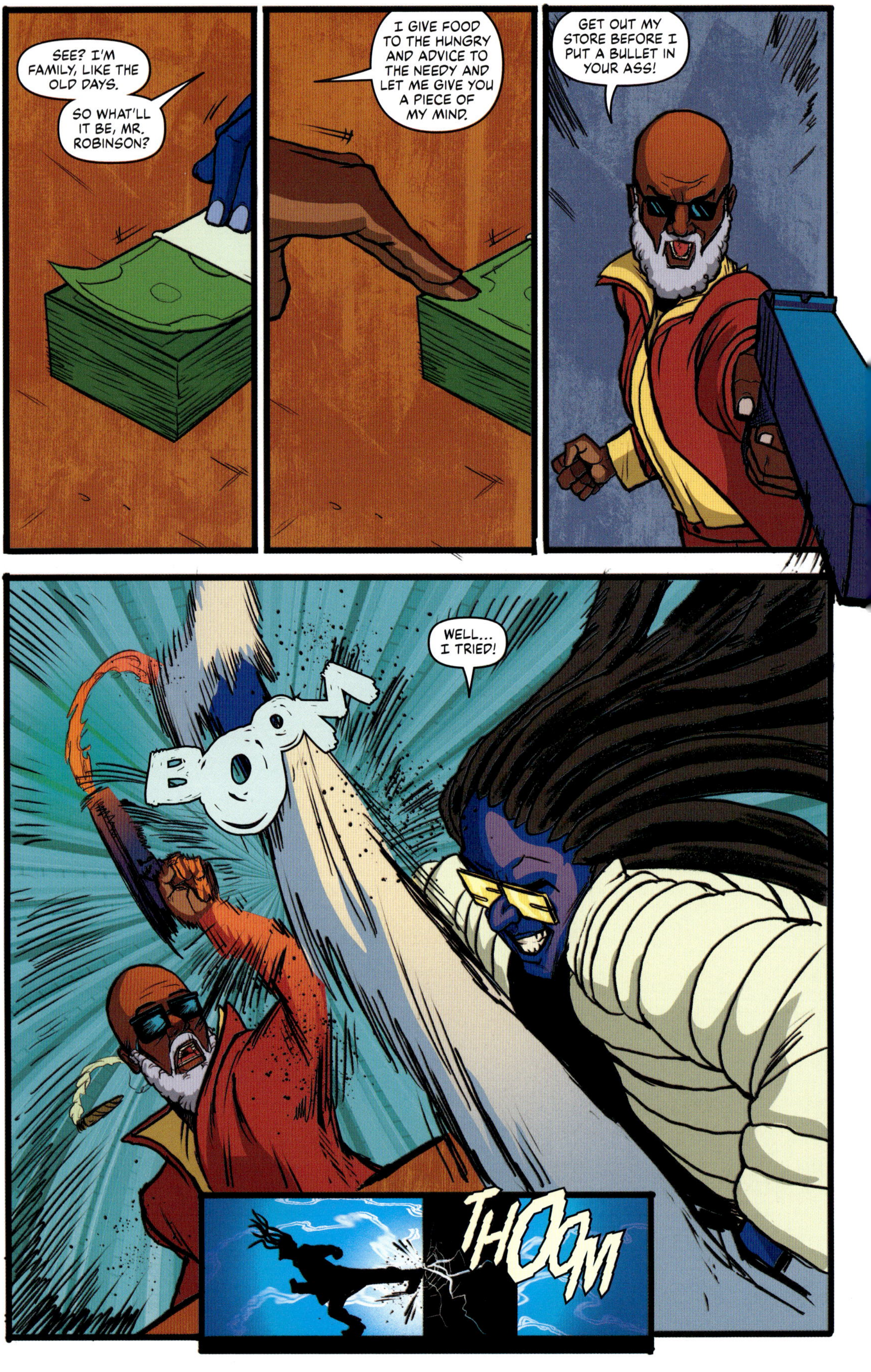
SEE? I'M FAMILY, LIKE THE OLD DAYS.
SO WHAT'LL IT BE, MR. ROBINSON?
I GIVE FOOD TO THE HUNGRY AND ADVICE TO THE NEEDY AND LET ME GIVE YOU A PIECE OF MY MIND.
GET OUT MY STORE BEFORE I PUT A BULLET IN YOUR ASS!
WELL... I TRIED!
BOOM
THOOM

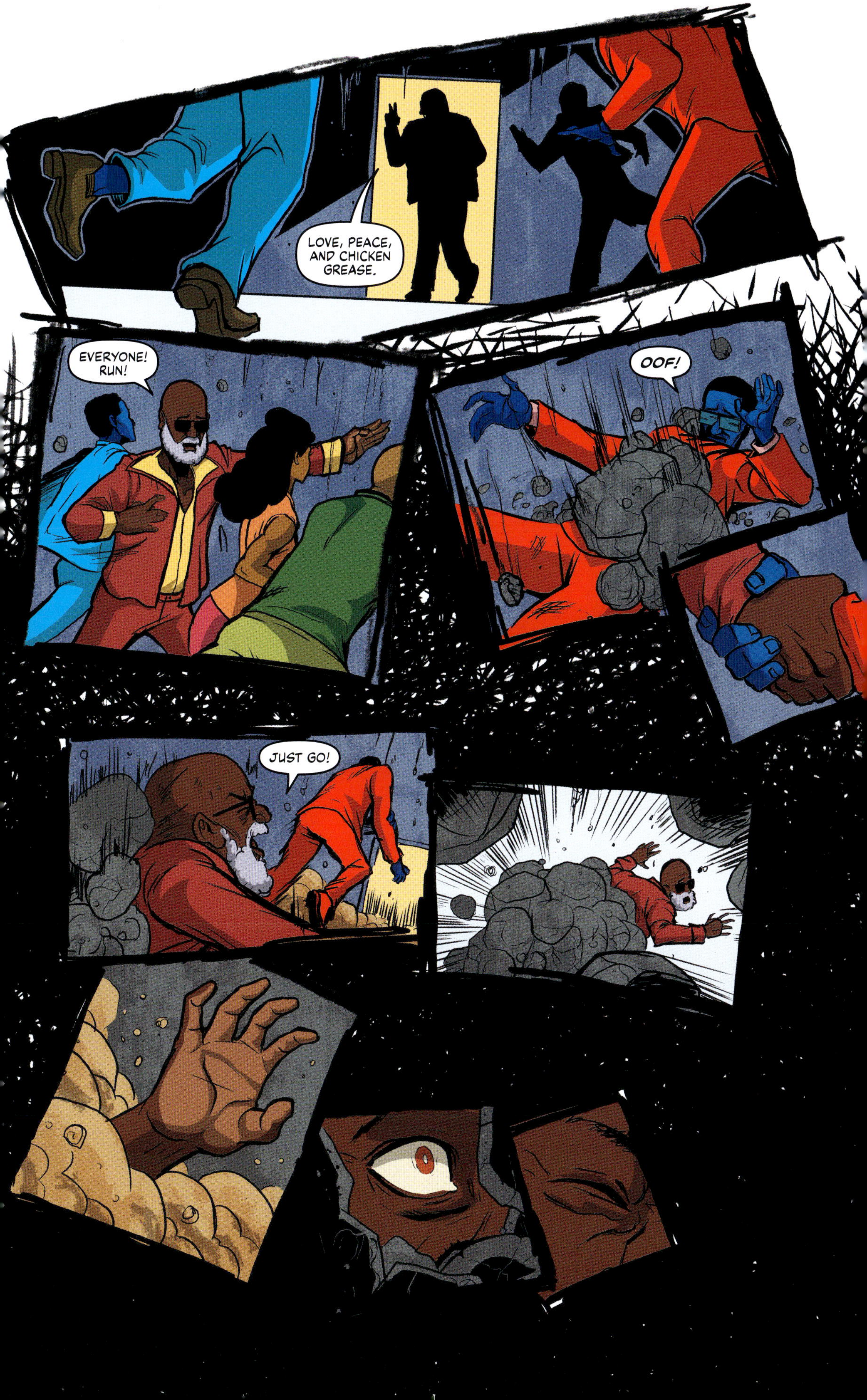
LOVE, PEACE, AND CHICKEN GREASE.
EVERYONE! RUN!
OOF!
JUST GO!

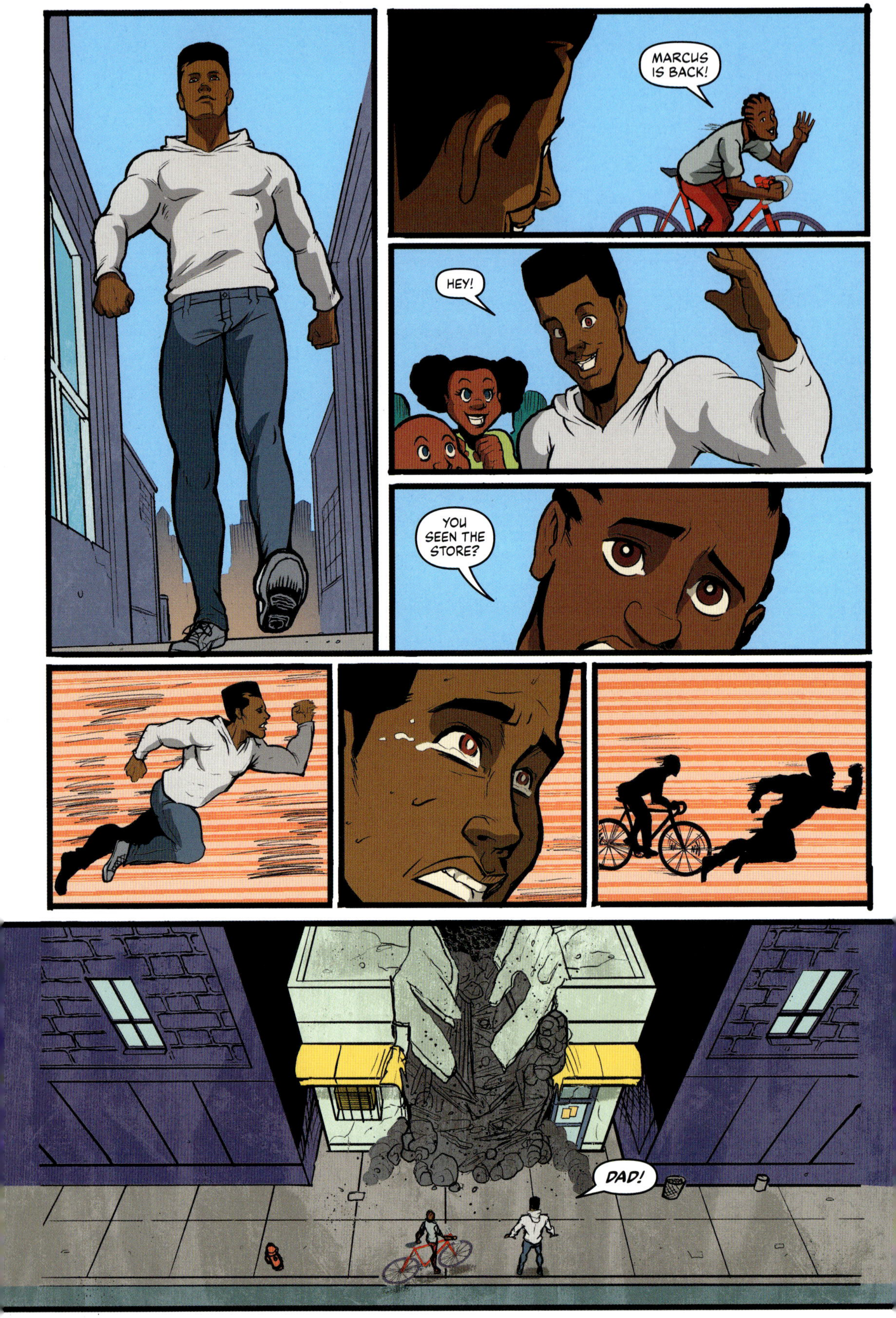
MARCUS IS BACK!
HEY!
YOU SEEN THE STORE?
DAD!

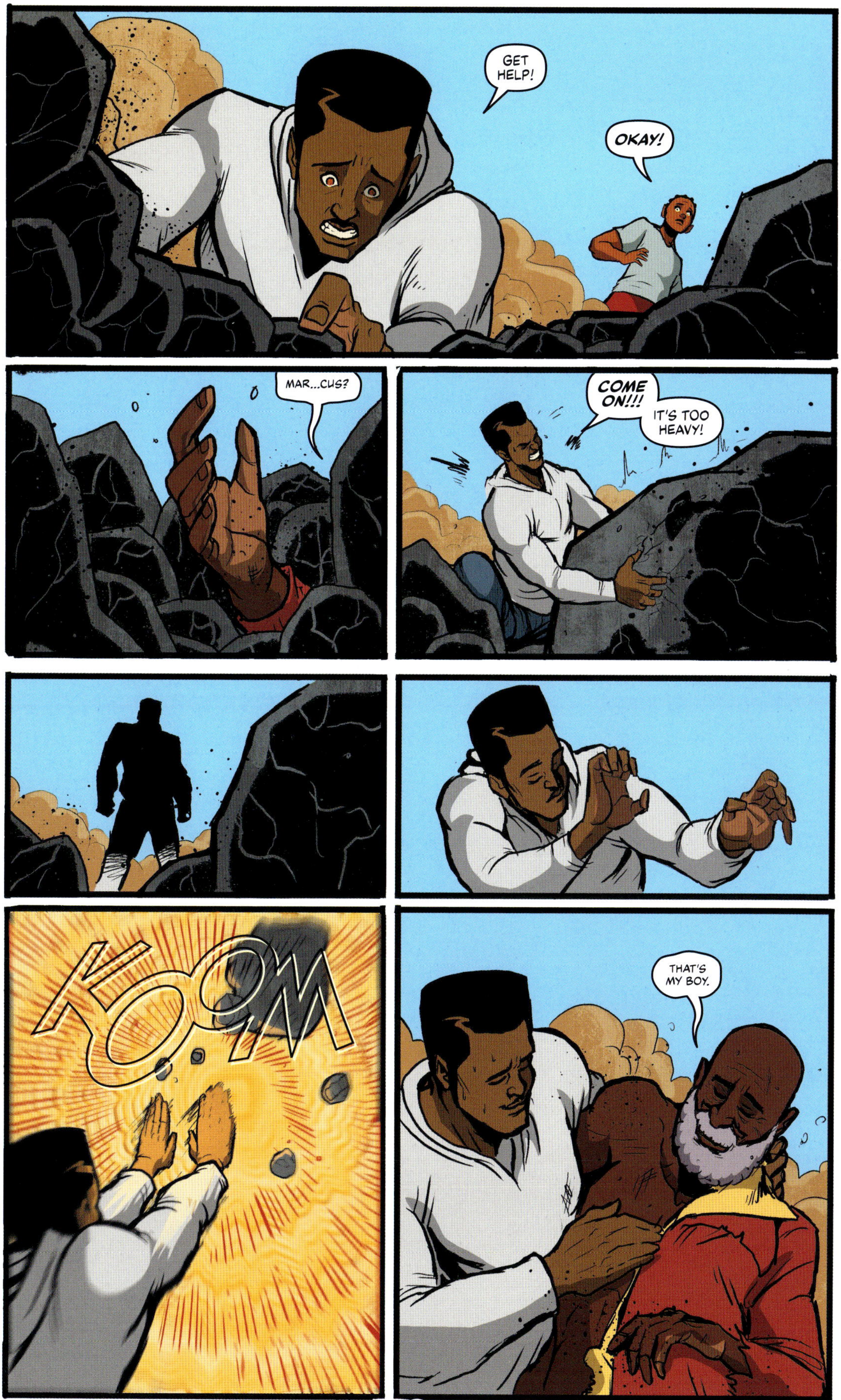
GET HELP!
OKAY!
MAR...CUS?
COME ON!!!
IT'S TOO HEAVY!
KOOM
THAT'S MY BOY.

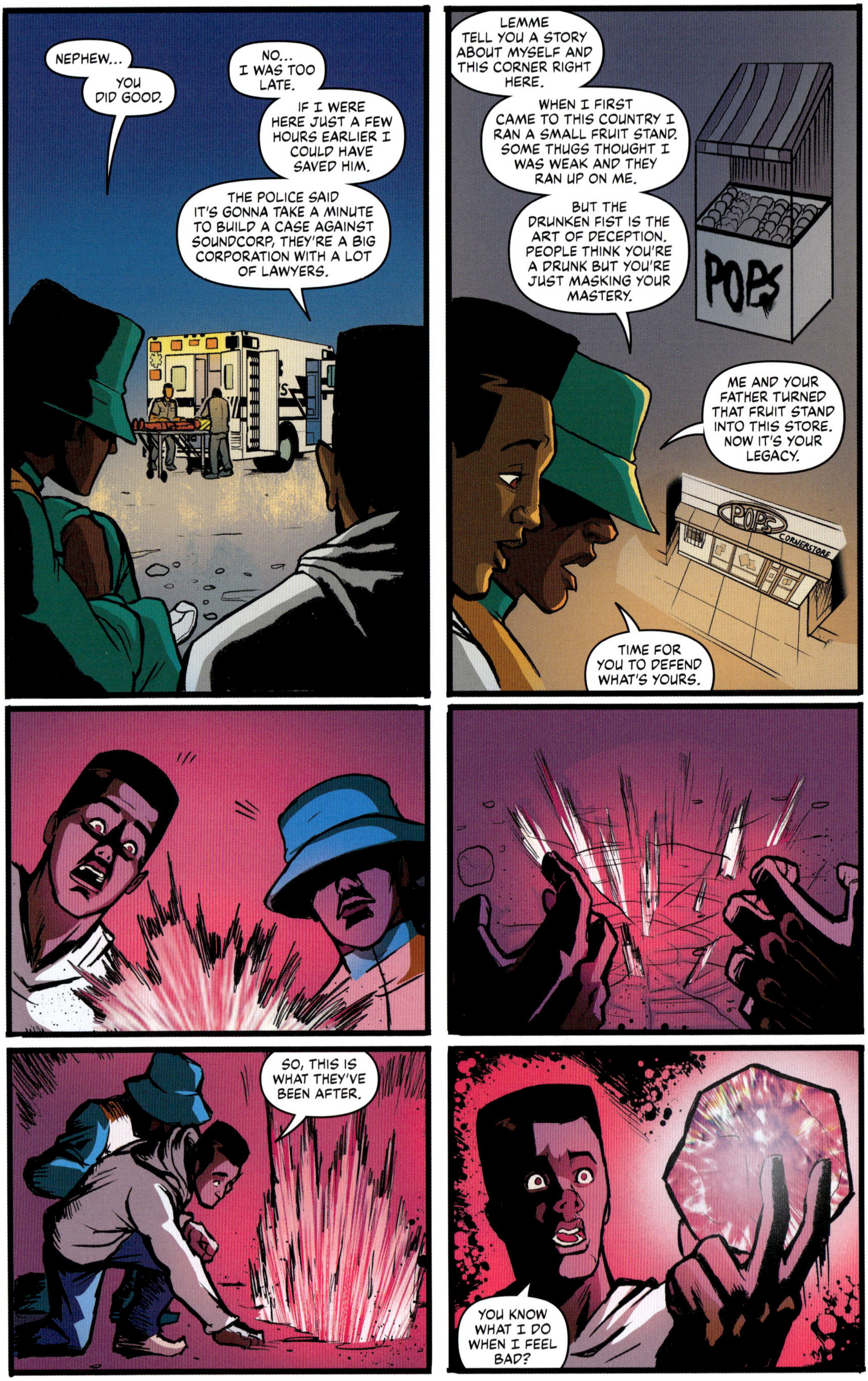
NEPHEW... YOU DID GOOD.
NO... I WAS TOO LATE.
IF I WERE HERE JUST A FEW HOURS EARLIER I COULD HAVE SAVED HIM.
THE POLICE SAID IT'S GONNA TAKE A MINUTE TO BUILD A CASE AGAINST SOUNDCORP, THEY'RE A BIG CORPORATION WITH A LOT OF LAWYERS.
LEMME TELL YOU A STORY ABOUT MYSELF AND THIS CORNER RIGHT HERE.
WHEN I FIRST CAME TO THIS COUNTRY I RAN A SMALL FRUIT STAND. SOME THUGS THOUGHT I WAS WEAK AND THEY RAN UP ON ME.
BUT THE DRUNKEN FIST IS THE ART OF DECEPTION. PEOPLE THINK YOU'RE A DRUNK BUT YOU'RE JUST MASKING YOUR MASTERY.
POPS
ME AND YOUR FATHER TURNED THAT FRUIT STAND INTO THIS STORE. NOW IT'S YOUR LEGACY.
POPS
CORNERSTORE
TIME FOR YOU TO DEFEND WHAT'S YOURS.
SO, THIS IS WHAT THEY'VE BEEN AFTER.
YOU KNOW WHAT I DO WHEN I FEEL BAD?

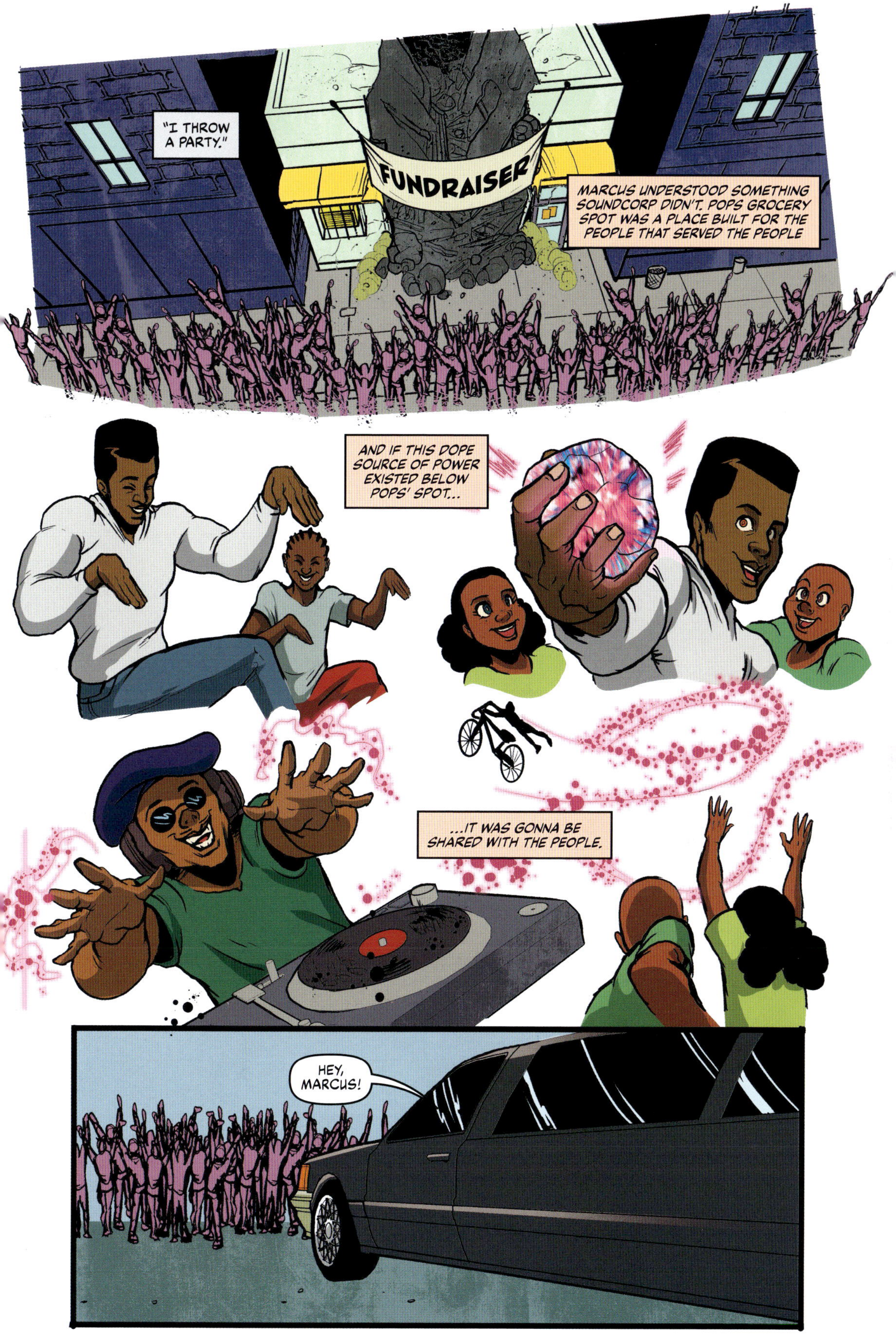
"I THROW A PARTY."
FUNDRAISER
MARCUS UNDERSTOOD SOMETHING SOUNDCORP DIDN'T. POPS GROCERY SPOT WAS A PLACE BUILT FOR THE PEOPLE THAT SERVED THE PEOPLE
AND IF THIS DOPE SOURCE OF POWER EXISTED BELOW POPS' SPOT...
...IT WAS GONNA BE SHARED WITH THE PEOPLE.
HEY, MARCUS!

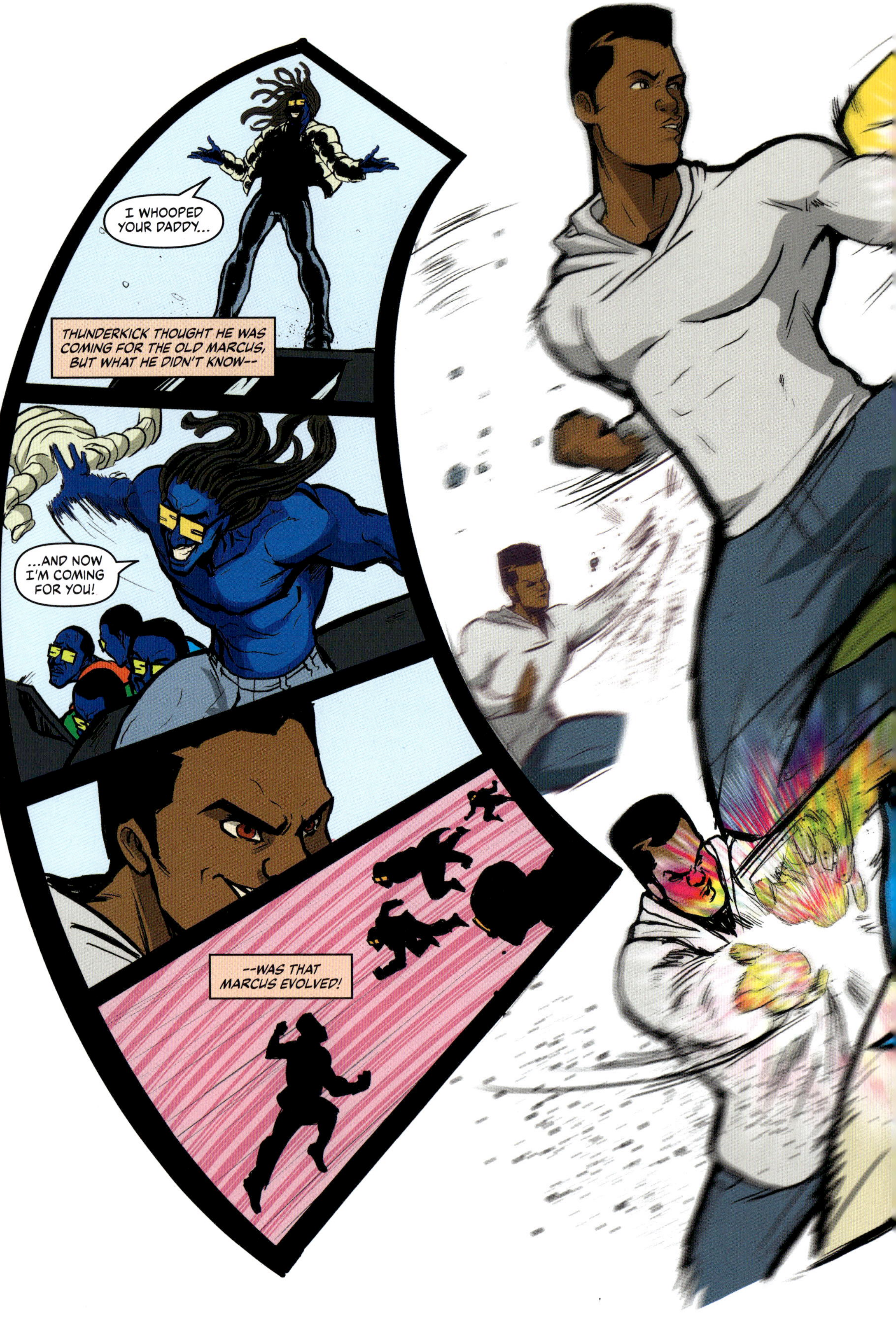

I WHOOPED YOUR DADDY...
THUNDERKICK THOUGHT HE WAS COMING FOR THE OLD MARCUS, BUT WHAT HE DIDN'T KNOW--
...AND NOW I'M COMING FOR YOU!
--WAS THAT MARCUS EVOLVED!

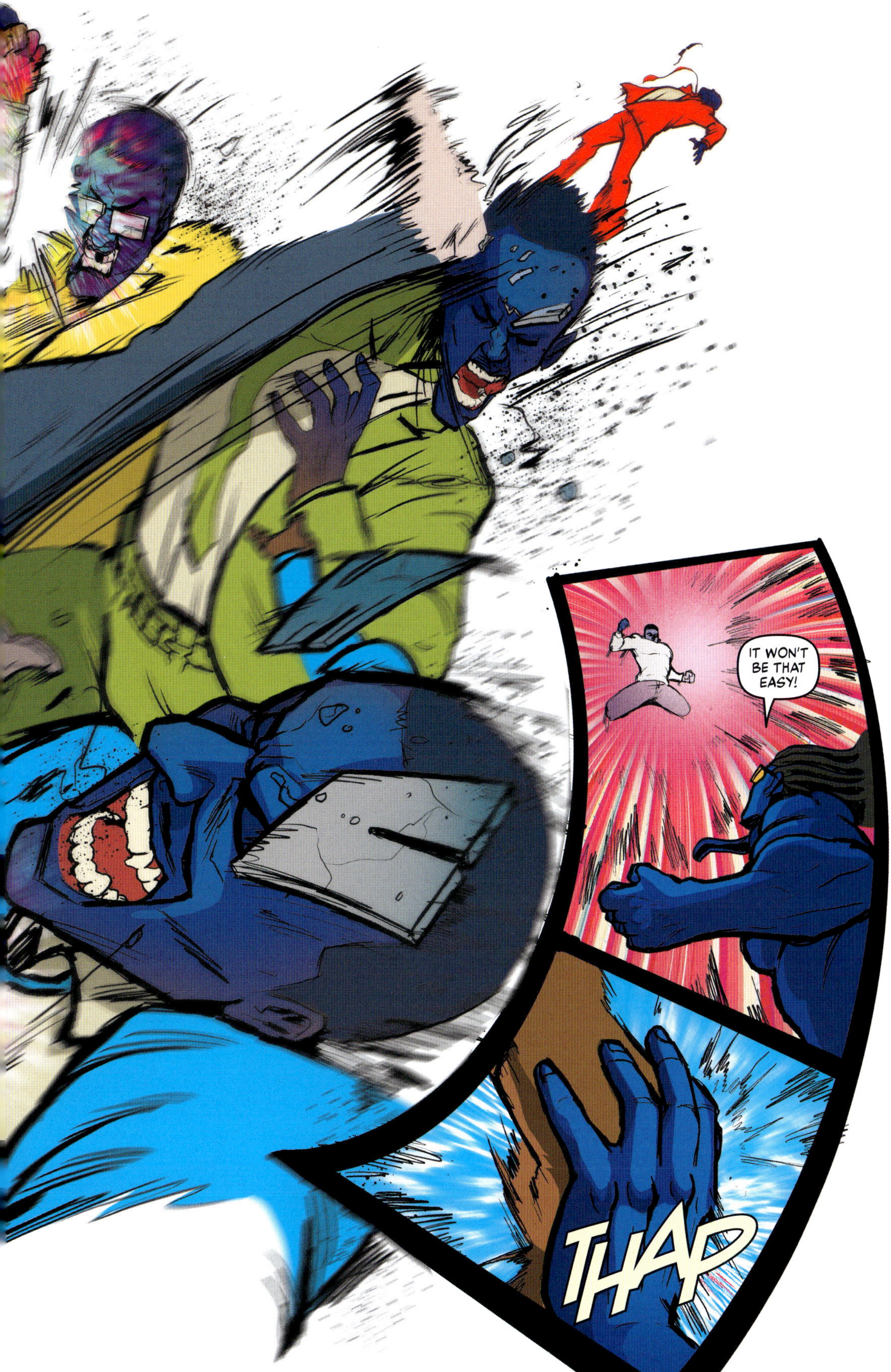
IT WON'T BE THAT EASY!
THAP

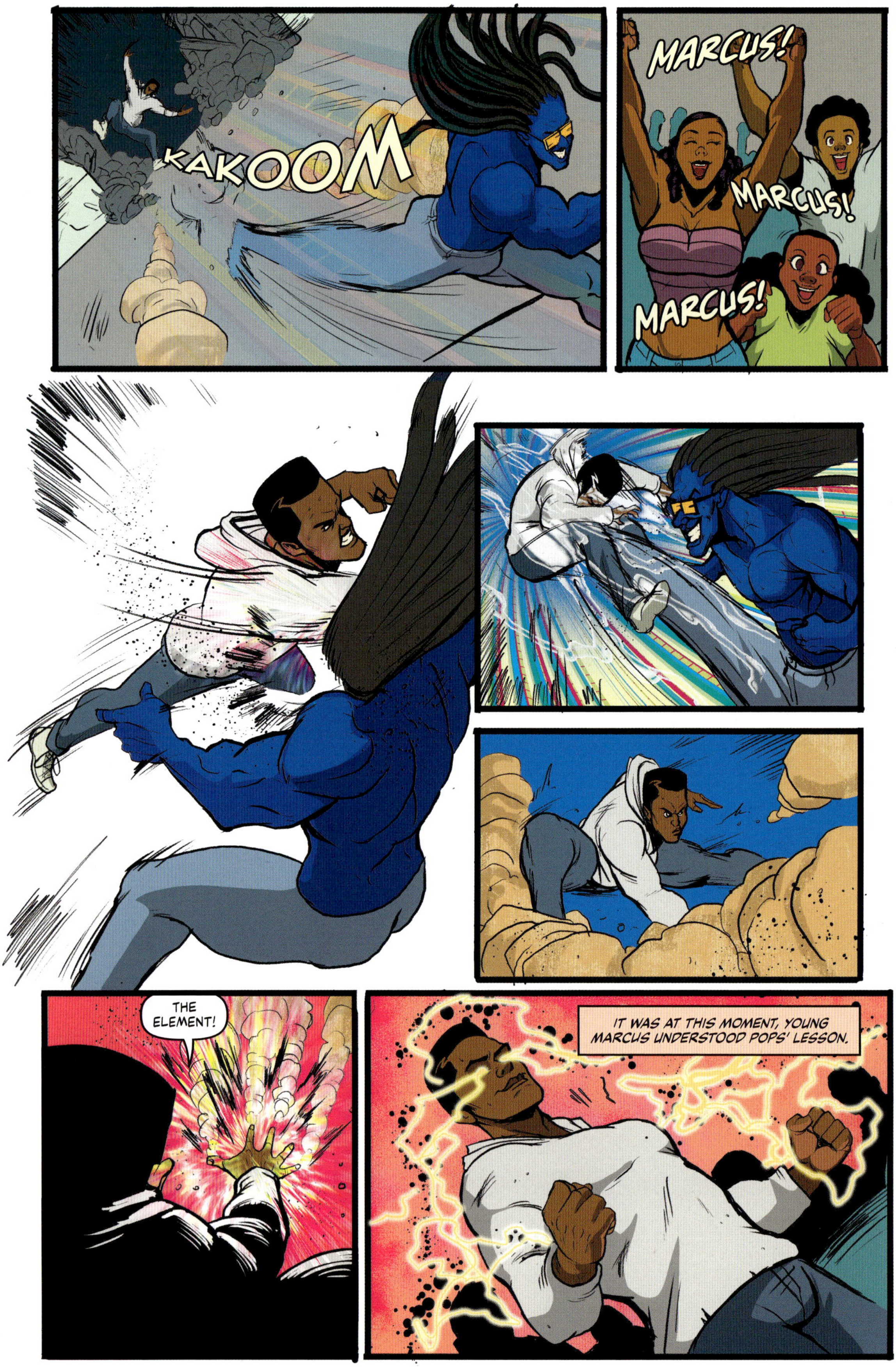
KAKOOM
MARCUS!
MARCUS!
MARCUS!
THE ELEMENT!
IT WAS AT THIS MOMENT, YOUNG MARCUS UNDERSTOOD POPS' LESSON.

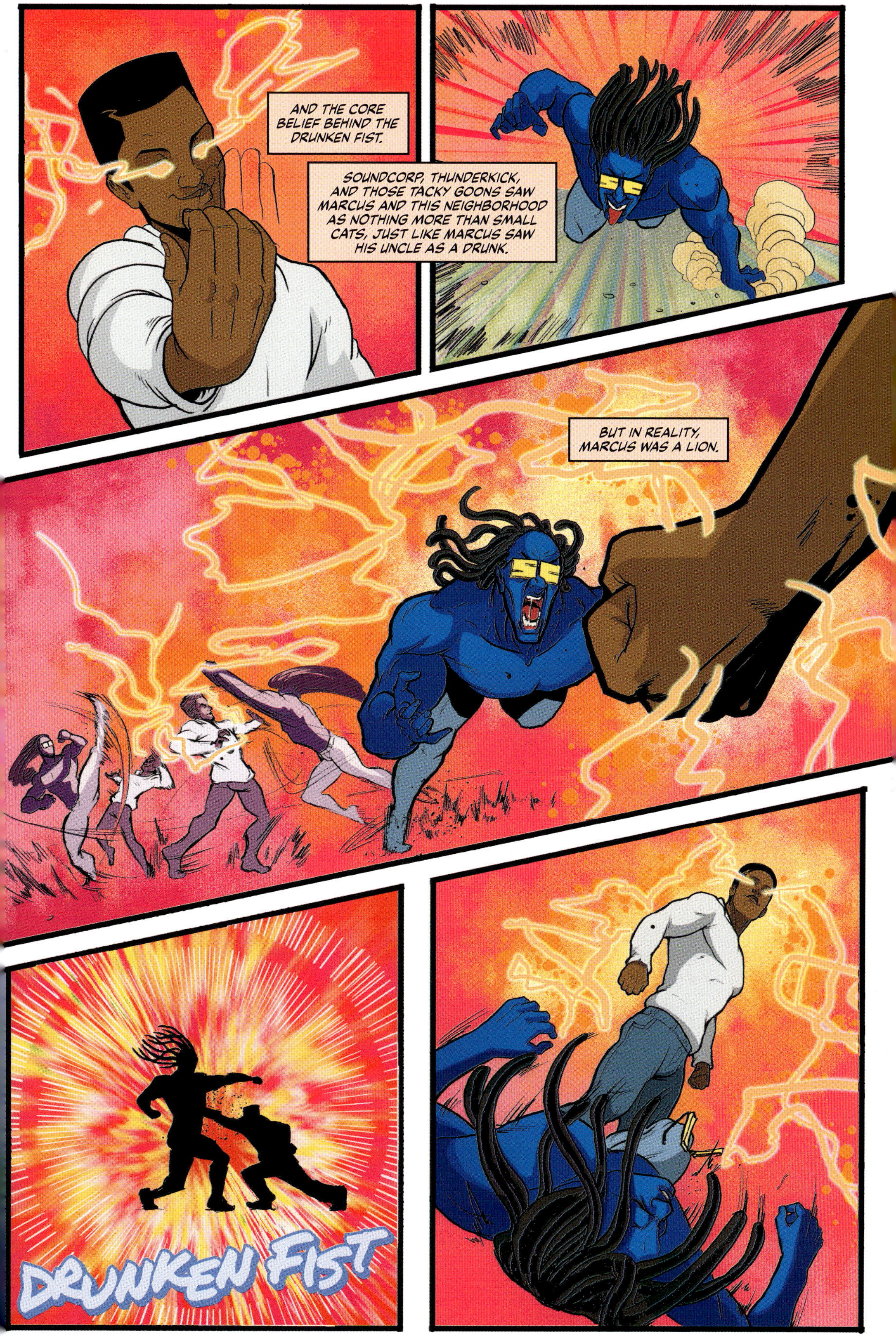
AND THE CORE BELIEF BEHIND THE DRUNKEN FIST.
SOUNDCORP, THUNDERKICK, AND THOSE TACKY GOONS SAW MARCUS AND THIS NEIGHBORHOOD AS NOTHING MORE THAN SMALL CATS, JUST LIKE MARCUS SAW HIS UNCLE AS A DRUNK.
BUT IN REALITY, MARCUS WAS A LION.
DRUNKEN FIST

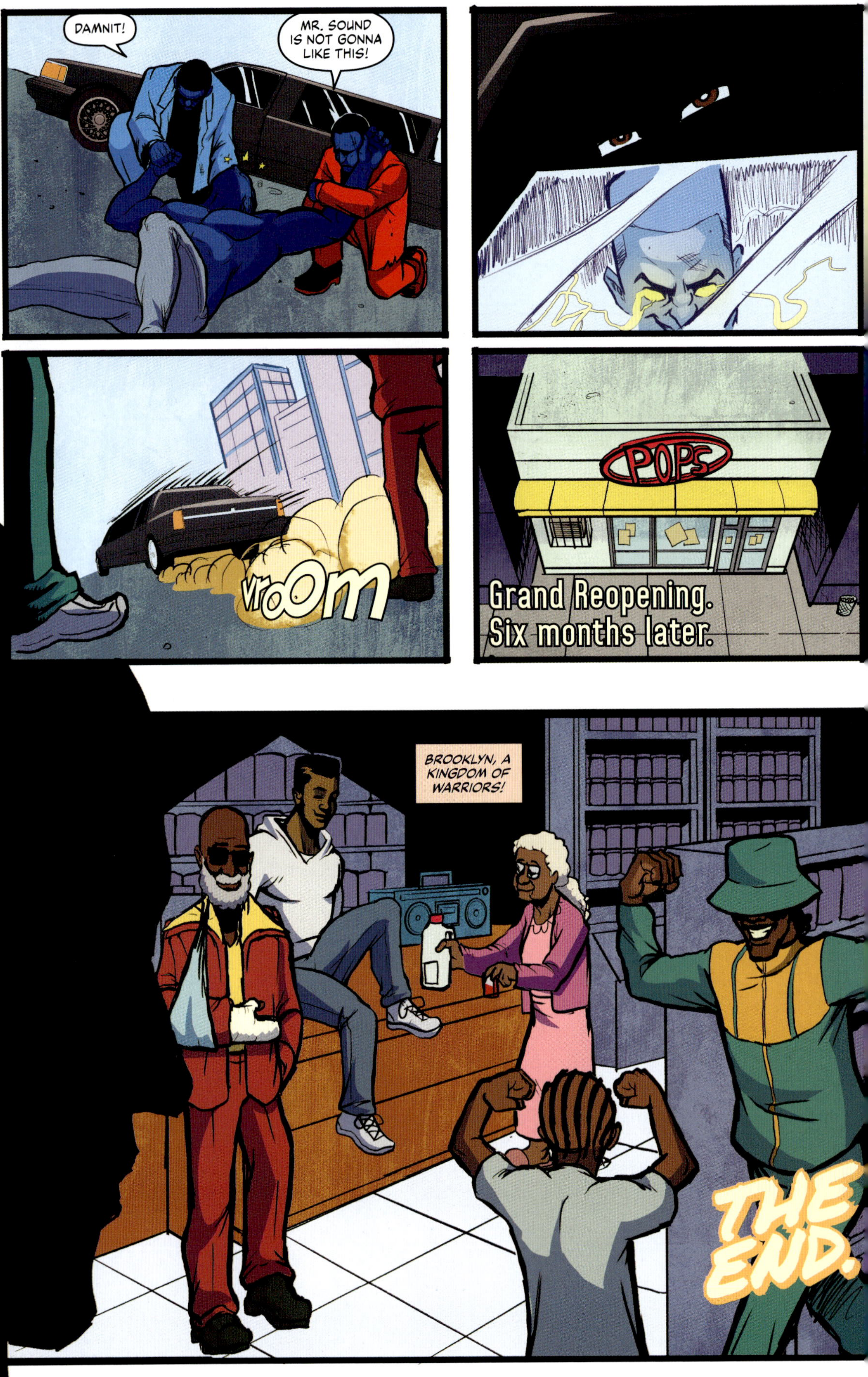
DAMNIT!
MR. SOUND IS NOT GONNA LIKE THIS!
VROOM
POPS
Grand Reopening.
Six months later.
BROOKLYN, A KINGDOM OF WARRIORS!
THE END.

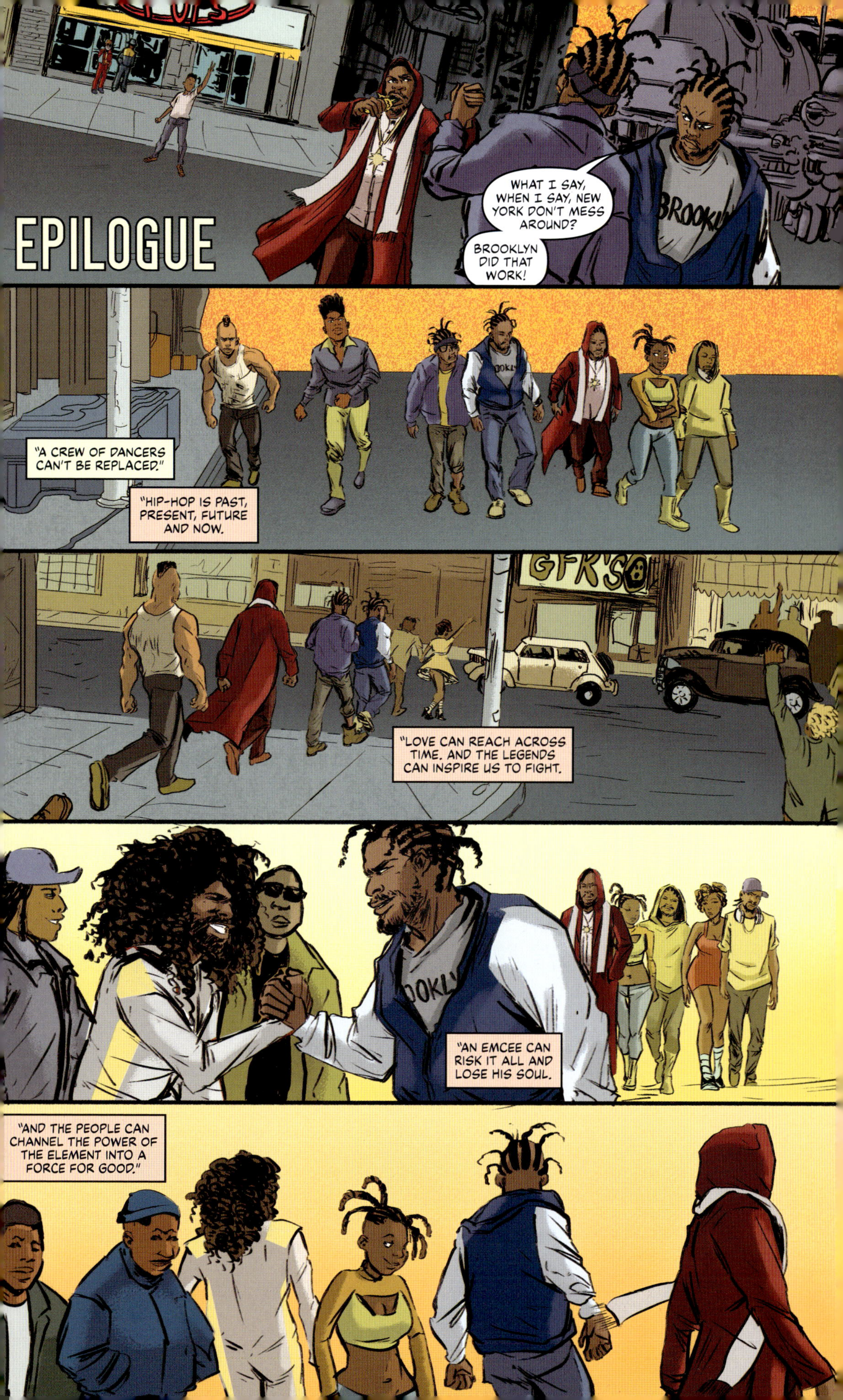
EPILOGUE
WHAT I SAY, WHEN I SAY, NEW YORK DON'T MESS AROUND?
BROOKLYN DID THAT WORK!
"A CREW OF DANCERS CAN'T BE REPLACED."
"HIP-HOP IS PAST, PRESENT, FUTURE AND NOW.
GFR'SO
"LOVE CAN REACH ACROSS TIME. AND THE LEGENDS CAN INSPIRE US TO FIGHT.
"AN EMCEE CAN RISK IT ALL AND LOSE HIS SOUL.
"AND THE PEOPLE CAN CHANNEL THE POWER OF THE ELEMENT INTO A FORCE FOR GOOD."

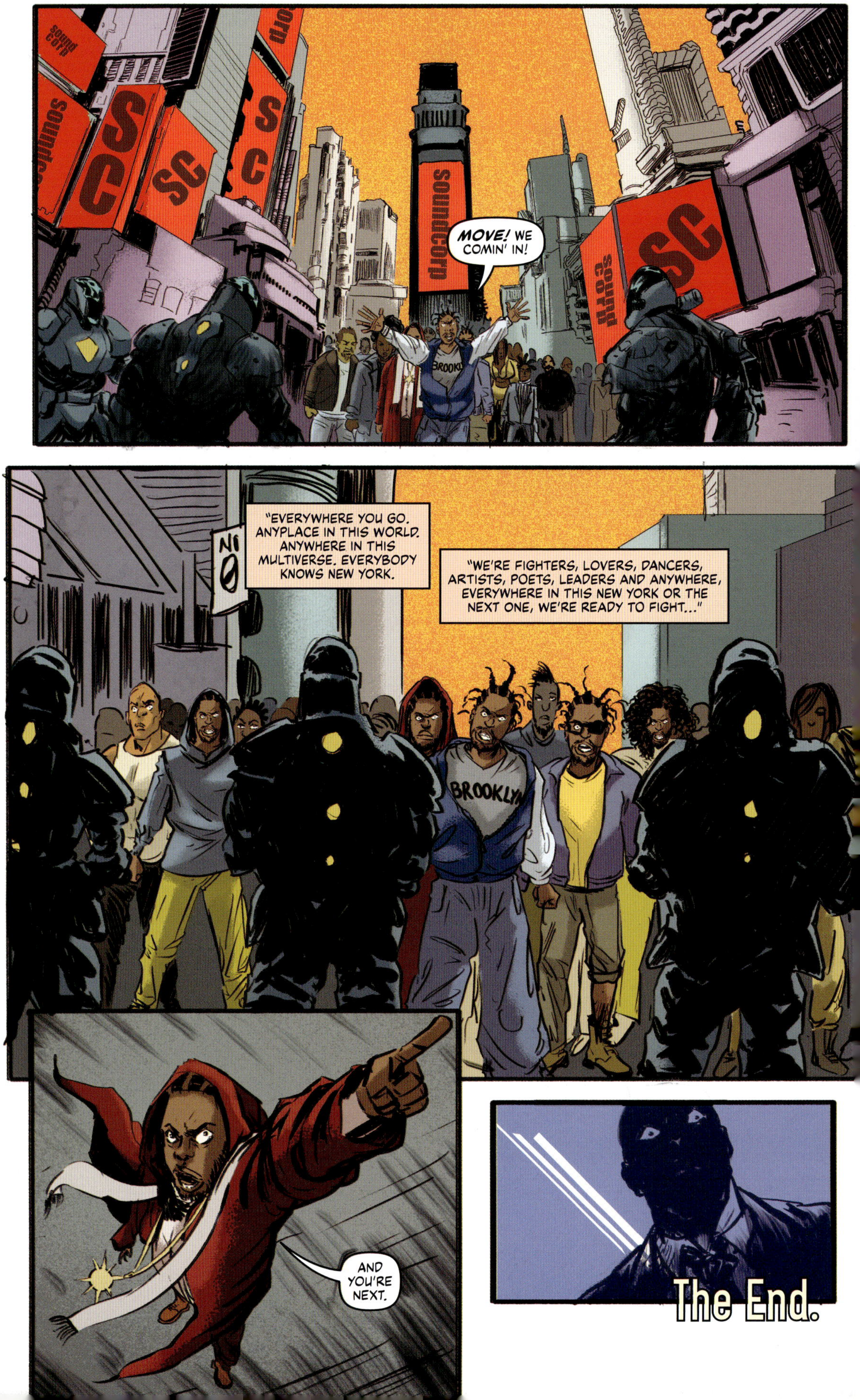
soundcorp
MOVE! WE COMIN' IN!
"EVERYWHERE YOU GO. ANYPLACE IN THIS WORLD. ANYWHERE IN THIS MULTIVERSE. EVERYBODY KNOWS NEW YORK.
"WE'RE FIGHTERS, LOVERS, DANCERS, ARTISTS, POETS, LEADERS AND ANYWHERE, EVERYWHERE IN THIS NEW YORK OR THE NEXT ONE, WE'RE READY TO FIGHT..."
BROOKLYN
AND YOU'RE NEXT.
The End.

AFTERWORD

A Lyrical Ruckus in the City was a huge collaboration between storytellers and artists. The catalyst for the book was twofold. First, Jaxson Beckett Williams, Messiah Jacobs, and Nicole Beckett of Four Screens started writing a story entitled *Sword of the Cypher* in the early days of 2020 when COVID hit. There was little to do but watch superhero movies and read comic books while huddled in our respective houses awaiting the world's fate. It was an apocalyptic moment where we needed a real-life superhero to come and save the world. During this time, our minds ran wild.

Jaxson, Nicole's son, was 10 at the time, and full of imagination. Jaxson was set on creating a truly fantastic hip-hop hero to go alongside his favorite icons of the medium. Inspired by *Across the Spider-Verse*—a fantastical orchestra of art, action, and New York flavor—Jaxson, Nicole, and Messiah began to write. Thus, *Sword of the Cypher* was born.

Secondly, in the midst of their writing sessions, they were devastated by the tragic and highly televised death of George Floyd, prompting civil unrest and protests throughout the country. It became clear to them that *Sword of the Cypher* must have a mission bigger than the anticipated superhero strife. Our hero had a deeper undertaking now: realizing social justice, community building, and elevating Black excellence.

Set in New York City, *Sword of the Cypher* was a story ready to connect with others, and so, joining forces with Icelene Jones, administrator of the estate of ODB, and David Steward II, CEO of Lion Forge Animation, we were able to create *A Lyrical Ruckus in the City*—an entire universe: a world of fact and science fiction, all laid out in the five boroughs of New York City, narrated by the outrageous ODB.

It was in this mad collaboration among ODB's immediately recognizable persona, the unshakable connection to our team members' Messiah Jacobs and Chris Robinson's birthplace, and a need to highlight people's universal virtues that *A Lyrical Ruckus in the City* was born.

We created a universe immersed in the five boroughs, reflecting everyday people as heroes: in Manhattan, our heroes dance-battle with artificial intelligence against cultural appropriation ("LaGuardia's Steppers"); in Brooklyn, our hero is up against gentrification sweeping his neighborhood ("Marcus and the Drunken Fist"). Over in Queens, we see a young rapper's struggle with ambition and authenticity in hip-hop ("Demon Flow"); and in Harlem, we experience time-crossed lovers united by the historically diverse music scene Harlem celebrates ("Love in the Mix").

Our team set out on a mission to include as much talent of color as possible to reflect our New York heroes. We strove to include greats like Paris Alleyne, Ron Wimberly, Chris Robinson, Ike Reed, and David Gorden. We also brought in young and burgeoning talent like writer Jaxson Beckett Williams and illustrator Chris Gooding. All of this talent brought the heart and authenticity our culture exudes.

A Lyrical Ruckus in the City shows our heroes in all facets of life and grappling with a rapidly changing world, reminding us that everyone can make an impact. Ordinary becomes extraordinary. We hope that when you immerse yourself in *A Lyrical Ruckus in the City*, you can see the real-life superhero within you.

—The Estate of Russell Jones

■ BIOS

OL' DIRTY BASTARD, born Russell Tyrone Jones, was an American rapper and founding member of the legendary Wu-Tang Clan. His eccentric style, raw energy, and innovative storytelling made him a standout artist in the hip-hop landscape. His debut solo album, *Return to the 36 Chambers: The Dirty Version*, spawned hits like "Brooklyn Zoo" and cemented his status as a pioneer in the genre.

Meet **IKE REED**, the comic world's answer to a superhero without a cape. Co-founder of Lion Forge Comics and the brain behind hits like *Quincredible* and *TriMaxx*, Ike's the guy turning pages into adventures. When not crafting epic tales in comics and manga, he's penning scripts for *Drawn In* on PBS. Now he's cooking up some secret sauce for Big Fat Hero and Composition Media. His writing? A cocktail of sci-fi, superheroes, and a dash of street smarts. Spoiler: He's as legendary as his characters!

DAVID GORDEN is a creator, writer, and sequential artist who specializes in the creation of intellectual properties. Born and raised in St. Louis, Missouri, he fell in love with art, particularly visual storytelling, at a young age. He began making his own comic strips and submitting them to the *Post-Dispatch* at the age of eight. The *Post* very graciously turned David down, with the editor at the time sending him a rejection letter that encouraged him to continue to pursue his dream of becoming a cartoonist. David went on to become a professional graphic artist and cartoonist and was a founding member of legendary St. Louis art crews Air Assault and later Mach One. David knows that today's world has become predicated on people's attention being captured by engaging stories and eye-catching visuals and has over two decades of experience applying his skills in character creation, sequential art, storyboarding, script writing, and concept creation, and he is also a founding member of Big Fat Hero, a social media hub and outlet for short stories, podcasts, geek culture, and production. David has written and created IP for Lion Forge Comics, Rampage Jackson, Scott Steindorff, and Nick Cannon. His creative credits include *Rampage Jackson: Street Soldier*, *Trimaxx*, *Quincredible*, *Sympathy for the Soul* (script adaptation), *Make Believe* (script adaptation), and more. David is the creator of Kwame Hightower and Quantum University. He released his first independent OGN, *Kwame Hightower and the Man With No Name* in late March of 2018. David has recently begun work on his next graphic novel, *Kwame Hightower and the Exiles of Kalatheaa*, and is actively promoting his books through touring, posts on social media, speaking engagements, and teaching workshops on visual storytelling.

JASON PIERRE is a Los Angeles–based filmmaker and writer born to first-generation Jamaican immigrants and raised in the South Bronx. He received a BFA in creative writing from Brooklyn College. He was a production supervisor for BuzzFeed Motion Pictures, where he produced videos across several BuzzFeed YouTube channels and series. He has written four episodes of BuzzFeed's animated *The Good Advice Cupcake Show* for Facebook Watch, and all the episodes of *The Era*, BuzzFeed's Cocoa Butter channel's show on Facebook Watch. He was then a staff writer on Season 3 of the CW show *In The Dark*, and co-wrote episode 6, "Arcade Fire." He returned for Season 4 and wrote episode 8, "Tequila Mockingbird." His 2018 short film, *Existential Donut*, follows a man on a quest to help a donut find its hole, and has screened at 13 film festivals. He has a passion for art, animation, science fiction, and discovering '80s movies he never knew existed.

TROY-JEFFREY ALLEN is a comics writer, video producer, Internet personality, and host. He is known for his work on *MF DOOM: All Caps*, *Chuck D Presents Apocalypse '91: Revolution Never Sleeps*, *Fight of the Century*, and the Harvey Award–nominated *District Comics: Unconventional History of Washington, DC*.

A pioneering figure in the comic book industry, **REGINE SAWYER** wears multiple hats as a writer, editor, and the founder of Women in Comics NYC Collective International. Her creative talents have given life to works like *The Rippers*, *Eating Vampires*, and *Ice Witch*. Sawyer is the driving force behind Lockett Down Productions, a small press that exclusively features female comic book artists, with a particular focus on women of color.

CHRIS ROBINSON is the writer of Vince Staples's *Limbo Beach* and indie darling *Werewolf Frankenstein*, as well as the editor of *All-Negro Comics 75th Anniversary Edition*. Formerly, he edited *Black Panther*, *Moon Girl and Devil Dinosaur*, *Ghost Rider*, and much more for Marvel Comics. Learn more at CROB.info.

DAVID BRAME is the Eisner Award–nominated comic artist of *After the Rain*, whose art for the graphic novel was hailed as "bold and arresting" by *Publishers Weekly*. He was also a contributor to the graphic novel anthology *Young Men In Love: A Queer Romance Anthology*, which earned the GLAAD Award for Outstanding Graphic Novel or Anthology and the American Library Association's award for Great Graphic Novel for Teens. David lives in Alaska with his two dogs. For more information, visit David's Instagram @amazingdavidbrame.

DOJO GUBSER is the creator of popular webcomics such as *Rot8ion* and *Paisley Brickstone*.

MAAN HOUSE is a comic book artist with a passion for creating dynamic and expressive imagery that brings stories to life. He is known for his trademark style, which has been seen in a variety of titles, including *Godkillers*, *Devil Within*, and *20 Degrees Past Rigor*. House's work has garnered recognition and praise from both critics and fans alike, earning him a Ringo Awards nomination for Best Cover Artist.

FELIPE SOBREIRO is a Brazilian artist and colorist. He has worked for all major comic book publishers, including Marvel, DC, Image, Dark Horse, IDW, Heavy Metal, and others, with titles ranging from the creator-owned hits *Luther Strode*, *Spread*, and *Local Man*, to Marvel's *Generation X* and Ahoy's *Justice Warriors*. Felipe lives with his wife in Brazil's capital city, Brasília, in a house they share with a horde of cats and a dog.

CHRIS GOODING is a comic book artist with a passion for storytelling. With a background in animation and motion comics, Chris has a keen eye for detail and a talent for bringing characters to life. He has worked on a variety of projects, from superhero epics to indie graphic novels, and is always looking for new ways to push the boundaries of the medium. His work has been praised for its dynamic style, vivid colors, and emotional depth.

MIKE JC is an artist of boundless passion and creativity. With two fine arts degrees in his arsenal, he embarked on a captivating freelance journey. Mike's expertise shines in the world of black-and-white illustration, comics, and the enchanting realm of pinups. His journey began in freelancing, where his unique style gained recognition. His art has graced the pages of industry giants like Antarctic Press, Archie Comics, BlueWater, and Oni Press. Notably, he's contributed as a penciler to iconic projects like the Madonna and Drake bio comics.

In Memory of Russell Jones
"Ol' Dirty Bastard"
1968–2004